A NIGHT OF *Indulgence* AND *Sloth*

VICTORIA PAULEY

ISBN: 978-1-7781022-2-6 (ebook)

ISBN: 978-1-7781022-3-3 (paperback)

Cover Art by: TRC Designs

Formatted by: Kismet New Moon Graphics and Design

Editing by Telisha Merrill

Contents

Content Warning

This book is classified under the dark romance category and includes themes which some may find triggering. The FMC in this story deals with trauma from her childhood which we see internally through monologue or flashback. It's intended for adults who enjoy dark romance with sexual scenes between 2-3 consenting adults (both inside and outside of the sex club), secrets, office romance, and other scenarios that could be harmful. Should the above make you uncomfortable, you may want to consider skipping this book.

If you need further clarification on any of the above listings, email me at authorvictoriapauley@gmail.com.

Club Rapture
Lock In

Chapter One

Liliana

The strong scent of horse dung and wood shavings overpowers everything else around me in the crowded cabin. It doesn't seem to matter that my younger sister, Calantha, is no longer mucking out the stalls and instead preps for bed after a long day.

I desperately wish for the chance to help her get clean, but she isn't afforded such luxury. Only those of us who serve the guests get to bathe properly, while the rest of my aunt and uncle's foster children have to wash up in the creek beyond the house.

"I've got to go, Calla. Uncle insists I not be late for their special visitor again, but I promise you, we're going to get out soon. Here. They don't feed you enough." I hand over the extra bread roll I stole from the kitchens earlier that day.

"You're the best big sister anyone could ask for," she says before taking a massive bite from the crusty bread. Luckily, the others in the cabin are preoccupied and don't notice the extra food, or else I'm sure they'd get us in trouble. Living here beneath the heel of my uncle doesn't allow *for false beliefs about the way people are. It doesn't take long to realize just how far someone will go to earn favor. But they'll find out soon enough that Aunt and Uncle don't appreciate tattletales.*

After one last hug, I head toward the door with every intention of doing my duty, when heavy footfalls sound on the steps outside. I freeze as the large wooden door bangs wide and my uncle steps into the cabin. He's rarely found out here this late at night, and my insides curl with worry.

"I thought I told you not to be late, Liliana, yet here you are, wasting time."

Despite every atom in my body begging me to cower under the weight of his stare, I stand tall. "Sorry, Uncle. I wanted to see my sister before she went to sleep. I was just about to leave."

He tsks, roaming his eyes along the row of bunk beds until he finds Calantha. To my surprise, she's hidden the hunk of bread and pasted a tired, weary look on her face.

"It's true, Uncle. She was just leaving, and I'm all ready for bed," Calla insists. Just like always, she backs up my stories, even though I'd rather she didn't. I'm supposed to be the one protecting her, not the other way around.

"If I couldn't tell from your looks that you were related, it's clear from the lies that spew from your foolish mouth." Uncle strides forward, gripping Calantha's arm so tightly that she winces.

"No!" I shout, racing forward to pull him off her, but it has the opposite effect. He holds her more firmly until a whimper escapes her, and I stop dead in my tracks.

"You thought you could steal from me? Give away my

offerings of food to someone else? That food is only avail-able for those who earn it, but she hasn't, has she, Liliana?" He pulls her toward the door, shoving past me until I'm knocked to the ground.

"It was my fault! She had nothing to do with this. Leave her alone!" I shout, desperate for him to turn his attention on me instead of my younger sister.

He stops on the porch, still holding on tight to Calantha as he turns to me. "She will earn back what you stole, and you will take her place in this cabin until I feel she's paid it off." His saggy old face shakes with his anger, but the gleam in his eyes tells me just how much he's enjoying this. "I was more than willing to hold off on inviting her to work at the main house, but you've forced my hand. She's doing this because of you. Remember that next time you try to pull one over on me." Then he shuts the door and locks it from the outside.

"No, no, no," I scream, pounding on the door with all my strength. The other kids watch, completely uncaring that my little sister is on her way to service one of their guests. And it's all. My. Fault.

"Lily!" Calantha screams as I continue to thrash against the door.

"Lily! Lily! Lily!" On and on she shouts, begging for my help, for my protection, but it's no use.

I've finally done it.

I've ruined her.

"Lily, wake up."

I lurch awake, scrambling back as my eyes focus on the person in front of me. Calantha sits on the edge of the bed, looking at me with a worried expression on her usually joyful face.

"Oh, thank God," I whisper before wrapping my arms tightly around my sister.

"The same nightmare?" she asks softly, and all I can do is nod, not ready to let her go. Her hands run gently over my dark hair and I focus on it. I've never been able to afford therapy, but from what I read online, it's best to pinpoint something tangible.

I take deep breaths to calm my racing heart, reminding myself repeatedly that the events of my nightmare never happened. My sister was never forced to submit to any of my uncle's deplorable *friends*. We weren't trapped with those vile people anymore. We escaped.

When the fear drains from my bones, I separate from my sister, and she hands me a hot mug of coffee. Despite everything we've gone through since our parents died, she's still the sweet, thoughtful girl I remember growing up with. Luckily, we'd gotten out before they'd forced her to bend to the whims of others, and even now she doesn't know all the things I'd had to do for their "guests".

She was in her last year of college to become a veterinary technician. Our aunt and uncle might have forced us to be their unpaid farmhands, but at least one good thing had come from being in their care. My sister's love of animals has grown into something remarkable. Our dark past never diminished that, and I was only too happy to help her claim her dream job.

I would never tell her just how much debt we'd

collected over the years though. As the older sister, it was my job to protect her from the bullshit things in life and, just like I'd done at the farm, I would shield her from whatever I could in the real world.

"The good news is that you'll soon have health benefits, and maybe a therapist will help you get past the trauma so you'll no longer have those nightmares. Plus, once I'm finished with school in a few weeks, I'll be able to get a job and help pay for things so you aren't so stressed out all the time." She gives me a genuine smile, full of hope. It's one of the things I love so much about her. Optimistic to her core.

A knock sounds at the door of our tiny apartment, and I jump at the sound. Calantha only pats my hand before striding with confidence toward the door.

"Make sure you—" I start, but she interrupts me.

"I know, Lily. I'll check the peephole before opening the door. I promise."

Standing from my bed—which is also our living room couch—I stretch, hoping to relieve some of the stiffness from my muscles. My body is always coiled tight after a nightmare, and it usually requires at least an hour of calming yoga to loosen up again.

"Who is it?" I ask, curiosity and a little fear slamming through my insides.

"Breakfast!" she singsongs, bringing a bag of food to the coffee table along with a beautiful black envelope. "I almost forgot. This was in the mailbox when I checked it last night." Her eyes shimmer with excitement as she hands it to me. Embossed in silver letters, my name stands out like a beacon against the black of the envelope. We usually only receive bills, so I'm equal parts excited and nervous to find out what's inside.

"Well, what are you waiting for? Open it!" My sister's enthusiasm spurs me into shoving down my fear and carefully breaking open the seal.

Inside is a thick piece of black cardstock with an elegant design on the top and words etched in pale blue. Tilting it slightly, the areas in blue turn almost white as they reflect light back at me. Flipping it over, I find only a single website on the other side.

"Oh my God," Calantha squeals, taking the card from my hands. "They accepted your application for the lock-in! You lucky bitch."

"Am I supposed to know what that is?" I'd never heard of Club Rapture before, and I sure as hell didn't apply for anything, so why would I be getting an invitation to any club? I was a certified homebody, only ever going out for work unless my sister was with me. Hell, I even made our grocery orders from the comfort of our tiny apartment.

"It's only the hottest, most exclusive club in NYC, Lily. Seriously, how have you never heard of it?" She hands the invitation back to me, and I read it over once again.

You're invited to the exclusive Club Rapture for a night of decadent sin and slothful debauchery. Leave your inhibitions at the door, and come explore the darker side of pleasure.

A shudder runs down my spine as I realize what this

is. A sex club. And this isn't just any event, but one that requires me to be locked inside. Memories of all those nights trapped with my uncle's special guests threaten to break through until my sister places her hand on my shoulder.

"I can't do this, Calla. Not after everything."

She pulls me into her arms, once again seeming to hold all my broken pieces together. "Do you remember the time we went to the zoo with mom and dad? I was terrified to go inside the feeding enclosure because of that kid who claimed he lost a toe to one of those creepy looking goats. And you know what you said to me? You told me that just because something is scary doesn't mean we should run from it, and that sometimes, it's the things we fear the most that bring us the greatest joy. I fed those animals with all the confidence I could muster, even though I was terrified, and that's when I realized I wanted to work with animals someday. I think this would be good for you, Lily. When was the last time you put yourself first? You know I won't force you, but I *really* think you should go."

Her words hit me hard, and my eyes prick with tears because she's right. Before our parents died, I'd been fearless. Well, maybe not fearless, exactly, but I never once let it stop me from doing something. After what happened at the farm, I'd become someone else. Someone who feared everything and would rather stay tucked away from the world than actually experience something.

"But I didn't even apply. They probably meant to send this to someone else, and it wouldn't be fair for me to take their spot." *Jeez, could I have come up with a lamer excuse?*

"So... don't hate me, okay? But I signed you up..." Her gaze darts around the room, never fully resting on me. "It wasn't guaranteed that you'd get in, but you did, and I really think you should go. It's alright to be a little selfish sometimes, Lily. Take care of yourself by going to this club and letting someone else take care of you."

Her words settle inside me like rocks at the bottom of the ocean, weighing me down and allowing me to really consider what she's saying. I can't go back to the person I was before, but maybe I can move beyond my fear. If Calantha is right, then this might just be the first step toward overcoming my past, a way to take back my sexuality and fearlessness until I recognize the person looking back at me in the mirror.

We might have been safe from the farm, but I was still trapped there. Club Rapture could be just what I need to break free of the hold my past has on me.

Chapter Two

Liliana

Today was the day, and I was a ball of fucking nerves.

Clearly, my usual routine of checking the mail once a week wasn't very smart. Now I was stressed as hell with no time to freak out. Even if I had checked it last week, it wouldn't have been enough time for the planner in me. And it baffled me that invites to something like this weren't sent months in advance, though I suppose I didn't have much experience with exclusive parties. Maybe this was how they usually worked, but it left me a jittery mess. Part of me wished that Calantha would have told me she'd signed me up, but deep down, I knew I'd have only used the time to talk myself out of it. The fact that I had to sign a non-disclosure agreement when submitting my R.S.V.P made chills run down my spine, but Calla assured me this was only for my protection and the club's too.

The event started at ten pm, and I had absolutely nothing to wear. All I had was lounge clothes or business outfits that I'd just purchased for my new job at Exalta Solutions.

I interviewed last week for the executive assistant position and received an offer on the same day. The company was new, only operating for about seven years, but that hadn't stopped them from accomplishing incredible things around the world. Not only were they active in the health sector, offering support for those in need of therapy and other medical and mental treatments, but they also helped create technology that kept children, teens, and young adults safe.

During my interview, I'd been shocked to learn that two men, Aiden and Kaleb, had started the company together after college. To my further surprise, Kaleb had joined us halfway through the meeting and spoke at length about their values and the future mission of the company. It was eye-opening and reminded me that this was exactly what I wanted to be doing, even if I was struggling to figure out how I'd work for two powerful men after everything I'd been through at the farm. Regardless of all that though, it was exactly the type of company I'd wanted to work for, and I was so excited to start on Monday.

Hopefully my plans tonight would only bolster my confidence so that I could do an even better job instead of the opposite. I sure as hell didn't need a traumatic breakdown mere days before starting, that's for sure.

Considering my lack of acceptable clothing, Calantha practically drags my ass out on Saturday morning to help me pick the perfect outfit. Before the farm, I'd never have believed my sister would be the one to help me choose a sexy outfit or convince me to attend a sex club, but damn, how things have changed.

The moment we enter the boutique, she takes charge, and before I know it, I'm whisked into a dressing room and dumped with at least a dozen outfits. Every single piece of clothing looks more like a scrap of fabric than anything else, but I'll try on a few just to please her.

I grab the one with the most fabric—a neon pink romper with well-placed cutouts—and nearly laugh out loud at my reflection in the mirror. I swear these dressing room mirrors are the absolute worst. More often than not, they appear warped, almost like what you'd find at the circus.

Hesitating, I step from the dressing room, and my sister practically squeals.

"Damn, girl. Look at that body!" She motions for me to do a spin, and the moment my back turns to her, she slaps my ass.

"Calla..." I say, more embarrassed than annoyed. "There's absolutely no way I'm wearing this out in public. My ass practically hangs out at the bottom! Isn't there anything with, I don't know, a little more coverage?"

Right then, I noticed a woman with a lanyard hung around her neck standing near the dressing room. She comes a little closer, assessing me.

"Actually... we just received a new piece that would look absolutely gorgeous on you. It's a little more modest than that but still very sexy. Just give me a second."

I nod, retreating into the dressing room and taking off

this godforsaken outfit. Clad only in my bra and under-wear, I peruse the rest of the outfits hanging in my stall and cringe further. Why had I let my sister talk me into this?

Footsteps approach, and suddenly there are two articles of clothing being passed over the door. "Here, try these on."

The top is a satin bustier with spaghetti straps and corset-style ribbing down the bodice in the color champagne. It tapers in near the bottom, exposing the curve of my hips when I put it on, and even though my moderately-sized breasts are on display, it's still considerably more coverage than the last outfit.

A pair of leather shorts accompanies the outfit, and while still shorter than I'd usually wear, at least they cover my ass. I feel sexy for what could be the first time in my entire life.

With a smile, I unlock the door and step out. Even if Calantha doesn't like it, I'm already determined to buy this one. The entire thing is still a step outside of my comfort zone but not enough to throw me into a full-blown panic. A compromise.

It turns out that I have nothing to worry about though, as my sister starts a slow clap. "Holy shit! You're a knockout."

"This is the one," I say, confidence lining my every word. The associate is nowhere to be found, so I turn back to the dressing room. Before I can lock the door, I hear a panted, "Wait!"

She's out of breath but hands me a pair of boots.

"These sneaky devils were trying to hide from me, but I finally found them. It's our last pair though, so hopefully you're a size seven."

Excitement fizzles through my veins as I stare at the black, knee-high boots. The heel isn't very high, just an inch or two thick. I sit on the cushioned bench and pull them on. I knew the shoe size would fit me, but in my experience, the shoe size and the calf size don't always match up, so I had no clue if these would work.

The boots go a little higher than my knee, leaving a creamy expanse of flesh between them and my shorts. Once again, this isn't an outfit I would have ever chosen for myself, but it makes me feel strong, confident, and ready to put my trauma behind me.

On top of our shopping trip, somehow Calantha had snagged appointments for us at the spa. She confessed to having booked these after applying on the off chance I was accepted, and my heart swells at how loving she is. Not only would I be arriving at the club with a fresh blowout, but I'd also be buffed and waxed until I felt shiny and new.

I couldn't have thanked her enough for this, and truthfully, it was exactly what we both needed. After our conversation yesterday, I realized we hadn't truly been living. Sure, we couldn't exactly afford weekly spa days, but we could splurge now and then.

With this new mindset, I was ready to make some changes. It would be easier once I started working for Exalta Solutions because the pay was almost double what I made before at the family-owned textile company, not including the employer paid benefits and extra time off allowance. Once I made it past the probation period, we'd have more days like today.

As the nail technicians put the finishing touches on our pedicures, doubt rears its ugly little head. Should I really be leaving my sister vulnerable and alone just so I can go to this sex club? How had Calantha even heard about it anyway? It could be a trap... some gross trick played by my aunt and uncle to remind me just how much they owned me.

It wasn't exactly logical, but I couldn't get my brain to shut off. Calantha must have noticed, since she leans over to grab my hand. "Whatever your brain is telling you right now, *stop listening*. Everything will be fine, Lily."

"I'll be locked away all night... What if you need me? If something happens to you and I wasn't there because of some stupid sex club, I'd never forgive myself."

Her only response is a scoff as we slip our sandals back on and head out to the car. Once inside, she turns to me with a serious expression lining her face. "I promise you, I'll stay inside all night. As much as I want to drop you off to make sure you don't bail," her eyes narrow, letting me know just how much she believes I might ditch it, "I'll stay home, watch a movie, and eat popcorn. Stop trying to find excuses, and remember how fucking hot you looked in that outfit."

I roll my eyes as she starts the car and pulls into traffic. She's right. Again. When the hell did my baby sister grow up into such a sensible person anyway? Though I was happy to see our past at the farm didn't chain her down. That's all I'd ever wanted, really. But now I had to face the fact that I wasn't alright. I'd never let myself move past it, and as scared as I was for tonight... I needed it too. Fuck, change was scary.

By the time we arrive home, I only have an hour until the doors lock. Just enough time for me to put on a bit of makeup—Calantha insists that I wear a darker shade of lipstick than I'd usually wear, yet I can't deny how good it looks—and before I know it, my cab is outside.

I take one final look in the mirror and place the strap of my handbag on my shoulder. The woman looking back at me is barely recognizable. My black hair hangs loosely around my shoulders, the soft strands shinier than I'd be able to do on my own. There's a glint in my eyes too, something that screams 'sexual goddess'. *As if!*

"They aren't going to know what hit 'em," Calantha says, hugging me at the door.

I ignore her comment—because what the hell would I even say to that? —and ask her a question instead. "You'll lock the door after I leave? And stay in all night?" Before she answers, the sound of corn popping in the microwave fills the space.

"Yes, yes, yes. Now get going. You're already cutting it way too close. Ah! Have so much fun!" She hugs me, placing a quick kiss on my cheek, and then shuts the door.

The lock clicks into place, and I hear a muffled "Go!", a clear indicator that she knows me way too damn well. I rush outside and into the waiting cab, giving them the address to Club Rapture with a shy smile.

Either they don't know what goes on there or they

don't care, because the ride is silent. My mind races with both scary and intriguing thoughts. This will either be the night of my life or a fucking disaster. As much as I fear the latter, I'm also hopeful that it'll be just what I need.

The cab pulls off the main road toward a large building with the number twenty-two printed on the side in gold lettering. The smooth, black concrete walls stand out from the nearby buildings but otherwise give nothing away about what goes on inside. We drive past the valet area and the cab stops. Pulling some cash from my wallet, I pay the driver and step out into the cool night air.

Can I truly do this? Once I step inside, there's no going back. Surprisingly, that doesn't terrify me as much as I thought it would.

I take a deep breath, steel my spine, and walk toward the gold-accented red doors. Two men stand on either side, and the one closest to me holds out his hand as I approach. *What the hell does he want? A handshake?*

"Your invitation," he says gently, causing my skin to redden with embarrassment, but I dig it out of my handbag and show it to him anyway. Without glancing at it too long, he turns to the tray I hadn't noticed beside him and picks up a light blue bracelet before handing it to me.

Once I've got it on my wrist, he opens the door and gestures for me to go inside. I stare at the ground for a moment, breathing in deeply to steady myself before tilting my head up and catching a glimpse inside Club Rapture for the first time. The lounge area is enormous, with dark, jewel-toned seating areas and a bar along the back wall.

A drink is exactly what I need. With furtive glances at the other guests, I notice several well-dressed servers walking around with tablets and speaking to each person. So preoccupied with trying to figure out what's going on, I almost crash into an emerald couch and fall flat on my ass. I straighten on wobbly legs and let out a shaky breath. Holy hell, am I ever grateful that the heels on these boots aren't any higher, or I'd really have made a fool of myself.

When I finally make it to the bar—after putting extra effort in to watch where the hell I was going—I'm hot and in desperate need of something to cool me down.

Before I get a chance to order, the clock on the wall catches my eye, and I watch as the hour hand ticks to ten o'clock. Time slows down like in the movies when it seems as if all other sounds fade away except for the loud tick as the hands move. The doors are officially locked.

Just then, a well-dressed man with dark hair strides to the center of the room. He's tall and trim, exuding a powerful dominance that has the crowd falling silent.

"Welcome to a night of sin and debauchery like you've never experienced. My name is Steffan Lykaios. For those of you who've been a member of my club and delved into our sins previously, this night will truly be different from anything you've partaken in before. For tonight, every single person here will immerse themselves in the darkest depths of their sinful nature and not surface until dawn." His piercing green eyes drift across the crowd, landing on me for a split second before moving along to the other guests. One of his arms sweeps open, and I notice a row of elevators that I hadn't seen before. "As the lights flicker to a new color, one that matches that of your bracelet, let your inhibitions fall away and step inside the waiting elevators, for it's time to embark on your journey of sin and corruption."

Sensations run through me, and I expect to panic like I usually do, but I don't. This place is nothing like the farm. I'm not crammed inside a small room, forced to please a stranger against my will. This is consensual, a choice, and that alone lifts a weight from my shoulders. *Breathe, Lily. This is a new beginning.*

Once Steffan leaves, the light changes to purple, and I exhale the breath I was holding, grateful not to be first.

A bartender approaches me with a glass of water already in hand. "Can I get you anything?" she asks, her smile soft.

I nod while swallowing a large mouthful, then order a Bellini. She mixes my drink in a flash, handing me the yummy cocktail before backing away and leaving me alone once more. I take a sip, delighted by the light peach flavor. Drinking isn't something I do often—alcohol and anxiety don't really mix—but the prosecco and peach puree are exactly what I need to loosen up my tight muscles. The effects from the massage I had earlier are long gone.

The lights shift to green, and four men make their way toward the elevators. Once again, I'm glad to find that my color hasn't been chosen. While I might feel confident in this outfit, it's not enough to overshadow my nerves, and I can't help but fear what's coming. Once I step beyond those elevator doors, who knows what awaits me? I never used to fear the unknown, but now it was like an icy hand squeezed around my heart.

I swivel on the velvet-topped barstool, noticing that some of the other guests are gone, and one of the servers from earlier is heading my way. He's handsome, in a sophisticated sort of way, with symmetrical features on a soft face. Not exactly my type but, until tonight, I never really considered what that was.

"Good evening, miss. Have you had the chance to sign our Consent to Participate form? We require each guest to do so before going to their designated floor." He smiles, his eyes dropping to my hand, which trembles slightly.

"Oh! I haven't, but I'd be happy to." He hands me the tablet and reminds me to read it through before signing at the end. Once I've handed it back to him, I place both my hands in my lap and take a deep breath.

"Thank you," he pauses to read my name off the form, "Liliana. If at any point you want to leave, just speak up, and we'll make arrangements for you. This is a safe space, I assure you. Keep an eye on the lights. Once it turns light blue, you can head to the elevator and scan your bracelet."

A grateful smile pulls at my lips, and my eyes burn. He leaves, and I turn back to my drink, wondering if my trauma was that easy for people to see or if he said that to every guest tonight. Either way, it settles my nerves enough that my hand stops trembling.

The lights have changed again, this time to red, and the room is even emptier than before. After another healthy swallow of the yummy peach drink, I realize my glass is empty. I'm tempted to order another drink, anything to help soothe the jittery fear running through my veins, but I need to keep my wits. My aunt had always administered a sedative before she'd let any of her foster kids meet with their guests. She promised it was for my protection, that it would make things easier for me if I closed myself off from what was happening, but that was a crock of shit. Nothing about being forced by my own damn family to please their disgusting guests was easy, and in truth, the sedative only made those nights worse.

Shaking off the dark thoughts which threaten to spiral, I notice the lights have turned light blue, and I'm the only one left. My heart hammers in my chest, thrashing like a wild animal caught in a cage, and when I turn to hop off the stool, it skips a beat. An incredibly gorgeous man steps into the bar, his dark hair tousled in a way that looks effortless, but I'd bet he spent time on. His gaze meets mine, and as the smile parts his lips, my thighs clench as if on their own.

That's when I realize where he's headed.

Straight toward me.

Chapter Three

Aiden

The woman assigned to Sloth is a goddess.

Her silken black hair begs me to wrap it around my fist while I fuck her mouth, but tonight isn't about me. It's about her.

Liliana Sinclair. My new assistant.

Once I found out she was the same woman who interviewed with Kaleb, I should have had the club pick someone else. It wasn't exactly ethical to spend an entire night pleasuring the woman who would have to forward my calls and schedule my meetings. At least, not when she was ignorant of it all.

But here we are. Ethics be damned. Kaleb had mentioned her beauty, yet underneath it all, he had sensed she'd been through more shit than the average person. Then we read the application that her sister had filled out.

It was the longest application the club had ever seen, with photos and anecdotes shared about the type of person Liliana was. Her sister hadn't exactly detailed the trauma, but she'd alluded to it enough that we got the gist.

They hadn't been safe, but Liliana made sure her sister never experienced the worst of it.

This was a woman who needed taking care of. And not because of any high maintenance, self-centered personality, but because of the opposite. Based on the application, Liliana was selfless. She grew up protecting and loving her sister for years after their parents died and would rather sacrifice her own happiness to ensure that of someone she cared about.

We were hooked from there. So hooked, in fact, that I broke protocol by coming to escort her myself.

Her eyes, shocked and wide open, lock on mine as I approach. My steps are slow despite the beast inside me begging to hurry, to throw her over my shoulder and bring her upstairs. That would only spook her, though. What she needs is to feel safe and secure. Only then will we make her feel bliss in a way she's never known.

"Liliana." I let the name fall from my lips on a sigh. Her throat bobs as she swallows, nodding in response and still unable to look away.

"Wow," she whispers back before stammering, "I mean, yes, that's me." Her cheeks turn pink with embarrassment, though I only find her slip-up cute. *Wow* is exactly my thoughts as well.

"Technically, I'm not supposed to escort you, but I hope you don't mind." I hold my hand out, and after hesitating for only a second, she places hers in mine. Electricity zips through my limbs, sparking my desire further. At her shocked gasp, I know she felt it too.

"Do you have a name?"

"I do. For tonight, though, you can call me Wes."

We move in silence toward the elevator. The main floor of the club is eerily empty now that the other guests have gone to their floors. It's strange being here instead of waiting upstairs, but with her, it feels right.

She fidgets beside me as we enter the elevator, her hazel eyes darting to mine before looking away almost sheepishly. It's fucking adorable. "You just need to scan your bracelet," I say in a hushed tone, afraid I might spook her. She stands slightly in front of me, enough that I can see the goosebumps rise on her neck. Her brows furrow slightly as she glances down at the bracelet on her slender arm.

"Like this." I let my hand trail down her arm before wrapping it around her forearm and stepping us toward the scanner. She inhales, holding her breath until the soft click signals our success and the doors close.

But we don't move. Our bodies are close, so fucking close that I can feel the shiver that races down her spine. The scent of cherry blossoms fills my senses until I almost lose myself entirely. It's all I can do to stop myself from running my nose up the soft column of her neck just to get more.

Finally, she exhales, and as much as I don't want to move further away from her... I have to. Otherwise, I might just ravage her in this elevator. I don't stop touching her though, letting my fingers dance along her arm while she struggles not to look at me.

She's nervous, but her pebbled nipples push against the silky fabric of her top, giving away her desire. Never have I reacted so quickly to someone. How the fuck will I handle her as my assistant?

"Is this your first time at Club Rapture?" I already know the answer, but I'm desperate to hear her delicate voice again.

"Yes. I'm a bit nervous." Her laugh comes out light and breathy, like she's embarrassed to admit it.

"I promise we'll take good care of you, Petal."

"W-we?"

The doors open to the seventh floor, and instead of answering her question, I step out and beckon her forward. "Welcome to a night of Indulgence and Sloth, Liliana. Come and claim your pleasure." Desire and lust drip from my voice like honey.

She bites her lip, inhaling deep, and steps into the large open room.

Kaleb and I have worked on several of the floors at Club Rapture, but the seventh is our favorite. Sloth is a floor designated for the giving of pleasure. Not that the others aren't, but here, we indulge in it. Guests typically aren't allowed to put any effort into pleasing us. Instead, the focus is purely on them. Tonight, that focus will be aimed directly at the shy being in front of me.

Liliana peers around the room, taking in the vast array of items that could be overwhelming to someone who isn't used to it. A massive four-poster king bed sits in the middle of the room, with built-in cuffs and bondage gear offering an array of different options. Along the far wall are several sex toys, fetish gear, and other paraphernalia sure to bring pleasure.

I lead Liliana to the sensual lounger in the corner, urging her to sit. She does so without question, seeming unable to protest as her brain tries to take in everything. I run my knuckles along her cheek, grabbing her chin lightly until she's forced to finally meet my gaze.

"Our only focus tonight is pleasing you. By the time this night ends, we'll have wrung every single orgasm from this luscious body. Do you trust me?"

Once again, her cheeks flush and my cock hardens further at the sight of her innocence. "You keep talking as if there's more people than just you and I here..." Her nervous laughter sends another shot of desire through me, and I can't fucking wait to turn it into gasps of pleasure.

I trail my fingers down her neck, dipping over the swell of her breasts. "You'll enjoy the extra hands, I promise. So will you trust me, Petal?"

Her eyes widen as it finally sinks in that she'll have more than just me to please her tonight. Despite her nervous behavior, her body betrays just how excited she is.

Finally, she nods.

"I need you to say the words, Lily-love."

"Yes. I'll trust you."

"Good." I walk over to the dresser along the wall and grab a blindfold from the top drawer. She hasn't stopped watching me, so I know she's seen what I have in my hand. Once again, her teeth pull against her lip and, fuck me, I want to taste it.

I kneel so that I'm eye level with this gorgeous creature and slide my hands up the outside of her thighs. She sucks in a breath, letting her lip free at last.

"Every time you bite that lip, I want to taste it myself."

She clenches her thighs together, and a smile spreads across my face.

"You can," she says breathlessly.

I lean ever-so-close, forcing her to part her thighs and let me between them while bringing my hands up her body until they rest against her cheeks. Her eyelids flutter, lips parting in a delicious invitation. The scent of her arousal floods my senses, causing my mouth to water. I'm desperate to have her explode on my tongue, to push her body higher and higher until she comes at my command, but it's too soon.

Instead of leaning in to kiss her, I place the blindfold over her eyes, then drag my thumb along her bottom lip. "I'll be tasting more than just your mouth tonight, Petal."

Chapter Four

Liliana

After Wes blindfolded me, he left me on the comfortable lounger while he stepped away to do *something*. I tried to figure out exactly what he was doing, but it was useless. Half the instruments I saw strung up on the wall were foreign to me, so there's no chance in hell I'd know what they sounded like anyway.

My mind races once more at his use of *we*. Just how many people were showing up here? Could I even handle that? Fear threatens to immobilize me, but I push it farther into the recesses of my mind.

This isn't the farm. I breathe in. *You are safe.* I breathe out. *You chose this.* I breathe in again, but this time, I hold it. When I finally let it out, my body relaxes and my mind is once more firmly under my control.

With my sight removed, my other senses run wild. The soft, cool leather of the lounger provides ample relief to my overheating flesh. There's a low hum in the room, reminding me of the whir from an air conditioner. My heart beats a staccato rhythm, creating my own personal soundtrack as I wait with bated breath. A shiver runs down my spine in both anticipation and chill. I trace my hands up and down the seat beneath me, concentrating on the grainy texture of the leather to distract me from the lustful nerves racing through me.

Footsteps approach, and I freeze. Squinting behind the blindfold, I try desperately to catch even a silhouette, yet all I see is inky darkness. Somehow I'm not scared. The Liliana of last week wouldn't have stepped foot in here without having a full-blown panic attack, yet even though I'm effectively trapped in here with a stranger—and possibly *strangers*—I feel at ease.

The lounger shifts seconds before hands gently graze my ankle, running up my boots until they meet the bare skin at my thigh. I gasp, jolts of electricity shooting straight to my clit at the feel of warm hands on my sensitive flesh.

"I'm going to undress you now, Petal."

"Okay," I breathe out as he pulls the zipper of my boot down slower than necessary. Every move he's made so far tonight has been unhurried and gentle, as if he's scared to spook me. Like he can see into the very depths of my soul and truly knows just how broken I am. Yet under his touch, I don't feel broken.

When my boots come off, he trails his fingers along my ankle and calf, and then up my thighs until he lifts me straight off the lounger.

"Oh!" I gasp, mentally off-balance, yet loving the feel of his solid body. Tentatively, I place my hands around his neck and push my fingers through his short, dark hair.

He releases a low growl of approval that seems to vibrate through my very soul.

Setting me down, he holds my hand to steady me before placing it on what must be the bed as he moves to unlace my top. The touch of his fingers through my hair as he moves it out of the way brings goosebumps to my flesh. He drops kisses along my shoulders and back, around to my collarbone as he finally removes my shirt. I almost shift to cover myself and, as if sensing that very thought, he says, "So beautiful."

He places his hands on my waist, unzipping my shorts. My heart hammers in my chest, blood boiling as I realize I'm more turned on than I've ever been before.

Ever so slowly, he pulls my shorts down. I don't move, can't move, until his hands touch the back of my knees. Placing my palms on his shoulders to steady myself, I step out of the shorts until all I'm left in is a lacy thong.

Time stands still, yet he doesn't rise. Instead, he stays on the floor in front of me with his fingers playfully caressing my legs. My nerves skyrocket once more. Maybe he doesn't find me attractive? God, wouldn't that be embarrassing...

"Fuck me," he groans, placing a kiss on each thigh. "You're so wet for me already, Petal."

My pussy clenches hard as the need in his voice urges mine on further. His hands roam around to my bare ass, squeezing the fleshy mounds, but another sensation distracts me. Cool air meets my panties, and I realize he's blowing softly. My nipples pebble painfully as I stand here, almost naked and on the verge of begging for more.

Then his mouth lands on me, placing a kiss over my panties as he inhales deep. A soft moan escapes me at the contact, causing him to chuckle against my soaked underwear.

He pulls away, slipping two fingers into the sides of my thong and pulling it off me. My thighs are wet, slick with my arousal, and it should embarrass me, but all I feel is need.

"On the bed for me, Petal. On your stomach."

Without hesitating, I move onto the silky sheets and lay down. Part of me had hoped that the blindfold would shift as I placed my head on the pillow, but I'm left in darkness.

"Do you still trust me?" Wes asks, his hand trailing over the globes of my ass.

"Yes," I whisper. Just then, a door opens from somewhere to my right, and I realize what I just agreed to.

Footsteps approach, accompanied by soft-spoken curses. "She's delectable." The new voice isn't as deep as Wes's, sounding more carefree but just as arousing. Seriously, Lily? You don't even know who he is or what he looks like, but you're attracted to his voice? Who the hell are you?

"My colleague, Fitz, and I will take excellent care of you tonight, Petal."

Suddenly, there's another set of hands on me, roaming over my back with what feels like warm oil. They sit on the bed on either side of me, each working an arm and a shoulder until they share my back. I lay there, completely at their mercy and surprised to find that I'm loving every minute of their attention. Long fingers trace the feather tattoo along my spine, sketching each intricate line with a tenderness I've never experienced before. My heart clenches deep inside my chest with the realization that these two complete strangers fill a hole inside of me that I never even knew existed.

Four hands massage my limbs, spreading the oil around and coating my entire backside with it. It's relaxing enough that I know if I wasn't so fucking turned on, I could probably fall asleep beneath their soft strokes.

That is, until they move to my thighs. Hands roam up my inner thighs as my core floods with the idea that they'll finally touch me, only for them to stop and head back down my legs. Again and again, they tease me until I'm practically panting.

I'm seconds away from mustering the nerve to ask for more when it happens. Fingers graze against my pussy, and I gasp. When they trail back down my leg, another set of fingers brush against my core instead.

With how wet I am, I know they must be coated with proof of how turned on I am. Hell, I've probably made a damn puddle on the sheets beneath me, but I'm too strung out to care. My only concern is getting off.

Both of their hands leave me at once, and I whimper.

Wes chuckles while Fitz says, "Such a greedy little thing."

Their hands return, shifting me until I'm flat on my back. I try to breathe normally but it comes out ragged, as if I've run a marathon instead of just laying here, kept on the brink of bliss.

More oil gets spread over my limbs, but they're careful not to touch the places that I want them to. They only tease, acting as if they'll touch my breasts only to shift at the last second and go around.

Desire turns into frustration until, finally, it happens all at once. Both Wes and Fitz glide a hand over my breasts, squeezing and tweaking my nipples at the same time. Their other hands move lower, down my stomach and thighs before they each pull a leg out toward them until I'm exposed. Each palm trails up the inside of my thigh while they continue to play with my nipples.

Inside, I'm screaming, begging them to let me fall off the edge they've kept me on for so long. As if hearing my thoughts, they don't stop. Sensations roll through me until I can't tell whose fingers are on my clit and whose are inside of me, but I don't even care.

I've been coiled so fucking tight for far too long, and now it crashes over me like a storm. I cry out, my chest arching off the bed as lights spark behind my eyes. On and on my orgasm flows, unending and ever growing.

As it fades, their hands slip from my body. My own lay limp by my side, and all I want to do is rip this goddamn blindfold off so I can see them. I want to touch them and return the favor.

Before I can panic that they've left me, the end of the bed dips as someone sits there and spreads my legs further apart. Something wraps around my ankles, a soft click echoing around me.

"What's that?" I ask, my throat dry.

"We're just keeping your legs out of the way, Petal,"

Wes says, gripping the back of my neck and lifting me up so that I can drink the water he's brought. It's cool on my tongue, soothing an ache I didn't realize I had.

After a few healthy swallows, he retreats once more.

My legs are spread wide, bound by the built-in shackles on the bed. Instead of inciting fear, it excites me. A feeling I never thought I'd experience around sex again.

And the night has just begun.

Chapter Five

Kaleb

How in the fuck am I supposed to work with this beauty on Monday morning now that I know just how sensitive her body is? It'll be torture. Though Aiden has it much worse. He might have given her a shortened version of his middle name, Wesley, but there was no way she wouldn't recognize him at the office. At least for me, it wasn't likely that she'd figure out the man named Fitz is only an abbreviation of my last name, Fitzgerald, without having seen my face. That's the hope anyway. The plan had always been to keep our identities hidden, but Aiden got a little too excited.

That was an issue for tomorrow. Today, my only focus was her.

Her small mews of pleasure are music to my ears, and I'm desperate to take off her blindfold. I wanted to watch her eyes light up while in the throes of bliss, but I also wanted her to see just how much I enjoyed bringing her there.

Aiden lay between her bound and spread legs, focusing on her pretty pussy with a look of hunger written on his face. She's been soaked for us all night; her tangy scent hanging in the air and making my mouth water. But I'd have my chance to taste her soon.

"I promised earlier that I'd get to taste you, Petal. Are you ready?"

"Yes," she whimpers, her hips rising slightly from the bed.

"Good girl."

Knowing Aiden, he has no intention of tasting her anytime soon. At least, not while she expects it. He'll toy with her until she's putty in his hands, and then he'll claim her orgasm. Probably multiple, if the past is any indication.

I shift off the bed and step toward the table along the back wall where I had lit a massage candle earlier. The lush scent of coconut permeates the air as I approach. Blowing out the flame, I pour a little of the oil onto my wrist, checking the temperature.

When I return, Aiden is kissing Liliana's thigh while stroking her pussy, actively avoiding her clit. Ever the tease.

"This is going to be warm, Liliana. Do you still trust us?" I ask.

Aiden chooses this moment to insert two fingers inside her, so her answering 'yes' comes out more of a moan.

I hold the jar over her body and let it drip over her breasts and down her stomach. She sucks in a breath, her hips bucking.

With my free hand, I massage the oil into her body

while Aiden continues pumping his fingers inside her. At my signal, he pulls out of her and spreads her pussy wide, blowing a puff of cold air. The sight of her squirming and wet for us nearly has me undone. I stare, trying to capture this perfect fucking image in my mind forever, and then I pour a small amount just above her clit.

"Oh fuck," she murmurs as Aiden spreads the oil around her hips and inner thighs before spreading some of the warm oil onto her clit with his fingers. She shudders, her hands fisting in the sheets at her side, and I can't help but smile.

Placing the melted candle on the bedside table, I climb back onto the bed and suck one hardened nipple into my mouth. Her body responds to the slightest touch, and I'm almost positive we could get her to come from nipple play alone.

Aiden and I make eye contact, nodding to one another as we prepare for our next move. He blows another shot of cold air on her clit, changing the temperature once more, while I place kisses up her neck and onto her cheek.

She turns her head toward me as if she's seeking exactly what I'm about to give her. Little puffs of air escape her parted lips as she grows ever closer to ecstasy once more. Then I move.

Unable to hold back even a second longer, I descend and place a scorching kiss on her lips at the same moment that Aiden stops blowing cold air on her clit and sucks it into his mouth. Her jaw falls open, giving me the perfect opportunity to change this chaste kiss into something more.

Our tongues twirl in a dance that almost seems choreographed, as if we'd been taking lessons on how to kiss each other our entire lives. She sucks on my tongue, causing my cock to grow harder in my slacks.

I tweak her nipple, rolling it between my fingers as Aiden flicks his tongue against her clit and suddenly, she's breaking. Falling apart into a million pleasure-filled pieces in front of us, and it feels like we're the only people who know how to put her back together.

Her legs shift, catching against the bonds as she tries to close her knees and stop Aiden's torturous assault on her clit, but he doesn't let up.

Breaking the kiss, I shift further down the bed. "I think you can give us one more, Blossom," I say as Aiden pulls one of his fingers from her to make room for two of mine. She's soaked, drenched through the sheets, and the sight of it almost makes me come in my pants.

He continues his onslaught on her clit while pumping his finger in and out of her. Instead of matching his rhythm, I hook my two fingers inside her, rubbing that sweet spot until her moans grow even louder. I suck her nipple into my mouth again, grazing my teeth against it while she thrashes beneath us until she lets out a scream and her cunt floods with another orgasm.

"That's our good girl."

Chapter Six

Liliana

Soft arms envelope me, stroking my hair as if I'm a prized childhood toy. *Where am I?*

Memories flash behind my eyelids, but in my groggy state I can't quite put them together. The hands are more masculine than Calantha's, so I know it's not her. But that must mean...

I jolt in bed, turning to see Wes's stormy gray eyes as he lies on the bed beside me with a smile on his face. Then I remember. The club... my screams... their hands all over my body. But I don't see Fitz anywhere. It's only Wes and I left.

"It's okay, Petal. You're safe. You had a much needed nap, and now I'd like you to have some water. How do you feel?"

I take the water from him, grateful for his offer as I swallow every drop of liquid in the glass. He watches me as I drink, his gaze darkening with each shift of my throat, and a blush creeps across my cheeks. "I'm a little sore. Is there a bathroom somewhere?"

He nods, motioning toward a door that's now ajar. "I've already got a bath started for you. Come."

We hop off the bed and head toward the bathroom, where the subtle scent of vanilla bean grows stronger. Inside, there's a large soaker tub filled with steamy water and bubbles with a wooden tray resting across it. There's another glass of water on top, along with some grapes, cheese, and little chocolates.

"Do we still have time?" As much as I want to enjoy the tub, there's a part of me that doesn't want to waste even a moment on trivial things like eating. My body might be sore but it craves their touch, and after tonight... everything will go back to normal.

He steps forward, pressing me against the counter as he trails his nose up the column of my neck before biting my earlobe. I release a shuddering breath, my stomach fluttering as arousal flows through me.

"We're nowhere near done with you." Wes pulls back, holding my face almost reverently, and his eyes drop to my mouth where I *may* have been biting my lip. Heat builds between us as the seconds tick by, and then his lips are on mine in a kiss that engulfs my entire body in flames.

This kiss is different from the one I shared with Fitz but no less potent. All I want is for him to fuck me against this counter, for Fitz to come back and join him until all three of our souls blend into one.

But he pulls away.

"Enjoy your bath, Petal. And make sure you have at least a few bites of food. You'll need your energy for what we have planned next." He places one last kiss on my lips and then exits the room.

I release the shuddering breath I didn't know I was holding and quickly empty my bladder before stepping into the soaker tub. I found a scrunchy on the counter and put my hair up so it wouldn't get wet. Was it these men who were thoughtful or is it just club protocol? I quickly shake that thought away and pop a grape into my mouth instead. My teeth tear through the skin of the grape, filling my mouth with cold, flavorful juice, and I relax into the tub as I toss another sphere into my mouth.

My body aches deliciously, and as I think about their plans for me, I can't help the excited chill that goes through me.

After a few more grapes and a piece of cheese, I place a thin piece of milk chocolate on my tongue and let it melt. I'm not hungry for food. I'm hungry for them.

***

Wes knocks quietly before stepping through the door. Our gazes lock, sparking a heat far hotter than the bath I sit in. He grabs a towel, walking toward me with confident, determined strides.

I stand, exiting the bath and letting him dry me off. It's far more sensual than I could have anticipated. Even something as mundane as this has my core tightening and my pussy on high alert. She was far greedier than I'd ever expected, and I wonder if it would have been like this with anyone else.

Without a word, he leads me out of the bathroom and back into the main room, which has shifted. It isn't a big change, but there's now a large wooden cross in the corner where there hadn't been before. He pulls a blindfold from his pocket as we stand in front of the cross, and I notice the massive bulge in his pants. My mind spins with the knowledge that it isn't only me who feels this way. He wants me too.

After placing the blindfold over my eyes, a door opens on the other side of the room and someone enters. Wes doesn't seem to care as he latches a pair of cuffs around each wrist before bending low to do the same with my legs. I wait for fear to strike as I stand here, exposed and vulnerable but it never comes. My lust for these two strangers overrides all logical thought.

The air moves around me, signaling another presence. Somehow, my body knows that it's Fitz and responds without conscious thought, my neck extending toward him. He claims my lips, pressing his body flush against mine until I feel the hard wood of the cross behind me, chafing against my naked skin.

God, I want to touch him. To wrap my legs around him and feel his hardness against my flesh, but I'm trapped and at their mercy.

"You look ravishing, Blossom," Fitz says after pulling away. He kneels low, sucking each nipple into his mouth before licking the seam of my pussy. I push my hips out, to beg him without words not to stop, but he only chuckles.

Another pair of hands join in, trailing softly over my

breasts and teasing my nipples. It's torture and rhapsody all at once, but I don't want them to stop.

"Your nipples are so responsive, Petal. How about we test just how far we can push you?"

Questions pass through my mind but fly out the window as both Fitz and Wes lavish attention on my nipples, sucking and massaging them until I'm out of my mind with the sensation.

"Take a deep breath," Fitz says, and I follow his instruction. An odd sensation, like silicone instead of fingers, pinches against my hard nipples when Wes adds, "Now exhale."

I do as I'm told, trying to figure out what they've put on me. "What are these?" I ask, shifting slightly and causing whatever hung from my nipples to dance with my movement. A soft tinkling sound accommodates the exquisite sensations, driving me wild.

"Nipple clamps," Wes says, running his finger over the tip of one of my nipples.

"Is it enough pressure, Blossom, or can you handle a bit more?" Fitz's voice is seductive, filled with challenge, and I consider his question before responding.

"A little more, I think." Heat rises to my face, and I hope the blindfold hides my blush. They tighten both clamps slightly, and I release a soft moan.

"If it ever gets to be too much, we can remove them."

Then, as if working in sync with each other, they remove their hands. Once again, I wish I didn't have to wear this stupid blindfold. I wish I could see what they were doing so at least I could know what's coming. I listen to their footsteps, the rustling of toys along the back wall, and their whispered words.

"She's so fucking gorgeous."

"Do you think she's ready for our cocks?"

I whimper. Fucking hell, am I ever ready. Images flood my mind of all the different ways they could share me. Could I take two cocks at once? The thought alone causes my core to ripple and my thighs to get slick with my arousal.

Shit, what are they doing to me?

A low hum starts, and I jerk my head around as if I can find the source. I no longer hear their voices or the shuffling of feet, only the subtle hum and my frantic breathing.

There's a light tug on the clamps, causing me to cry out at the same moment a finger trails along my center. Then something soft and smooth replaces the finger, and I realize where the hum was coming from.

A vibrator set on low presses through my wetness, rising closer to my clit but never settling long enough to throw me over the edge. I shift, trying to hold it more firmly against my clit, but it's always moving, dancing, roaming everywhere but the place I crave it the most. At such a low vibration, I need the pressure. I need more.

"Please," I beg, my inner walls contracting with the need to come as frustration mounts inside me. "More, I need more."

"You're insatiable, Blossom. But we aim to please." Fitz's voice is so close that I can feel his hot breath against my neck. I don't know whether he's controlling the vibrator or Wes, but whoever it is finally rests it on my clit. I cry out, realizing they've upped the vibrations, and it's all too much. Sensation floods me, causing my body to jerk against my bonds as I teeter on the edge of insanity.

Then I feel it. One man stands on either side of me, grazing their teeth along my neck while gently flicking the clamps on my nipples, and I shatter.

My pussy clenches, empty and needing to be filled as I realize this isn't enough. I want them, need them to finally claim the part of me I've not allowed anyone else to have since the farm.

"Fuck me," I pant, my tone desperate. "Please, I—"

"As you wish, Petal."

Chapter Seven

Liliana

They've freed my arms and legs but haven't removed the clamps from my aching nipples. My legs wobble in the aftermath of my orgasm, and my clit throbs, little jolts of electricity flying through me as I'm led to the bed.

"On your knees. Yes, just like that." Wes's praise slips over me like a balm, and I eagerly follow his instructions as the bed dips around me.

Hands roam my body, and I can't tell where Fitz or Wes are until someone's bare flesh presses against my back and there's an unmistakable hardness between my thighs.

"Oh God," I pant, unsure if he'll fit inside of me but so desperate to try. Then, before I can worry too much, someone kisses me, and I forget about my fears.

"This is going to be cold," Fitz says from behind me, and my brows draw together in confusion. What the hell is he talking about?

Then I feel it. Something cold and wet slides down the crack of my ass. No one has been there before, and if I had any reservations about how he'd fit inside my pussy, he definitely won't fit *there*.

As if sensing my worry, Wes soothes me while Fitz spreads the liquid around my puckered hole.

"It's only a small plug, Petal. For beginners. You're not ready for our cocks there yet." He places small kisses across my cheeks, my forehead, and my nose before settling on my mouth again. But I can't focus on his kiss while Fitz's fingers toy with my ass.

Wes flicks one clamp, then the other, until I cry out. At the same time, Fitz pushes the plug past the ring of muscles until it's fully seated inside me. I don't move as my body struggles to accommodate the foreign object. It's not an uncomfortable sensation, only a new one. And with everything else I'm feeling right now, I know it won't be long before I'm thrown headfirst into another orgasm.

"Good girl. You're perfect. Are you ready for my cock, Blossom?" Fitz asks as Wes pushes two fingers inside my already-soaked pussy.

I open my mouth but no sound comes out, so I nod vigorously while Wes says, "Oh, she's more than ready." He removes his fingers, rubbing them against my clit while Fitz lines up with my entrance from behind. I grip Wes's shoulders to steady myself as Fitz teases me with his cock, circling my entrance until he finally pushes in barely an inch and stops.

"Fucking hell. The way this tight little cunt strangles my cock," Fitz groans.

I push my hips back, trying to take more of him, but he only laughs and thwarts my attempt. With Wes still stroking my clit, I'm close, so fucking close, but something's missing. I know exactly what it is, but they seem reluctant to give it to me.

"Come for us, pretty girl," Fitz commands as he plunges to the hilt inside of me, and the added plug inside my ass has me feeling fuller than I've ever experienced. My inner walls contract, pulsing around his hardness while I teeter on the precipice of release.

Wes suddenly removes the nipple clamps and I enter sensation overload as blood rushes to the tender peaks and Fitz thrusts long and deep. I tumble, somersaulting through a seemingly endless orgasm as Wes licks and sucks on my nipples while Fitz fucks me from behind.

When I think I'm finally coming down from my high, Fitz shifts the plug in my ass, pressing against it to make shallow pumps, and I'm once again thrown into euphoria.

He groans behind me, shuddering as he comes, joining me in internal serenity. But I'm not offered any peace yet. Fitz pulls out, trading places with Wes, then kisses me deeply. I sink into him, unable to hold myself up any longer.

Wes gently removes the plug and then pushes his cock through my slickness, coating it with our combined releases.

"You look so good with my cum dripping from that perfect pussy," Fitz says after ending the kiss. Wes holds me up while Fitz shifts on the bed until his face nestles between my legs.

"Move forward, Petal. You're going to ride his face while I take you." My insides contract at his dirty words, but I follow the orders willingly. I should be exhausted and in pain, but all I want is more. I want to claim every piece of them, just as surely as they've claimed every piece of me.

Wes pulls away, pressing a finger inside me before pulling it out and bringing it to my mouth.

"Taste what you do to us." I open my lips without question, swirling my tongue around the salty taste of our mixed pleasure. He tries to remove his finger but I stop him by sucking gently, and he growls behind me.

"Brace yourself on the bed. That's perfect, just like that," Fitz commands, his mouth inches from my core. Every order they make of me, I follow without question. Dick-whipped. I think that's the word for it.

Is it even possible for me to come again? Surely there's a limit, there has to be. Yet I'm not ready to stop. I'm more than willing to test my limits with these two.

"Feel just how much we want you." Wes presses his tip to my opening, and holy shit. His cock feels thicker than Fitz', like he might actually split me in two. Part of my brain screams that it would be a good way to die, speared by these two men into oblivion. But the other part knows I'm not ready. Not when I've only now realized just how good this can be.

"I don't think it'll fit," I pant, my limbs shaking as Wes pushes his monster cock in further.

"We'll make it fit, baby. This pretty pussy is about to be stretched out and filled with my cum. Relax and focus on Fitz."

Fitz, who had been planting soft kisses along my thighs, switches direction and heads toward my swollen nub. He's gentle, lapping against me softly, like he knows just how tender I am. I feel like a prized possession as he treats me like a queen, and the moment I relax, Wes sinks deeper.

"So tight," he groans, grabbing hold of my hips and shifting further. My walls spasm around him, and he shudders. "Choke my cock with your cunt, Petal. Just like that."

He thrusts faster at the same moment that Fitz puts more pressure on my clit. His fingers spread me wide, and I can't do anything but take every ounce of pleasure they offer me. Tension coils tightly inside me, almost painfully, but it only urges me higher.

Wes pulls me up, curling his hand around my throat as he whispers, "Who owns this pussy?"

"You," I whimper as his thrusts turn savage, and I swear I can hear angels sing.

"And Fitz?"

"Yes. Both." I can barely speak, barely breathe as my pleasure mounts to uncontrollable heights.

"That's right, Petal. We do. Now come for us one more time. Show us how well we own you."

Fitz sucks on my clit, his fingers moving toward my cunt where Wes' cock fills me entirely, and as his finger presses against my opening, I shatter.

I am nothing, no longer a person at all and instead, only pure feeling. Tears stream down my cheeks as my bliss ebbs and flows like the ocean, rising higher and higher like a tidal wave before crashing me against the shore.

In that moment, life and death merge into one, and I wonder if maybe I have died. Maybe this is what heaven feels like, cherished and loved beyond anything I could have ever dreamed.

Chapter Eight

Liliana

Sounds filter in through my mind, but nothing seems real.

Someone places a warm, wet cloth against my skin, and beside me, water drips into a bucket as someone rinses another cloth.

Club Rapture.

I open my eyes only to find that the blindfold still hinders my view.

"Not yet, Blossom," Fitz says, grabbing hold of my wrist to stop me from removing it. "You've been through a lot. Just relax, and let us take care of you." He kisses my knuckles and continues to clean me.

"You were so good tonight. So, so good." Wes brushes the hair from my face as he trails the cloth over my neck and up to my cheeks. Likely wiping away my tears from earlier.

"Thank you. Both of you," I whisper, my lip wobbling.

Tonight was a revelation. Before coming here, I had only been an empty shell of a person, content to live out my days in complete and utter safety. But now, I see that I wasn't living at all. My heart might have been beating, pumping blood to my organs, but that was the extent of my life.

I don't want to go on that way. I want more of this feeling. Of pleasure, yes, but I want to return it. To find someone who makes me feel the way Wes and Fitz did and to lavish them with just as much attention as they did me.

"It was our absolute pleasure. Now rest, Liliana. Enjoy our last few moments together."

Calantha was right. It's okay to be selfish sometimes. It doesn't mean that I'm a bad person or that I can't set boundaries, but I don't always have to put others first. And I can finally understand that the only one who will ever put me first is me.

I walked into Club Rapture as a scared, terrified woman stuck in her past, but I'd be walking out as someone else. Someone strong and sure of herself.

A brand-new Liliana Sinclair.

"Do I smell crepes?"

Calantha stumbles into the kitchen, rubbing the sleep from her eyes while I pour her a hot cup of coffee. Her shirt says, 'If you love me, let me sleep' and I know for a fact that's exactly how she really feels. Before our parents died, we always had matching pjs. Our parents usually chose ones with cute flowers and garden puns on it – if their daughters' combined nickname of Calla Lily didn't give away their love of plants, our clothes would. Now that we were older, we still bought matching sets whenever we could and dubbed Sunday afternoons as Sister Sunday. We'd throw on our most ridiculous pair of pjs, slap on a face mask, and watch a romantic comedy.

I have a feeling today might be a little different.

"Grab a seat, Calla. Breakfast is almost ready."

She takes the coffee from the counter before heading toward the small table on the opposite wall. It's more of a breakfast nook than a dining room, but it serves us just fine. On the table is a plate of crispy bacon, fruit, syrup, and a can of whipped cream. Since we both can't function without coffee, I didn't bother pouring any orange juice, though I had heavily considered making mimosas to celebrate my new outlook on life.

Once the last crepe is done, I add it to the pile I'd kept warm in the oven, grab the scrambled eggs, and bring everything to the table.

"Someone's in a good mood," Calla says, waggling her eyebrows.

Despite it coming from my sister, a blush still rises beneath my skin. Hell yes I was in a good mood. How could I not be?

"Calla... I..." Tears build behind my eyes and I try to shove them back. I told myself I wouldn't cry, yet here I am, blubbering like a fool. After taking a deep breath, I try again. "Thank you for last night. I don't know how I'll ever repay you."

She grabs my hand, squeezing slightly. "Oh shush,

Lil. All I want is for you to be happy. Whatever I can do to help, you know I'll do it."

I nod, swallowing the lump in my throat and focusing on the food in front of me. How goddamn lucky was I to have someone like Calantha on my side? Honestly, I felt bad for anyone who grew up as a single child. There's nothing quite like the bond of a sibling, even if she used to annoy the hell out of me when we were kids.

The farm might have fucked us up in more ways than one, but at least it brought us closer. Our bond was that much stronger, and as long as we had that, nothing could hurt us.

"Okay, spill," Calantha says, placing her fork and knife down on her empty plate.

I grin behind my coffee mug, taking a long, slow sip just to annoy her.

She tosses a blueberry at me. "You're the worst, Lil."

I pick up the yummy fruit and pop it in my mouth before standing to clear the table. "It was surreal, actually. Like if my body didn't ache right now, I might not believe that it really happened."

"Gah! I'm so jealous." Calantha pouts, putting the leftover fruit back in the fridge. "Was he cute? Or was it a she? You've got to give me more, Lily. Come on!"

I bite my lip, remembering Wes's handsome face and wishing I knew what Fitz looked like. Something told me he was a little less reserved than Wes, more carefree, so maybe his looks encompassed that.

"Well, actually..." I peek over my shoulder, catching my sister's eyes before turning back toward the sink.

"There were two of them. Both guys. Though I only saw one of their faces."

Our apartment falls into complete silence. I turn to find Calantha staring at me, her eyes filled with suspicion. Without adding more to the conversation, I continue rinsing the plates and adding them to the dishwasher while she stands there unmoving.

Finally, she says, "Oh my God. You're not joking, are you?"

"Not even a little."

"Who are you, and what have you done with my sister?" she teases, grabbing a dish towel and snapping it at my leg. "No wonder you ache after spending the entire night with *two* men!"

"It still hasn't really sunk in. But I also feel different somehow, like now I know it can be good and not so bad that I need a sedative." I laugh, even though the joke isn't funny.

Calantha steps forward and pulls me into a tight hug. "Our uncle and his gross friends can't touch you anymore. Never again, Lily."

We pull apart, and I catch an odd look on my sister's face. "What is it?"

"It can wait. I don't want to kill whatever buzz your body must be on after all those hot orgasms." She laughs, but it comes out forced.

"Well, now you have to tell me, otherwise you know I'll overthink and end up at the worst plausible scenario." We are polar opposites in that regard. Where Calantha can compartmentalize her thoughts and worries, all of mine stand at the forefront of my mind, screaming and compounding on each other until I'm on a first-class trip to anxiety station.

"Fine. I heard from Detective Briggs yesterday. You can guess what he said, since it's been the same every single time we've made an anonymous tip. Apparently they looked into our accusations on the farm but couldn't find anything incriminating."

As shitty as it is to hear, I'm not exactly surprised. We'd tried to shed light on what was happening at the farm at least twice in the years since we escaped, and each time, we'd been shut down. I knew my uncle worked with some pretty important people, but I never would have guessed he'd have law enforcement in his pocket too.

"We might need to find another tactic, since clearly he's got friends in high places. Thanks for telling me. I'd love to expose him, but at this rate, I'm worried he'll figure out who the anonymous tips are coming from, and that's the last damn thing we need."

"You're right. We've got enough to focus on now, anyway. Between your new job and my upcoming final exams, we'll barely have enough time to search for those two hunks you spent the night with." Calantha slaps my ass on her way by and rushes out in a fit of giggles.

Try to find Wes and Fitz? I couldn't. There had to be some rule to protect the club and its staff. I might not have been a stalker, but I wouldn't doubt there were people who would go searching with bad intentions.

Would I even know what to do if I ever saw them

again? Probably not. Half the reason I did okay at the club was because I knew it was a one night thing. No expectations. No judgment. And no pressure.

No. I couldn't think about that. Regardless of the aches in my body serving as a constant reminder of the incredible, passion-filled night I just had, I had to focus on making a good impression at my new job tomorrow.

My newly awakened libido could wait.

Chapter Nine

Kaleb

The events of Saturday night are ingrained in my mind, playing on repeat ever since we left the club.

Liliana Sinclair was more than we could have expected, and despite the sexual nature of our interactions that night, I was wholly convinced she's exactly what we need at our company.

Smart and determined, with a shyness that only added to her charm. I couldn't wait to be near her again, to get to know her with her clothes on and find out more about her.

She was an enigma wrapped up in a cloud of doubt, and all I wanted to do was clear it for her. I wanted her to see what I could already tell was behind that fear and doubt; a confident, capable woman.

It was insane to think I knew someone so well after such little time spent together, even more so when the majority of that time had been without words, but the connection I felt to her was deeper than I'd felt with anyone else in years.

Whatever terrible thing happened in her past, those demons had a firm grip on her, but after being with us, I caught a glimpse of who she is without them. Aiden and I got past her defenses and watched her blossom into one incredible fucking creature.

I just hope to fuck today goes smoothly. When she realizes that Aiden and Wes are the same person, how will she react? Will she somehow put the pieces together and figure out that I was Fitz? Fuck. There were too many unanswered questions and variables for my liking. I wanted to punch Aiden for risking everything by going off script and putting us in this position.

With only ten minutes before she's set to arrive, I try to focus on my emails instead of the million questions flying through my mind. If all I focused on was the bad shit, surely it would find me. There was no point worrying about things beyond my control anyway, or at least that's what I try to tell myself.

The phone on my desk rings the usual tone for reception, and as I answer, my heart rate picks up.

"Yes?"

"Mr. Fitzgerald, you have a visitor in the lobby. Shall I send her up?"

"Sure. Thanks, Pam."

Heading toward the elevators, I straighten my tie and wait for what feels like an entire hour before the elevator finally reaches the twenty-fifth floor. The doors open, and out walks the stunning woman from Saturday night, except this time, she's wearing a matching skirt and blazer combo that drives me fucking wild. Shit, shit, shit. My dick grows hard in my slacks, and that's the last goddamn thing I need right now. *Come on, Kaleb. Get it together!*

"Ah, Liliana. So great to see you again."

"Likewise, Mr. Fitzgerald." The smile she gives me sends my heart into overdrive. Fuck. I wonder what this moment would have been like if Aiden and I hadn't spent the night ravishing her curvaceous body.

"Please, call me Kaleb. As it's your first day, we'll start off slow. I'll give you a quick tour of this floor so you know where the kitchen and bathrooms are, then there's, unfortunately, a slew of paperwork from Human Resources that you'll have to go through. We'll do a full tour later this afternoon, and Aiden should be back by then as well. Sound good?"

"Sounds perfect."

We walk past several offices, and I give a brief overview of the floor as we go. "This floor is mostly for high-level executives and directors. On the lower floors is where you'll find HR, Accounting, IT, and our other departments. You'll get to meet everyone later this week, but hopefully you'll feel right at home."

She nods but doesn't look at me, too busy scanning the offices we pass and making note of who sits where.

"Here's the kitchen where you can keep your lunch. There are tables set up along the windows if you don't want to eat at your desk and a coffee machine over there." I lean in close and lower my voice conspiratorially. "We've got an espresso machine near our offices though, which makes significantly better coffee. You're welcome to use that one as often as you'd like."

She places her hand on her chest, feigning a swoon. "You had me at 'espresso'."

I chuckle, leading us away from the kitchens, down the hall, and past the bathrooms before entering the area where Aiden and I do most of our work when we're in the office.

"This is your desk. Aiden and I share this office, though we end up traveling quite a bit. As I mentioned in the interview, sometimes you may need to travel with us, but all company travel is fully paid for, and we'll do our best to provide you with plenty of notice."

She places her bag on the floor and runs her hands along the desk, beaming. "Wow, I'm in awe of your building." Her eyes glance behind her desk to the espresso machine, and I lead her over.

"Have you ever used one?"

"My last job only had a machine with the pods, so I'm way out of my league here." A beautiful rosy blush spreads across her face, reminding me of just how shy she was on Saturday night, even after she opened up to us.

"Well, luckily for you, I haven't had a coffee yet this morning. I'll walk you through it while I make mine, and then you can make one for yourself while I shadow. Are you in?" *Okay, so I absolutely already had a coffee this morning, but nothing would stop me from staying with her a bit longer.*

"Deal! Let the training begin."

I go through the motions, slowing down the steps and explaining how everything works while Liliana watches on with a clinical gaze. After I finish, I show her how to froth the milk and then clean the machine for the next person to use it. "Since Aiden and I travel so often, we usually only keep a small carton of milk in here so it doesn't go bad, but as you'll be here daily, you can order whatever you need. If you're feeling extra fancy or creative, there's also a shaker of chocolate powder to decorate the top with as well." I lower my voice again, "Honestly, it's the best part, even if my designs always look like shit."

Her laugh is contagious, brightening my day infinitesimally until I can't imagine having another shitty day as long as she's around. Without hesitating, she grabs a mug and gets to work, making herself a cappuccino like a pro.

"Damn. Do you learn everything else this fast or just food-related things?"

She chuckles, shaking her head before grabbing the chocolate powder. "Since you're my boss, I should probably tell you how quick and perfect I am. But you'll see for yourself in a minute just how much of a lie that would be."

Fuck me, this woman is a breath of fresh air. For whatever reason, she doesn't appear intimidated by me, and I can't even begin to explain just how refreshing that is. Yet I wonder how much that would change if she knew who I was.

As she finishes with the chocolate and steps back, I

have to stop myself from snorting. Whatever design she was trying to make definitely fell short of hitting the target. Unless she *had* been attempting to create a vagina, in which case, she knocked it out of the park, but something told me that isn't her style.

"Oh God," she whispers, digging through the cabinets until she finds a stir stick. Quickly she swirls the coffee around, destroying the beautiful piece of art she'd worked so hard on.

"If I were nice, I'd pretend I didn't see that, but since we're being honest here... what exactly *were* you trying to make?"

She throws the stick in the garbage and covers her face with her hands before mumbling something I can't understand.

"What?"

"I was trying to make a flower, but I definitely won't be making that shape at work again."

Despite her embarrassment being utterly adorable, it pains me to see her so uncomfortable. "Well, I thought it was perfect. But it probably wouldn't hurt to save that particular design for Saturday mornings at home." She chokes on her coffee, and I let the grin grow wider on my face. "I've got a call in five minutes, so I'll let you get settled. Your temporary login is in this folder, along with a list of the internal procedures and training HR needs you to complete. Email me if you need anything, otherwise I'll see you in a bit."

"Thanks for the coffee lesson, Kaleb."

"It was my pleasure."

I walk into my office and close the door behind me, realizing this might just be the first time I've wanted to say screw work and continue talking with the beautiful woman just beyond the door.

What the hell is she doing to me?

Chapter Ten

Aiden

Usually I hate Mondays. As much as I enjoy working, I still think the weekends are far too short, and Mondays alway suck. But not today.

Today could either go really well or really fucking shitty. Part of me was excited to find out which, even if I dreaded the answer. If she quit because of me, because of what happened at Club Rapture, Kaleb would be pissed. Hell, I'd be pissed at myself. Our plan had never been to reveal ourselves, but I'd let my desire get the best of me, and now we both had to deal with the consequences.

I'd worked from home this morning for as long as I could, hoping that she'd fall in love with the place and not care who I was, but I couldn't wait any longer. I had to see her. It was time to find out once and for all how she'd react.

Kaleb told me he hadn't been able to give her a proper tour of our building, and while it may not have been the best decision, I wanted to be the one to show her around. Call me cruel, but this way she wouldn't have a choice but to be in my company. She didn't strike me as the type to make a scene either, especially if we were around unfamiliar coworkers. But I needed enough time to show her that what happened at the club didn't change anything with her position here.

As much as I daydreamed about Kaleb and me fucking her raw in our office, I wouldn't act on it. Not unless it was what she wanted. Though that didn't mean I wouldn't try to make her want it if she stayed around.

I walk down the hall on silent steps, careful not to be seen unless I want to be. All I could spot of our new assistant was the back of her head while she scrolled through a training document on her computer, completely oblivious to the predator stalking nearby.

She faced the glass wall of our office, where I could see Kaleb talking on the phone. We'd been trying to wine and dine a new client who was proving to be rather hard to nail down. One highly intelligent scientist who insisted they had the cure for some pretty deadly diseases but was trying their best to avoid us. Either they were all talk or we were up against other wealthy companies who wanted to get their hands in the pot too. You'd be surprised how many people tried to profit off of someone else's misfortune. It's one of the reasons we started this company in the first place. Our own personal 'fuck you' to the assholes who wanted to make a quick buck off someone else's health problems.

Kaleb looks up and nods at me, a devious smile spreading across his face before he says something to the person on the phone and hangs up. Of fucking course he'd want to witness this. Despite the smile on his face though, I can tell he's just as nervous as I am to find out how this will go.

"Ah, you must be Liliana." Regardless of the very unprofessional images running through my mind, I keep my tone authoritative, like I would when talking to any other employee.

The beautiful smile that lit her face just a moment ago vanishes when she turns to look at me. She immediately darts her eyes over to Kaleb, who thankfully isn't glancing our way, before moving them back to me.

Her mouth opens and closes several times, but words never escape as she stares at me, completely horrified.

Extending my hand toward her, I keep my smile bright and cheery. "I'm Aiden Daniels, co-owner of Exalta Solutions. Sorry I couldn't join Kaleb in your interview, but I must say, your resume was exceptional. I'm excited to see you in action."

"O-oh, Mr. Daniels. It's nice to meet you," she finally squeaks out. Her cheeks turn a stunning shade of red, and as she bites her lip, all I want to do is take it into my mouth, just like I did at the club.

I don't, of course. Even though it causes me physical pain, I keep things professional.

Kaleb comes out of the office then, pretending to be oblivious to the very noticeable discomfort on Liliana's face. "Good! You've both met."

"Only now. For the first time," she replies, and it takes every ounce of willpower not to burst out laughing. But it gives me another clue as to what this woman is like. Clearly, she's a terrible liar.

Kaleb gives her a quizzical glance but continues. "Admittedly, Aiden is stricter than I am, so it's completely understandable if you think I'm the best." The smile he graces her with is pure charm, and her discomfort eases a little.

Fucker.

"I'm about to head into another meeting. Were you able to procure that contract?" He directs his last question to me, and I nod.

"Just arrived this morning. I've emailed it to you. Don't let them give you any shit, yeah?"

He laughs and turns back toward his office. "Enjoy the tour, Lily."

A moment of silence passes after Kaleb leaves and her unease returns.

"Are you ready?"

Chapter Eleven

Liliana

He can't be serious right now. My new boss, who also happens to be one of the men who tilted my entire world on its axis mere days ago, wants to take me on a tour of his building. Alone. Could things get any more awkward?

Shit. Okay, I guess they could. At least Kaleb wasn't tagging along, or Sharon, the nice woman from HR. They'd have to be blind and deaf not to notice how unbelievably flustered I am. Thank God I only had a light lunch.

"Oh, you don't have to take me on a tour. I'm sure you're very busy." I try to smile, though I'm sure it appears more like a grimace.

"I am, but this is part of my job. Come on, let's get started."

Maybe I could fake being sick? Pull the fire alarm? Trip and fall down a flight of stairs even. Anything to get me out of spending time alone with this man. Did he even remember, or was I already a distant memory?

After another moment of silence hoping he'd drop it

and leave, he still stands there with a smile on his face as if he didn't fuck me senseless two days ago. The more I watch him, the more I think that maybe he does remember. Maybe the memories flashing through my mind are similar to the ones going through his, and that's why he wants to take me on this tour.

Embarrassment hits me like a bat, scorching my face further as his smile grows. Fuck. I'm so not prepared for this. Calantha is going to have a field day when I get home.

"If you're sure," I say finally, standing and smoothing down my unwrinkled clothes for something to do.

"Perfect. Very practical not to wear heels, Liliana. We'll take the stairs down to each floor instead of the elevator. That way we have more time to discuss any questions you might have."

My office phone rings as we walk down the hall, and I almost run back to answer it — though not quite running and screaming like I envision in my head. Aiden, or as I'll call him to his face, Mr. Daniels, sees the temptation in my eyes though and reassures me that the call can go to voicemail.

He introduces me to the other staff on our level before we start our descent. We make our way through each floor, starting with HR, then onto accounting and IT, until I'm trying so hard to remember the names of everyone I've just met that I don't have a second to think about who Aiden is.

Well, shit. At least I hadn't thought about it until now.

He hasn't made a move to touch me or bring up Club Rapture, so that's something at least. Despite the many distractions, I can't help but notice how my body buzzes beneath his gaze. My pussy practically chomps at the bit to get another night with his talented fingers and tongue.

"We're going to skip the rest and head straight to the main floor. The ones we're skipping are our medical labs or treatment facilities. If you'd like to visit them in the future, we can arrange it."

"I would, actually, thank you."

Our steps echo throughout the stairwell as we head toward our destination. The silence breaks as we enter the lobby, and the sound of ringing phones and answering receptionists fills the space.

When I showed up here this morning, I thought this floor was strictly a lobby with maybe a warehouse or loading dock behind it. Aiden takes me towards a set of doors past the reception desk and scans his key card.

He catches me eying his card. "There should be one of these on your desk when we get back. You'll need it to enter each floor, though you won't have access to all, as a precaution."

Before I can respond, we walk through another set of doors and into a wall of warm, humid air. There's a fucking pool on the premises.

"No way," I whisper, in awe of the massive pool. I step closer to read the measurements written on the side. With a shallow end of four feet and a deep end of ten feet, this pool is perfect. There are two individual lanes sectioned off for swimming laps, but the rest of the pool is open.

Crouching down, I dip my hand into the cool water and sigh at the contrast to the muggy air. As sweat forms on my brow, all I want to do is dive in. When Calantha and I were at the farm, we worked every single day except for Wednesday afternoon. We had three short hours to enjoy ourselves, and we spent every one of them in the lake. Thankfully, we'd learned to swim before our parents died, but not all the kids were that lucky. We tried to teach those who wanted to learn and spent the rest of the time racing or splashing with each other. She'd fucking love this.

"Can I use it?" I stand and turn toward Aiden with every ounce of enthusiasm currently running through me. It ends up being a bit too forceful and my foot slips propelling me backwards.

Hands flailing, I try desperately to stop the inevitable. The last goddamn thing I need today is to go back to my desk looking like a drowned rat. Especially in front of *him*.

Just as I resign to my fate, preparing to sink below the cool surface of the water, warm hands wrap around mine, pulling me to safety.

The crisp scent of his cologne fills my senses as our eyes lock. We're close. So close that I can feel the hard lines of his body pressing against mine, reminding me of our night together. He's just as attractive in a business suit as he was in low slung jeans.

His gaze travels to my mouth, watching as I chew on

my bottom lip, and I recall his words on Saturday night. *Every time you bite that lip, I want to taste it myself.* My stomach flutters at the memory, reminding me just how carefree I'd been.

But we're no longer at a sex club. This is my boss. Fuck, it's my first day at work. What the hell am I doing? Part of me thinks I should just cut my losses and resign, but I need the money. *We need the money. It's not just me I have to consider.*

I clear my throat and attempt to step away, only to realize I have a pool at my back. He holds on to me a moment longer, seeming to press me more firmly against his body before his hands fall away and he retreats.

With the distance between us, my breathing returns to normal, even if my body doesn't want to cooperate.

"As an employee of Exalta Solutions, you'll have access to this pool whenever you wish." The deep rumble of his words startles me until I realize what he's said. Is he really not going to say anything about what just happened? Hell, do I even want him to? No, this situation is already a disaster. If he's giving me an out, I'll take it.

"Is it staff only?" I ask before I can think better of it.

"As long as she's with you, your sister is more than welcome to use the facilities."

My gaze darts from the pool back to him, shocked at his intuition. "How did you know?"

He smiles, his gray eyes darkening with lust and reminding me that he knows far more about me than I do about him. Instead of responding, he motions me toward a wall of glass overlooking the pool. Behind it stands an array of gym equipment with everything from free weights to a squat rack. There's even a fresh juice station near the entrance. Holy shit.

"Through those doors you'll find a sauna, and beyond the gym is a quiet studio for meditation or yoga, should that interest you. With your key card, you'll have access to all of this. Please use it as often as you'd like."

It all feels too good to be true, like a dream I'll wake up from at any moment and this will all vanish. I pinch my arm for good measure, even though I know it's silly. Aiden watches me, his eyebrow raised like he doesn't know what I'm doing. But I don't buy it.

He confirms my suspicions when he says, "There's no need to harm yourself, Liliana. This is real." He checks his watch, holding his hand out for me to move toward the lobby.

I follow along in silence, my thoughts spiraling in so many directions that I start to get dizzy. Today could not have been any more unexpected and still, despite the whole Aiden-is-Wes bomb, I can't deny how I feel. Like I belong.

We wait for the elevator in silence. His gaze bores into me the entire time, like he can see into my very being. He doesn't pry, and I don't offer anything. Somehow, the silence isn't awkward. It's comfortable.

The door opens, and we make room for people to exit. Sharon waves, wishing us both a good night and that she hopes I'll come back tomorrow. Then it's just us, alone in the elevator.

We both move to press the button for the twenty-fifth floor, our hands brushing against one another, and it's like déjà vu. Club Rapture. The bracelet.

My skin heats as a blush rises to my cheeks and lust fills my veins. I drop my hand, not even sure if either of us managed to press the button until the elevator starts moving. All I can think about is the feel of his fingers roaming over my body, plunging inside me. The way he and Fitz worked in tandem to bring me over the edge again and again.

I risk a glance toward him and instantly regret it. His gaze is scorching, like he holds the entire strength of the sun inside him, and I'm about to get burned. Just like Icarus. Aiden is my sun, and I won't risk my position here regardless of how much I crave the way he makes me feel.

Resolve settles the lust in my gut and the elevator doors open, saving me further discomfort.

"Ah, Aiden. There you are. Do you have a moment?" Dean, the Director of Innovation, asks.

Aiden nods in response, and I hurry out of there before he can say anything more, tossing a quick, "Thanks for the tour," over my shoulder.

I nearly ran back to my desk, desperate to get my things and get home to Calantha. She's bound to have some ingenious idea of how to handle this, or she should, seeing as she's the reason I'm in this mess. Alright, fine. So it's not her fault. I'm just a hot mess all on my own.

"Lily. How was the tour?" Kaleb exits his office with a smile on his face, but it falls the moment his eyes meet mine. "What's wrong?"

Too quickly, I plaster a smile on my face and rack my brain for an acceptable response. "Nothing! I'm just excited to get home and tell my sister about how great my first day was. Thank you so much for welcoming me in today. It means a lot." *Laying it on thick, huh, Lil?* Shit. But it's not like I could come right out and say, 'Nothing's wrong, except for the fact that your friend was one of two men who fucked me senseless on Saturday, and for a split second, I wanted him to do it again.' Not a chance.

"I'm glad to hear it, and we're all looking forward to working more with you. Here's your key card. You'll need it to get upstairs tomorrow."

He hands it to me and just as I'm about to thank him, I sense Aiden and stiffen.

Without a word, he brushes past us and enters his office. It stings a little, even though I know it shouldn't. Kaleb acts confused too, and I take that as my chance to collect my things and get the hell out.

"Thanks, Kaleb. I'll see you in the morning."

The scent of roasted potatoes and sautéed mushrooms envelopes me as I enter our apartment. Where I excel at baked goods, Calantha dominates in the main dish department. We're obsessed with watching the Food Network and trying out at least one new dish a week, depending on our budget.

As soon as she notices me, she grabs a bottle of champagne from the fridge and two glasses.

"Awe, you know you didn't have to do all of this." She really is the world's best sister. And I'll have to remember it later when she falls apart laughing at my incredibly embarrassing day.

"Oh, shush. We don't turn down a reason to drink good champagne, Lil. You know that. Now pop this sucker and spill."

I untwist the tiny metal clasp and remove the foil before carefully twisting the cork free. This part always looks so damn cool in the movies, but for whatever reason, it freaks me out. With my luck, I'll end up taking someone's eye out with a wayward cork.

Thankfully, there are no injuries, and I pour us each a glass while Calantha checks the food. Good. I'd rather she stay distracted than give me her full focus.

"I'll start at the part I know you'll love. They have a freaking pool on the main floor of their building, Calla. And a gym, juice bar, and sauna. It's surreal!"

"No fucking way," she says, turning the burner down and grabbing her glass of champagne.

"Yup. And I even confirmed that you're allowed to use it. As long as I'm with you."

She squeals, clinking her glass to mine. "Best. Company. Ever. Are bikinis allowed, or do I have to cover up the goods?"

I laugh and picture us swimming laps while wearing full body water suits. Until I remember Aiden, and my mood quickly sours.

Noticing the shift, she asks, "What?"

"Hmm? Nothing. What seasoning did you use on these potatoes? They smell incredible."

She ignores my attempt to change the subject and serves me with her best *nice try* stare.

I down the champagne and pour myself another, refilling hers for good measure. Then I take a sip, wasting more time as if I'm completely clueless to the eye-daggers she's impaling me with.

"God, Calla. I don't even know where to start. The company is amazing, and I really think I'm going to enjoy working there. Everyone was really nice and welcoming, but..."

"But what, Lil? You've literally not said a single bad thing so far. What happened?"

I inhale, ready to share every detail, and then I drain my glass of champagne instead.

"Lily!" Calantha says, her tone grating with annoyance.

"One of the guys from Club Rapture owns the company." There. I said it. Out in the open with absolutely no taking it back.

She just looks at me, blinking, and then the worried expression which lined her face only seconds before shifts, curling into a traitorous grin.

"No. Wipe that look off your face, Calla. This isn't good news!" I all but growl the words. There's a small part of me, the part that doesn't care about consequences and throws caution to the wind, that relishes the idea in the same way that I know my sister does, but I'm not that girl. I might have been at Club Rapture, but not here in real life.

Calantha rushes toward her laptop on the coffee table and opens it. "What's his name?"

"You're not seriously going to look him up, are you? Ugh, Calantha, this isn't a joke. I could lose my job."

Ignoring me, she types away and shouts, "Got it!" before scrolling through the Google Image search of Exalta Solutions' two owners. "Damn, they're both hot. Which one? And really, Lil, if he didn't fire you today, he's not going to. Plain and simple."

"We don't know that. And I sure as hell don't know how to act around him."

"Oh my God. You're tempted by the boss, aren't you? You little minx! I say go for it. Or if you must insist on denying yourself, at least give working with him a real shot. Don't give up just because you're scared."

"Do you know how annoying it is to have such a wise little sister?" I gripe, plating our food and bringing them to the table.

"Oh, just shut up and eat."

Chapter Twelve

Kaleb

She didn't quit.

Even after learning that Wes and Aiden were the same person. And that only made me want her more.

The image of her flushed face reappears in my mind. She'd practically rushed out at the end of the day, and after talking with Aiden, we knew a little distance between the two might help her comfort level.

We both wanted her. Not just as our assistant either, though it seemed like she'd be able to handle us both in that regard. Just like she did at the club. But we also knew that whatever the hell she'd gone through, whatever demons clawed at her insides, we didn't want to cause any more unease than she was already experiencing.

This meant changing up our current travel schedule so that Aiden would meet with clients this week while I stayed at the office. After how she reacted to only half a day with Aiden present, we both doubted she could handle an entire week with only him. Hell, if we did that, she'd probably quit before the week was out.

So instead, I'd forgo the travel and show her the

ropes. She still hadn't figured out that I was Fitz, and if I was a less confident man, I'd be worried. We'd never planned for her to see our faces and now that she knows about Aiden, we're in unfamiliar territory with just how to handle this.

I had expected to find her letter of resignation on my desk when I arrived on Tuesday morning, but instead I found her there early, going through our client contracts.

"Good morning. You're here early," I say, unlocking my office door and heading inside to set down my things.

She blows out a breath, slouching slightly. "I came early, hoping to use the pool or gym downstairs, but ended up forgetting my card. By the time I went home and grabbed it, it made more sense to just start going through these contracts."

"If you're not used to the card, it's definitely an adjustment." I chuckle, leaning against the doorframe of my office. "If it happens again, just ask someone at reception for a temporary card. If they aren't there, shoot me a text. I'm usually here early anyway."

I stride to my desk, snatch up one of my business cards, and head back toward her, grabbing a pen to put my personal cell number on it. "Here. Most of the staff have a lanyard or retractable clip for their cards too. Feel free to order one from the company account."

She blushes, accepting the card from me and placing it inside her purse. "Thank you. To be honest," she says, fidgeting with the strap of her purse, "being alone up here gave me a chance to try out that machine without an audience."

Lily shoots a glare at the espresso machine, and I can't help but laugh. "Oh no. What did he do this time?"

She leans back, grabbing the hem of her shirt and pointing out a wet spot. "He spat on me." Defeat lines her voice, yet her eyes spark with challenge and, goddamn, it's hot.

I turn toward the machine, giving it what I hope is a disappointed dad look and promise her I'll talk to him. Fuck, this woman does things to me. We're talking about a machine as if it's a kid, and I should feel embarrassed or awkward, but it just feels normal. Like she not only understands my quirky nature, but appreciates it too.

"Can I watch you make one? Maybe I'll do better if I watch how you handle him again."

"Sure. Come see the master at work."

The week passed in a blur. When I wasn't in meetings, I spent most of Tuesday with Lily. We went over the calendar, our alternating travel schedule, and I answered her questions about the client contracts she'd been reading.

It was amazing to observe the way her brain worked, firing on all cylinders to process new information and always asking questions. This was a curious woman, one who wanted to understand everything, to help find new ways of doing things, and was always willing to lend a hand.

Wednesday had been brutal. The only saving grace was the accidental meet-up with Lily before work. I'd been doing laps in the pool when she showed up in a one-piece swimsuit that would have knocked me straight off my feet if I hadn't been treading water. Even with a bathing cap and no makeup, she was gorgeous. How she managed to fit all of that dark hair under a little cap was beyond me.

We swam before work today too, this time even racing a little before I got out to put in a few reps with the weights. She'd been so excited to try out the juice bar after each swim as a little reward. The moan that escaped her pretty mouth when she'd tried their special Watermelon Wiggle smoothie damn near had me exploding on the spot.

After that, work kept both of us on our toes, but Lily proved once again just how integral she was to our team, and it was only her first week. She took it upon herself to get things for us before we even knew that we needed them. Not just for me, but for Aiden too. When she found out that he was trying to wine and dine a very important potential client of ours, she dug deep and uncovered information that ended up saving us from a total disaster. It's definitely not a good idea to take the deathly-allergic-to-seafood client on a private deep sea fishing tour. It was too soon to tell, but she might have just saved our asses and won us a client.

A knock on my door has me looking up to find Lily behind the glass. At my nod, she opens it.

"Someone from City Council is on the phone for you. Shall I patch them through or tell them you're unavailable?"

"Tell them I'm unavailable until tomorrow afternoon, if you don't mind. I know what they want, but I don't quite have all the pieces together yet."

"On it!"

She exits my office, leaving me with a smile on my face and completely unfocused from whatever the hell I'd been working on. Fuck, I had to get my shit together.

I pick up my cell, dialing Aiden and not really expecting him to answer, so I'm surprised when he does.

"This is Aiden."

I groan. "Every damn time. You have caller ID, dude. You don't have to tell me who I've called."

"If I break habit every time someone I know calls, it'll spiral. Deal with it. What's up?"

"Just wanted to give you a heads up that City Council is up our asses again. I've put them off until tomorrow afternoon, so we'll have to decide how we're going to play it before then." In our seven years of operation, this wasn't the first time we had to play ball with the stiff shirts at City Council, but this time it was someone new. Until we figure out where their allegiances lie, we have to play it safe.

"Do we have a name yet?" Aiden asks.

"No. Not officially, anyway."

"Alright. I'll make sure I'm around for the call tomorrow, and we can deal with it then. How are things with Liliana?" His voice softens when he says her name, and I know this week has been hard on him. Hell, I've struggled to be away from her, and I was here. It was going to suck when I was the one traveling next week.

"Really good. She's been enjoying the pool before work and usually treats herself to something from the juice bar. The sounds she makes with a Watermelon Wiggle smoothie are absolutely deadly." Just thinking about her made me hard. Even if she hadn't been at the club, I think we'd have both wanted her.

"Bastard," Aiden growls. "She really saved my ass with Alliance Medical, so clearly her discomfort with me isn't affecting her ability to do her job."

"I thought the same. Any news on that contract?"

"Sounds like the decision is between us and one other, though they were tight-lipped about which company it was. We just have to hope we've done enough to seal the deal."

"Well, we didn't kill him on a fishing boat, so that's got to count for something."

Chapter Thirteen

Liliana

"I can't believe you're already through with your first week!"

Calantha and I decided to get lunch today since she was in the neighborhood. She set her sights on an excellent animal hospital close to the building I work in. Because of her high grades and a very generous referral from her professor, she landed an interview earlier this morning, so we met at a little taco shop in between the two locations to celebrate.

I swallow a bite of taco and lift my glass of diet Dr. Pepper to cheers. "Well, I can't believe you only have three exams to finish before you graduate and a potential job opportunity."

She stuffs another piece of her burrito bowl in her mouth and clinks her sugar-rimmed margarita glass against mine. "I don't want to jinx anything but... Shit is finally falling into place for us, and I am totally here for it."

We finish the rest of our meal in companionable silence, watching passersby from the window as they rush off in a hurry. It's one of the things I love about New York City. When we left the farm, we wanted to get as far away as possible, but with no money and a target on our backs, we didn't end up very far. Still, it's nice to know we're in a city with millions of people instead of some secluded farmland. There might be plenty of scary people here, but it still feels safer than the farm.

"Want to come to the office with me tomorrow for a swim?"

"Like that's even a question, Lil. Of course I want to. Any chance I'll get to meet the two hunks you work for?" She wiggles her eyebrows at me, but I ignore her taunt and focus on pulling out some cash for our meal.

My phone vibrates with an email from Kaleb asking me to meet him in his office once I'm back from lunch. Uh oh.

"What's wrong?" Calantha asks, noticing the alarm on my face.

"I've got to get back. Kaleb wants to meet me in his office."

"From the sounds of things, it's probably to offer you a raise already. Or maybe he's just hungry and wants to eat *you* for lunch." She winks, likely joking, but I can't stop the flood of heat that enters my veins.

It's ridiculous, really. I've already slept with one boss, and now I'm attracted to the other one. Ever since Club Rapture, I've been amped up like a sex-crazed fiend. Is this what it's like for everyone else, or does someone have a voodoo doll of me with vibrators stuck in it instead of pins?

"Thanks for meeting me for lunch, Lil. Text me if I was right, okay?" She hugs me before strolling off to catch the subway, leaving me alone with my thoughts as I head back to work.

I'm nervous as I ride the elevator, but I can't figure out why. Aiden is the one who makes me nervous, not Kaleb. So why are my palms sweaty? It has to be what Calantha said. Her joke about Kaleb wanting me as his meal. Ever since she said it, I can't get the image out of my head.

But it's not just the picture of Kaleb feasting on me that's playing out in my mind. Someone else keeps popping up too. Aiden, watching us through the glass. What would he do if he found us like that? What would Kaleb do?

Fuck. Club Rapture spoiled me. Now I couldn't find two men attractive without automatically hoping they'd share me. How was I supposed to move on?

Veering off into the bathroom, I splash cold water on my face to stop my thoughts from racing. All week, he's been a beacon of light in the office. Someone who made me feel valued, whose mere presence didn't make me nervous, like with Aiden. And if I wanted that comfort with Kaleb to continue, I had to get my mind firmly out of the gutter and focus on my job. On taking care of Calantha and putting myself first more often.

Once I get my shit together, I head to my desk. Kaleb sits alone in his office with a thick stack of papers in front of him. Whatever has him transfixed allows me a moment to study him. His curly brown hair is neatly styled, though I bet if he didn't keep up with regular haircuts the curls would become unruly. I wonder what it looks like in the morning. Do the curls stay intact, or does it become a frizzy mess? *No. It doesn't matter what his hair does in the morning, Lil. He's your boss.*

He glances up then, his lips curving into a dazzling smile.

Shit. The way he looks at me brings me dangerously close to lusting after him all over again. *Okay, fine. So what if my nipples pebble beneath the weight of his stare? It doesn't mean I'm going to do a damn thing about it.* Shaking my head, I grab a notebook and pen, then stride into his office.

"You wanted to see me?"

"I did. How was lunch with your sister?" He closes his laptop and pushes away the stack of papers, giving me his undivided attention.

"It was great. We went to this little taco joint a few blocks over, and it was better than I expected."

"Macho Taco?"

"Yes. Have you been?"

Instead of Kaleb answering, Aiden's smooth voice sounds behind me.

"We have. It's maybe third on our list, after Los Tacos No. 1 and Ponche Taqueria," he replies, entering the room and handing me a smoothie. "Here. Kaleb told me you really liked this one."

"Thank you. I-I really appreciate it." As much as I

spoke the truth, because it really was sweet, I couldn't help but feel put on the spot. It would have been fine if he'd brought everyone smoothies. But he didn't, and now it's like there's a neon sign over my head that reads '*I fucked your friend once.*' Kaleb can't find out that Aiden and I knew each other before this, even if only for one night. Fuck! *Ugh, stop overthinking, and enjoy your damn smoothie. He's more likely to figure it out if you start acting weird. Get your shit together, girl.*

I set it down on the small table beside me, not bothering to take a sip just yet. "How was your trip?"

Instead of going to his desk, Aiden sits his ass on the side of Kaleb's desk with all the confidence of a man who gets shit done. It almost makes me smile to witness how Kaleb reacts, or his lack of a reaction, I should say. He doesn't seem fazed in the slightest, as if it's normal for Aiden to perch there. Not for the first time, I wonder how these two became friends. In some ways, they're so similar, but in others, they seem miles apart.

"It could have been a disaster if you hadn't saved the day."

He gazes at me with such intensity, it's as if he can see past my clothes and the walls I've built up inside myself to the very core of my being. It's unnerving. "Seriously, it was nothing. I'm just glad it worked out."

"It wasn't just *nothing*, Liliana. Thanks to you, Allegiance Medical has agreed to sign with us, exclusively. Apparently, the gift basket you sent went a long way in securing favor. We're hoping you'll agree to assist with more clients in the future."

"That you saved them from possibly dying of anaphylactic shock would have gone a long way too, I'm sure. But we'll keep that as our little secret," Kaleb adds with a wink.

I nod, a blush heating my face along with a sense of satisfaction. This job, it felt like home, and despite whatever complicated feelings I might have for Aiden and Kaleb, I wouldn't want to be anywhere else. I'll fight my lust and desire every damn day for the chance to stay.

"I think this calls for a celebration. Dinner tomorrow night. What do you say?" Kaleb asks, his eyes bright with excitement.

"No, no. You guys don't have to do any of that, really," I hedge, not liking all the attention.

"Kaleb only worded it as a question for your benefit, but we've already booked the reservation," Aiden says, his voice so stern and commanding that I can't stop my pussy from clenching. *Shit. I really can't go to dinner with these two.*

"He's right," Kaleb replies, stepping from around his desk so that he can sit against it in front of me. "We've been trying to secure a contract with this company for the better part of a year. This is a huge win for us, and we couldn't have done it without you. Please say you'll come."

My eyes travel between them, from Aiden's deep gray gaze to Kaleb's electric blue one. Inside my head, I can practically hear Calantha scream 'just say yes!', so I pull up my big girl panties and nod.

"Perfect. We'll email you the details." Aiden stands

and strides toward his desk, taking his laptop from the bag on the chair and opening it.

"Now, for the initial reason I wanted to meet with you. If you recall, I mentioned special events in your interview." Kaleb goes back to his seat and pulls out a piece of paper from the top drawer. He hands it to me, and I glance down at the elegant script on the thick cardstock.

"A charity gala?" I ask, looking up at him.

"You'd be surprised how many functions we have to go to, though they're usually much less formal. We've secured a company table and would like for you to join us. Think of it less like a social function and more of a work thing. There will be plenty of people from the health sector there that you should meet."

Before I can respond, Aiden chimes in. "We normally have advance notice of these things, but since this is your first week, we wanted to make sure you were aware and could plan accordingly. It's black tie, so you'll need to dress the part as well."

Aiden's and Kaleb's gazes snake along my body, making my skin prickle. "I'm sure my sister will be quite happy to help me pick out another outfit."

Aiden's gaze shoots straight to mine. "Another outfit?"

Shit. Why did I even say it like that? My tongue seems constantly tied around these two. Thankfully, Kaleb doesn't notice, and when his phone rings, I take my chance to escape.

"If that's all, I'll get back to work." I don't give either

of them a chance to reply before I'm out the door and back at my desk.

Five minutes later, there's an email from Aiden with the details of our celebratory dinner tomorrow and another from Kaleb with the charity event details. I don't bother reading through them, not now. Not while I'm within view of these two powerful men.

Calantha is going to have a damn field day with this tonight.

Chapter Fourteen

Aiden

"He's late."

I sit stoically in the boardroom at The Plaza, wishing I could get up and pace. Kaleb sits beside me, his laptop open and his fingers moving across the keys. I know he's tallying up a list of all the things we know about this particular council member so far, even though there isn't much to go on without a name. But making us wait on a fucking Saturday doesn't make either of us happy.

"We give him ten minutes. If he's not here by then, we're leaving."

Kaleb nods his agreement before shutting his laptop and placing it back in his bag. We're due to have a nice meal with Liliana this evening and never should have booked this meeting. I don't want to bring my frustrations to dinner, not when she is already so tense around me.

For a moment, my mind wanders back to the night of the lock-in. To the feel of her body coming apart beneath me. To how she trusted us with her pleasure. This woman has a hold on me so fucking tight, sometimes it's hard to breathe. And she doesn't even know it.

"Incoming," Kaleb says, shaking me out of my thoughts.

The door opens and a thin, pale man walks in, followed by a robust older gentleman and what must be his two bodyguards. The protective detail stays outside after closing the door while the other two men take their seats opposite Kaleb and me.

The pale man breaks the silence first. "This is Burt Brandon, the City Council's newest elected member." He motions to the larger man beside him with such bravado that I half expect him to announce he's also the next prince of fucking Monaco or some shit.

His nasally voice grates against my eardrums, but Kaleb and I don't say a word. They wanted this meeting, so they can say what they need to say or not. It makes no difference to us.

"I appreciate your interest in meeting me, and I look forward to working closely with you both," Burt says, flashing us a winning smile.

Kaleb and I share a look before turning back to him. "What is it you hope to work closely on, exactly?" Kaleb asks, tilting the corners of his lips into a smile. He can plaster a smile on his face and fool almost anyone, but not me. I mostly just intimidate. I don't really see the point in false pleasantry, especially not when it's with a snake.

"All in due time, my dear friends." Burt stands and motions for his companion to open the door. "I'll call on you when you're needed."

Every cell in my body lights up with the need to pummel this man to the ground. Who the fuck does he think he is? To make us wait here on a Saturday, only to stick around for less than five minutes while talking in riddles. There's no chance in hell we'll be doing this again. My facial expression gives nothing away as Kaleb and I stand as well.

"A word to the wise, Councilman," I say before he leaves. "We don't tolerate tardiness. Don't waste our time again."

He sputters, completely shocked that anyone would dare talk to him in such a way, but neither one of us stops to soothe his bruised ego. He might want some sort of alliance with us, but we don't fucking work with little weasels like him.

Only once we settle inside the car waiting for us outside the hotel do we speak.

"What kind of name is Burt Brandon? It must be fake." Kaleb sends a text to our hacker friend, Elliott, asking for all the dirt he can find on the new council member. "What I want to know is how does a guy like that even get elected? We were barely in the room with him for five minutes, and I already hate him."

"Guys like him rely on fear and power. Chances are, he has friends in high places. We just have to figure out what the fuck that means for us."

"That's what you're wearing? You realize it's a celebratory meal and not a work meeting, right?" Kaleb takes in my dark gray suit with disgust.

"Well, I'm certainly not going to put on a pair of old jeans and worn out shirt," I reply, frowning at his outfit and knowing he'll take the bait. Not that he's dressed like a slob or anything, but I like to make him sweat from time to time.

He gestures to his dress pants and expensive polo shirt. "Neither of these are *old* or *worn out*, so fuck off, yeah?" Not bothering to fight me on it further, he gets up from his seat at the table and heads to the bar.

Because Kaleb and I have been friends for years, I know how to push his buttons and when to quit. Or at least I used to. With Liliana around, he seems different. Before her, he'd have bantered with me back and forth about our outfits, but now he appeared genuinely worried. Knowing I fucked up, I follow him to the bar to apologize.

"A glass of your best whiskey, please. Neat," I say to the blue-haired bartender currently mixing a Moscow Mule for Kaleb. She'd been trying to flirt when I showed up, though Kaleb was entirely oblivious to it, his mind solely on one specific woman.

I wait until she hands us our drinks before placing my hand on his shoulder. "I'm sorry about earlier. She's going to find you drop dead sexy, regardless of what you wear. You know that."

He laughs and takes a sip of his drink. "I don't know that. I can't manage to read her at all, and I feel ridiculous. Did you know that part of me hopes she'll figure it out? If she remembered me from the club—"

"If she remembered you from the club, she'd probably quit. And trust me, her knowing doesn't make it any damn easier. She avoids me like the fucking plague. We knew going into this that things wouldn't be easy, but we just need to have patience. Regardless of what happens with her in our personal lives, she's an asset to the team."

"I know, I know. I won't jeopardize anything. Don't worry."

"Kaleb, that's not my worry, and you know it. She's only been working for us for a week. We have plenty of time to woo her. Let's just focus on getting to know her and making sure she gets to know us. Deal?"

He lifts his glass, knocking it against mine before taking a drink. "Deal."

I would never admit this to him, at least not on purpose, but I have similar worries. Less about how she'll perceive me, since the cat's kind of out of the bag, and more about what it means that she knows. There was something about Liliana that took hold of both of us from the moment we laid eyes on her. Her soul called to ours like a siren, and I was starting to realize that with her, I wouldn't mind drowning.

Chapter Fifteen

Liliana

Calantha helped me pick out a dress since I had absolutely no sweet clue what people wore to fancy dinners. The classiest place I'd ever been was the Olive Garden. I've never even heard of the restaurant DANIEL before, let alone could afford it now that I'd checked it out online.

I walk through the main doors of the restaurant in my form-fitting black dress with a pair of heels I borrowed from Calantha. Did I spend all morning walking around in them to make sure I don't make a fool of myself? Yes. Did it work? Not quite. But I figured if I was worried about walking, I couldn't obsess over the fact that I'd be eating at a nice restaurant with my two incredibly attractive bosses. One of which knew my body intimately and the other that I very much wish did. *Yup. Focus on making your feet work, Lily.*

While I wait at the podium for someone to seat me, I take in the gorgeous area. There's a bar nearby where Aiden and Kaleb currently stand, having what appears to be a serious conversation. Aiden has his arm reassuringly placed on a frowning Kaleb's shoulder. There's a pull deep inside that beckons me toward them, begging to find out what's wrong. As hard as that pull might be, I don't give into it. If they want me to know what's going on, they'll tell me. We're co-workers, after all. Not friends. *Or anything else, for that matter.*

A stunning waitress with ash-blonde hair approaches me at the podium, her lips tilted in a fake smile. She looks me up and down, seeming unimpressed with what she finds. "Table for one?"

Okay, so she's pretty, but she's also a bitch. As much as I want to snark back with a comment of my own, I know better than to think I won't fuck up somehow. It's funny, really. I protected my sister at the farm and would easily fight any battle for her, but when it comes to myself, that fire just isn't there anymore. "Actually, I'm here for a reservation under Fitzgerald."

Suddenly, I hear Kaleb's voice as he appears beside me. "Ah, you made it."

I turn to see him smiling at me, looking devilishly handsome in a blue shirt that makes his eyes pop. He takes my arm, causing goosebumps to rise on my flesh, and glances toward the woman behind the booth. "She's with us."

To my surprise, she hides her shock well. Or at least better than I expected. Her eyes widen slightly, but her jaw doesn't hit the floor like I thought it would.

Aiden stands at my other side, dressed elegantly in a gray suit with matching tie and pocket square. He places his hand on the small of my back, and I think I might just faint. Warmth spreads across my flesh, sending a tremor of pleasure right to my core. I tell myself it's all an act. They must have heard the waitress' comment and are only trying to make her jealous. That's all. It's not like he wants to touch me. That would be inappropriate. *Right?*

"Come," Aiden says, striding past us and effectively dismissing the waitress. The blood pumping through my veins heats at that one word, reminding me of our shared secret. *Oh, I came for him alright.*

Oblivious to my internal musing, Kaleb leads me through a gorgeous mirrored archway that's so strategically placed that I almost don't realize it's a mirror. We walk past busy tables and other guests, but I'm too busy taking in the opulent room to pay much attention to them. The ceiling has wooden accents and lovely art on each tile. Based on the grandeur of this place, it feels as if it could have been painted by Michelangelo himself.

We don't stop here, instead passing through an arched doorway into a room with red walls and a much more intimate feel. Finally, Kaleb stops at a curved booth in the corner and gestures for me to sit.

I scoot in, fully intending to keep going all the way until I'm on the other side, but I don't get that far. Kaleb and Aiden each take a seat, cutting off my exits and leaving me stuck in the middle of the booth. Placing my clutch behind me on the seat, I swallow and try to hide my discomfort. Sandwiched between these two for any reason probably isn't good for me, though my body doesn't seem to have gotten the memo.

A server approaches the table to take our drink order,

and I welcome the distraction. I find the extensive drink menu, one that doesn't appear to have any prices next to the cocktails, so you know it has to be pricey, and let Kaleb and Aiden order first.

"I'll have the white cosmo, please," I tell him when it's my turn.

"Great choice, miss. I'll be back shortly."

He leaves and as much as I want to look up at my two companions, I don't. Instead, I take a sip of the water in front of me and peruse the menu. *I am so not cut out for this shit.*

"We were thinking of ordering from the tasting menu. Smaller portions, but it will give us a chance to try different things. How does that sound?" Kaleb asks.

"That sounds really nice." And I mean it, I do. Even if I don't stop my inspection of the menu. Plus, more plates of food meant more chances for the server to save me from any uncomfortable topics of conversation. Win-win.

"Here. There's a few options on this side." Kaleb reaches over to flip my menu, making it more than obvious that I hadn't truly been paying attention. Great. Just great. Could this evening get any worse?

I check out the selection, not at all surprised to find half of the words are much too fancy for me to know what they truly are. *What the hell is a vichyssoise, anyway?*

"If I remember correctly from your file, you don't have any allergies, right?" Aiden asks, and I freeze.

From my file? He can't seriously be referencing the application Calantha had filled out for Club Rapture, right? He wouldn't. Not in front of Kaleb. Fuck. What the hell is he thinking?

The blood drains from my face as I just sit there. Do I pretend I know which file he's talking about? Do I just ignore it? Neither of those options sound appealing, and if I keep silent much longer, they'll know something's wrong.

"I confirmed with HR before we made the reservation. As long as you were honest in what you filled out at work, you should be safe to get whatever you want from the menu," Kaleb tells us. My heart finally starts beating again as his words sink in.

Jesus. He meant my file at the office. I have to get my shit together, but my mind can't quite seem to forget what happened, and instead of going on with my life, I am hyper focused on that one blissful night. Was there even an allergy section in the forms I filled out at work? I don't remember it, but if Kaleb thinks there was, I'll go with it.

Just then, the waiter comes back with a tray of drinks. The guys each got what I'm guessing is bourbon, based on the amber coloring, but it's my glass that has me mesmerized.

"Wow, this is beautiful." This isn't just a drink, this is art. The liquid in the glass isn't clear, which I expected because of the white cranberry juice. What I didn't expect, however, was the gorgeous single ball of ice that appears to have a pink orchid trapped inside.

Before I have time to taste the striking drink in front of me, Aiden explains to the server that we'll be ordering from the tasting menu. He only specifies one item, as does Kaleb, and I realize the rest of the menu is set and only the dessert has options. I also notice that of the two options, I only know how to pronounce one of them. Shit. I should have paid more attention when they were ordering. Guess I'm choosing the chocolate dessert. *Woe is me, am I right?*

After the server leaves, Kaleb grabs his drink and raises it in the air. "To salvaged deals and new beginnings."

Aiden and I repeat his words as we lift our drinks, clinking them together before we each take a sip. The cool liquid hits my tongue, zapping my tastebuds with a tangy sweet concoction that packs a punch. Holy shit. How much alcohol is in this thing?

I make a mental note to take it easy on the booze, promising myself I'll only order water after this. No need to stumble out of here and do something foolish. Nope. Around these two, I need to keep my wits.

"Is this a typical Saturday night for you guys?" I ask, hoping to keep them talking about themselves so that I don't have to speak. Alright, fine. So I'm also curious about the answer. As much as I should probably keep things strictly professional, I can't help but want to know more about them.

"Nah, not really. We never wanted to be those stuck-up adults who work all the time, so we try to keep our weekends free," Kaleb says.

"Though we usually have some sort of function at least one or two weekends a month that we have to attend," Aiden replies, and I picture them at lavish balls and soirees.

"Or stuck at the airport. Fuck, there was one time Aiden ended up stuck in Hawaii for two extra days because of this wicked storm."

"Holy shit. Hawaii? I can think of worse places to get stuck." My gaze moves from a smiling Kaleb to a less than enthusiastic Aiden. He opens his mouth to speak but Kaleb interrupts.

"This no-fun oaf did nothing except sit in a board-room at the hotel."

"There was a category four hurricane. I was lucky enough to have power and a dry place to stay." Aiden rolls his eyes, and something about it tells me they've defi-nitely been over this a few times before.

"Excuses, excuses." Kaleb chuckles and leans his forearms on the table. "Back to your initial question. We usually try to relax as much as we can on the weekend. Go to the gym, watch a movie, visit family. Hell, some-times I don't even leave the penthouse."

I laugh, knowing exactly what he means. I won't lie, though. Part of me is a little shocked that they didn't spend their weekends at the bar or on lavish dates with women. They are both incredibly attractive, so it's not like it would be hard to find a companion. Maybe for Aiden, I suppose, if he frequently works at Club Rapture, though I can't see how with his company. Something that feels a lot like jealousy churns in the pit of my stomach at that thought, but that's ridiculous. So what if he spends his weekends pleasing women at a club? It's not like I have any claim to him.

"How about you? How does Liliana Sinclair spend her weekends?" Aiden asks, his deep husky voice igniting a fire in my veins. His words hold a deeper meaning, or at least I take it as such, because he knows exactly how I spent my last Saturday night. Ravished by two strangers, and now here I sit at an expensive restaurant with yet another two men. *Shit. Was this becoming a thing?*

I focus on his words as they are because I can't keep adding context to them on my own or I'll go mad. "Definitely not at places like this, or anywhere else, really. I usually save Saturdays for house work and relaxing, and Sundays are a special day for my sister and I."

"Special how?" Kaleb asks, leaning forward and giving me his undivided attention. I can't pretend I don't like it. Not when he looks at me like I'm holding the moon and the stars in my tiny palm. I shouldn't like it, but just like everything else so far with these men, I just can't help it. *My little secret.*

"It's silly." I take another sip of my Cosmo, trying to calm the sudden nerves surging through me.

"Even better," Aiden says, leaning forward.

I've never told this story to anyone, and to be honest, no one's ever asked before. It's not like I make a lot of new friends, but even at my old job, nobody ever asked me about my personal life. The cautious pessimist inside me shies away at any notion of sharing such intimate details with my new employers. She urges me not to give them anything they can hold over my head later. But just like I did that night before Club Rapture, I push her down. It's time I put a little trust in someone who isn't myself or Calantha.

"Fine, but no laughing. Got it?" They both nod and immediately their faces lose all emotion. I chuckle, take a deep breath, and spill our embarrassing Sister Sunday details.

To my surprise, neither of them laughs, and instead they regale me with stories of their own. When they were in college together, they were the perfect students every day of the week, except on Saturdays. That was their day of junk food, laziness, and video games.

"When was the last time you spent a Saturday like that?" I ask, noticing the server on the other side of the room with a tray full of plates headed toward us.

"Shit. I don't know. Seven years ago, maybe?" Kaleb looks at Aiden, who only shrugs, not knowing an exact date either.

"What! That's way too long to go without doing nothing. Even savvy businessmen like yourselves need a break, you know." As the words leave my mouth, a plan starts to form in the back of my head. If they won't make the time themselves, someday I'll give them a little push.

It's amazing to be around people who have their shit together, and not just that, but they don't seem held back by their past. I could be jealous – and let's be honest, I kind of am – but it's also refreshing. We spend the rest of the evening eating and talking, sharing little stories about ourselves and our hopes for the future.

I share things about myself that I never thought I

would. Not the farm, though. Never the farm. But I tell them about my parents, being raised by my uncle, and then moving out to NYC when I was only nineteen. They open up about their families too. I learn that Kaleb's favorite holiday is Easter and that Aiden's dad is his hero. I sense more beneath those little pieces of information but don't press further, totally content with the light conversation.

Despite the secrets between us, I can't deny how comfortable I feel with them. Maybe this will all work out after all.

Chapter Sixteen

Kaleb

I love traveling, even for work. That's why Aiden and I swap out who travels which week, because we both enjoy hopping on a plane to meet a client or check out a prospective new venture. But this time, it just feels different. Better. And there's only one reason. Lily.

The dinner on Saturday night went better than Aiden or I had expected. We had tried to keep it professional and friendly, which was a feat in itself considering the sleek black dress she wore and the fact that I couldn't help but wonder what she wore underneath. There'd been one moment of panic when Aiden had slipped up and mentioned her allergies on file. A file that we only had because of Club Rapture. Thankfully, I'd swooped in to save the day, and she appeared to have bought the cover story. As far as I knew, we didn't have that question in the paperwork.

I can't imagine what Aiden must be feeling now, stuck at the office by himself while Lily and I hopped on a plane to Canada. The office must feel empty without her radiance. Fuck. This woman had us wrapped around her finger already.

Apparently, she'd never flown anywhere before, let alone in first class, so although we don't have sleep pods or anything overly fancy, she had been giddy with excitement when we boarded. Aiden and I never thought to confirm that she had a passport, but luckily for us, she and her sister had made a spur-of-the-moment decision to get them earlier this year, hoping to go to an all-inclusive resort. That knowledge had ideas flowing through my head of us on a beach somewhere getting sand in all the places sand wasn't supposed to be. I'd have to talk to Aiden about the three of us visiting our contacts in Hawaii sometime.

I expect her to be frightened during takeoff, but just like she has so many times in the short time I've known her, she proves me wrong. Once the seatbelt signs are off, we order a glass of shitty in-flight wine.

"So, who are we meeting again?" Lily asks, fiddling with the empty pack of almonds one of the flight attendants dropped off.

"R.C.A. The Restorative Care App. They host one of the largest in-app counseling services in Canada and in the top five within the United States."

"Oh, I've heard of them, actually. I looked into using their services last year, but my insurance only covered in-person appointments."

Shocked that she just revealed something so personal to me, I tuck that little nugget away for future musings and focus on our conversation. "Wow. That's a pretty old school clause to have with insurance."

"Tell me about it." She chuckles, rolling her eyes before digging into her bag and pulling out a notebook. After writing the client's name, date, and location, she rests her gaze back on me. "Okay, and is this just a routine checkup, or is there some other reason we're visiting them?"

"Always so eager, Lily." I smile and finish the wine, not bothering to place any attention on the adorable blush that now lines her cheeks. "We want them to open a branch in the States in our building. The healthcare system is vastly different in Canada, and we want to make sure that we're being as specific as possible with what's offered."

She nods as she writes what I've said down and then starts adding her own ideas below. Her handwriting is neat, likely a requirement for the career path she's chosen and not shocking in the slightest. My sweet blossom gives her all to everything she does. Of course this would be the same.

"Do we know how open they are about operating directly from the U.S.?"

"We've brought it up casually a few times over the last couple of years with no luck. Aiden and I will push a little harder this time, though." It wasn't like they shot us down in the past, but they hadn't exactly been enthusiastic either.

"And the owners? What's their story?"

"Anita Sutherland. Her husband is an ex-RCMP

officer who struggles with delayed onset PTSD. She comes from a long line of therapists and psychologists who helped support her dream; to offer more affordable and attainable assistance."

"Wow. That's incredible." Her hand moves across the page, scribbling anecdotes and details with a wide smile on her face. "Do we have much time once we land before meeting them?"

"Only an hour, unfortunately," I reply, unable to look away from the concentration on her beautiful face.

"No worries at all. That's plenty of time."

Before I can ask her to elaborate, an announcement comes across the speakers.

"This is your captain speaking. We're flying through an area of turbulence, so please head back to your seat and fasten your seatbelts."

Worry lines her face as she puts her notebook away. "It's alright. This is completely normal, I promise."

She smiles, or tries to, but the plane shifts in that moment. Her hand flies to mine, gripping it tightly, and my heart stops. I hide the shock from my face, not wanting to give away just how much I crave her touch, and stroke my thumb in soft circles along the back of her hand. My skin tingles where it meets hers, and for a brief moment, I can't look away from our joined hands.

We hit another patch of turbulence, the plane jerking beneath us and snapping me out of my revelry. Her eyes are wide and full of fear. "Breathe, Lily. Focus on my voice." She closes her eyes, taking a deep breath, just like

I asked her to. "Good girl. Relax, and let me take care of you."

I move the armrest out of the way and pull her into me. She comes without hesitation, allowing my arms to weave around her and hold her tight just as the plane shakes again. A whimper escapes her, and I fight the urge to pull her into my lap.

I stroke her hair, talking in a low, soothing tone about absolutely nothing, yet to her, it's something. To her it's everything. She relaxes as I continue to comfort her.

"What's the difference between a rabbit and a plum?" I ask her.

"What?" she asks, confusion lining her voice.

"They're both purple, except for the rabbit."

A laugh bubbles up from her throat, and my heart soars, so I tell her another one as the plane shakes again.

"What's red and bad for your teeth?"

"A brick," she answers through a chuckle.

"Damn, how'd you know? Shit, you didn't eat bricks as a kid, did you? Are those even your real teeth?"

She slaps my chest playfully but doesn't pull away.

"Okay, one more. You ready?" She bobs her head against me. "What do you call a magical dog?"

"Umm, I don't know. What?"

"A labracadabrador."

"Those are all terrible," she says through fits of laughter.

"Maybe," I reply, not offended in the least. As terrible as the jokes may be, they were the perfect distraction.

A short while later, there's a soft ding that accompanies the seatbelt sign turning off.

"Is it over?" she whispers against my chest.

"It's over."

She pulls back, her eyes no longer holding the fear from before, and I sigh a breath of relief. "Thank you. Sorry for all that." She pulls her hand from mine and gestures to my chest.

"You have nothing to apologize for. Now, if you hadn't laughed at my jokes... we might have a problem."

This woman is a goddamn miracle.

After only one meeting with Anita, not only did Lily convince her to open a branch in our building, but she also made plans for her visit to NYC.

How the hell did Aiden and I function without her on the team? It truly baffles me, and I say as much to her over dinner.

"You've been in an almost constant state of growth since you opened seven years ago, Kaleb. I'd say you definitely functioned without me." She smiles at me, then turns her gaze to the sunset skyline.

We eat dinner at KŌST, one of the restaurants housed on the forty-fourth floor of the Bisha Hotel. The views from here are absolutely stunning. It's not yet dark enough for the lights on the CN Tower to turn on, but I hope for Lily's sake that we'll be out here long enough to see it.

"You don't take compliments well, do you? Either way, I'd like to toast today's success. May there be much more to come with you by our side." I raise my glass, and she follows suit, putting it directly in front of her face as if to hide from my praise.

The view from up here pales in comparison to her beauty. Sure, the skyline may be glowing as the day wanes, but nothing could shine brighter than her. Not for me. Fuck. I can't imagine what Aiden must be feeling. I'd be positively green with envy if our roles were reversed. And I know someday, they will be.

The rest of the meal passes in a mix of companionable silence, shop talk, and hearty laughter. Once the bill is paid, I take a deep breath and offer my hand to Lily.

"Come with me. I want to show you something."

She hesitates but eventually places her hand in mine, and I pull her toward the glass railing on the edge of the building. Darkness has descended around us, and any minute now, the CN Tower will be ablaze with the multi-colored lights that even I can admit are a gem to behold.

"Oh God, oh God, oh God," she whispers after looking down.

"Afraid of heights, are you?" I ask, placing my hand on the small of her back.

"Not usually, but this glass is really messing with me." She takes a step back, shaking her arms like that might help rid herself of the fear.

"I won't let anything happen to you, Lily. I promise." Our eyes lock for a moment that feels more like a lifetime. The need to pull her closer, to have her in my arms, consumes me, and I'm on the brink of throwing caution to the wind and just shooting my shot when clapping erupts around us.

We both turn toward the guests to see what's happening, but they aren't looking at us. The lights of the CN Tower are finally on.

Lily's shocked gasp tells me she's noticed, and we stand there, watching the lights flicker and change. But I've already seen the tower lit up a hundred times before. Why would I watch that again when I could settle my gaze on the beautiful woman at my side and catch the colors glinting in her eyes.

Only when more people join us at the glass railing do we realize just how long we've been standing there. We've got an early flight tomorrow, and a quick look at my watch lets me know it's long past time for us to head back to our rooms, even if I don't want to.

We're silent in the elevator, both stuck in our heads. My thoughts are on her and I wonder - no, I hope - that she's thinking of me as well.

Our rooms are on opposite sides of the hall, and as we stand at our respective doors, it feels like neither one of us wants to go our separate ways. But are we ready to take that step? For me, it's not even a question, but for her... I don't want to rush her. I don't want her too caught up in the beauty of this night that she makes a decision she'll regret in the morning. I can't risk her leaving us. She's too important.

With that in mind, I say goodnight, entering my room

and letting my door shut only once I know she's safe inside her own.

Releasing a shuddering breath, I rest my back against the door and tell myself again and again that I made the right choice. Even though it feels like half my heart is in the room with her.

My legs struggle to move, like they're no longer under my control, but I force them to action. Force myself away from the door and into the living room of my suite.

Away from the temptation that is Liliana Sinclair.

Chapter Seventeen

Liliana

The passage of time is fickle. When things go wrong, it feels like everything moves in slow motion. Like the world is working against you and trying to make things worse. But when life is good, time speeds up. Suddenly, weeks have passed, months turn into years, and you can't figure out where the time went.

For most of my life, it's felt like time was my worst enemy. Until now. Now I'm barely able to keep track of the days that seem to speed by me in the blink of an eye. The work I'm doing with Exalta Solutions is an enormous part of my recent happiness, but it's not just that. It's the people, too.

When I first realized who Aiden was, I almost quit. Fear had gripped me so tightly that I couldn't picture staying, not with him there, and certainly not after everything he'd done to me that night at Club Rapture. But now, I can't picture working for any other company or for any other owners. It feels like home.

Weeks have passed since that first day. Weeks full of challenges that keep me on my toes and some days, I even get to teach them a thing or two. When Kaleb isn't travel-ing, he joins me for a swim before work. More often than not, when Aiden isn't on the road, he's working out in the gym while we swim, and even though I thought things would be incredibly awkward with him, he hasn't explic-itly said anything untoward. He's definitely hinted at it on more than a few occasions, but even those have grown on me. I'm like a whole other person, and even Calantha has noticed.

Yesterday was her graduation day, so she's now offi-cially a vet tech and has one blissful week off before she starts her new job only a few blocks from my work.

Despite my inner turmoil, she went out with a few of her fellow graduates to celebrate last night and proved, once again, that I had nothing to worry about. I slept like total shit, despite all the progress I thought I'd made, but I wouldn't beat myself up over it. She still went out while I stayed home, which is already a step up from before.

Now that Calantha has a second coffee and every smell isn't threatening to make her throw up, we walk through the shops at Brookfield Place, hoping to find a dress suitable for the goddamn charity gala. Not that I could afford anything truly worthy.

I stop the fearful thoughts before they get started, not allowing myself to worry about what people will think and how easy it'll be for them to tell that I don't belong. Because I do. Aiden and Kaleb want me there, and that's enough for me.

I try not to let it go to my head. They want me there because I'm their assistant, and they bought a company table. That's all. Just because I can't stop lusting after them doesn't mean it's reciprocated.

"Oh, that dress is pretty," Calantha says, pointing toward a dress in the window of Adam Lippes before heading toward the store entrance.

Shaking off my thoughts, I focus on the task at hand. As much as I might wish I didn't care what others think, the hard truth is that I do. I want to fit in, so I'll do everything in my power not to stick out like a sore thumb.

As we walk into the chic store, I can already tell this place is way out of my budget, and Calantha figures that out as soon as she checks the price tags on the items we pass.

"Can I help you?" A rather snobby looking sales woman walks over to us, her face stoic and lacking warmth.

"No, thank you. We're just looking," I reply. Damn. I forgot this was why I never went shopping. Well, this and the lack of disposable income, but the snooty way some of these store clerks treated me was a damn fine reason on its own.

"Of course. We have a sale rack in the back if you're looking for something a little more... budget friendly." She looks down her nose at us once more before walking back to the counter.

"Even if we could afford this place, there's no way in hell I'd help pay that bitch's wage. Let's go find a place with more personable staff." Calantha waves her fingers to the rude woman as we leave, and we both giggle as we head off in search of a more affordable store.

"As much as I love New York, I don't think we could have picked a more expensive city to live in." I sigh, not wanting to admit defeat, yet knowing my heart just isn't in it anymore. I loved the idea of shopping, but I always ended up more disappointed than happy. Worries fly through my mind like eagles, diving fast and tearing apart any hope I have of making a good impression. If I don't find something suitable, I'll be letting Aiden and Kaleb down, and that thought leaves me more depressed than I care to admit.

Calantha grabs my hand, forcing me to stop and look at her. "Don't you dare give up now, Lily. We *are* going to find you a dress, and we *will* pay off the mountains of debt you've tried to hide from me. So what if we've failed so far at finding an outfit? It doesn't mean we give up. We never give up."

I stare at her with equal parts pride and awe in my gaze. She's right. Again. "How can you be wise and hungover at the same time?"

"It's a gift, I know. Now let's go find you a dress that'll knock your bosses' socks off."

"Aren't you going to be uncomfortable in that skirt today?" Calantha asks me as we ride the subway to work the following day.

"What do you mean?" I tug on the hem to make sure it's covering enough to be work appropriate. Sure, did wearing skirts cause me to daydream about the easy access my two bosses could have? Yes. But there's no way in hell I'd act on it. Those fantasies would live completely rent free in my head and only come out to play when I was alone with my favorite vibrator.

"Isn't today the day you're traveling with Aiden? You sure as hell wouldn't catch me wearing a skirt for a road trip with my hot boss. Not unless we were getting it on in the backseat." She winks at me.

I cringe, rubbing my palm against my chest. "Shit. I completely forgot that was today." *Note to self: keep a change of unflattering clothes at work.*

Calantha laughs, the glint in her eyes telling me everything I need to know about what she's thinking. "Oh, it'll be fine, Lily. It's about time you made him sweat a bit anyway."

It's not him I need to worry about. My thoughts churn for the rest of the ride to work, and the next thing I know, Calantha and I are parting ways.

"Good luck," she shouts, blowing me a kiss.

I send her a half-hearted wave, my mind still racing. I can't quite seem to get out of my own head. Would he be driving, or would we be in the back seat together? Fuck. What if I flashed him my coochie when I got out of the car? I bury my head in my hands as I try to think up a solution.

"Lily. Are you okay?"

I jolt and look up to find myself practically on top of Kaleb.

"Oh God, I'm so sorry," I tell him, wincing as I fiddle with the collar of my shirt. Warmth seeps through my blouse from where his hands are, where he physically had to stop me from running into him. I step back and he drops them, though the concern doesn't leave his face.

"Is everything okay?" He glances past me to the street, like he might find someone pursuing me.

"I'm fine, truly," I tell him, pasting a smile on my face and reaching behind him to open the door.

He eyes me skeptically. "Are you sure?"

"I'm sure. Honestly, it's silly. I forgot about the trip with Aiden today and regret wearing a skirt. I was caught up in my head trying to find a way around it in the future." We reach the elevator and Kaleb scans his card while I press the button for our floor.

Why the hell did I just tell him that? What is it about these men that makes me open up so much? Dammit.

At my words, his tense shoulders visibly relax. He peers down at the bag slung over his shoulder when a smile crosses his supple lips. "I've got a spare pair of sweats you could wear, though it might not go with that pretty top."

A surprised laugh bursts free of my lips as I picture it. "You know, I might have to take you up on that someday." Something coils deep in the pit of my stomach at the idea of wearing his clothes, and my mind quickly shifts to him pulling them off of me. *Get a grip, Lily. You might have two sexy as fuck bosses, but that doesn't mean you can have them both.*

The elevator doors close and he turns toward me. "Did you know that my penis was in the Guinness Book of World Records?"

"What?" I ask, laughing.

"Yup. But then the librarian asked me to take it out."

All of my problems vanish as I dissolve into laughter. Kaleb can always tell when I'm caught up in my own head, like he has a sixth sense or something. Not that I'm complaining. I welcome his brand of distraction. It's no surprise that when we exit the elevator onto the twenty-fifth floor, I'm laughing my ass off.

Isn't it funny how jokes work? Sometimes it's the worst ones, the ones that are so dumb and predictable, that make us laugh the most, and Kaleb has an arsenal of them.

"Thanks for the comedy, as always," I tell Kaleb as we reach my desk. I don't see Aiden yet, so I sit down to work through a few emails before we leave. Sure, I could do that on the car ride, but reading anything in a moving vehicle always makes my stomach queasy. *I'll just have to find some other way to occupy myself in the car...*

And just like that, I'm back to worrying about what will happen between Aiden and me in a tight space. Like a magician, he appears beside me as if summoned by my very thoughts. Thankfully, he doesn't seem to have actually seen the naughty images that crossed my mind. *This isn't a book, Lil, and he's not some Fae prince with the ability to read minds.*

"Are you ready, Liliana?" His soft, breathy voice catapults me back to the very first night we met.

I swallow once, then twice, before I finally manage to speak. "I'm ready.

Chapter Eighteen

Aiden

As a teen, I always dreamed of being rich enough to afford a driver. Whenever I'd watch movies, it always seemed like the coolest characters had a car on standby, just waiting for a summons. I'd succeeded, and the little boy in me still got a thrill every single time I saw that car pulled around for us. It never got old.

For today, though, I don't want a driver. I only want time alone with Liliana, so I opt to drive us to Haverhill, Massachusetts. The idea of us sitting side by side in the backseat has the blood pumping straight to my dick as I consider all the things we could get up to back there. And as much as I want all of that to happen, it won't help my cause. Half the time I forget what that even is, but today, it sits front and center in my mind. Don't make her so uncomfortable that she leaves. I still can't believe she hadn't quit after that first day, but I'll do everything in my power to make sure we don't lose her.

As soon as I see her outfit, I know I made the right choice. Having her in the passenger seat with her skirt riding up on her creamy thighs is enough of a temptation on its own. At least this way, I have the distraction of driving to keep the animal inside of me at bay.

The ride has been quiet, aside from the radio, with Liliana keeping herself occupied by watching the scenery pass us by. As someone who hasn't traveled much, it makes sense that she's so fascinated by the unfamiliar landscape, and despite the little voice in my head that tells me she's avoiding me, I know it's more than that.

Instead of checking into our accommodations, we head straight to Bright Point House, one of the in-care homes that Kaleb and I help fund. They frequently held biweekly grief counseling sessions for children, offered to the community free of charge, and today Liliana would get to experience it herself.

Kaleb and I try to visit at least once a year, and we almost always make sure our stay falls on one of these days. Grief, if left unchecked at any age, can be life changing. But we've always felt like youth don't have the proper tools to cope, at least they didn't when we were kids. With our company, we could help make a difference and arm the youth of today with the power to deal with that grief.

Bright Point House sits on a large plot of land with sprawling fields and a heavily wooded forest behind it. They have a garden the residents can tend to, a play-ground for kids to burn off energy, and a pond that is mostly used for feeding the ducks.

Unsurprisingly, the parking lot is almost full when we arrive. Kids run around the yard or hang from the monkey bars while their parents check in with staff. It always both amazes and saddens me with how busy these youth grief nights are. How fucked up must the world be to have so many children in need of help? And what would it take for people to realize it needs to change?

"This place is beautiful," Liliana exclaims as we walk toward the front door of the building. When we reach the porch, she stops for a moment, staring with unblinking eyes at the kids as they run and play, as if she's caught up in an old memory.

"What's wrong?" I place my hand on her arm, jolting her from whatever had caused that pained expression.

"Oh. Nothing, sorry. Seeing all of those kids kind of sucked me back in time. But I'm sure this place isn't anything like the farm." Her voice is distant, like she's trapped inside her head instead of standing beside me.

Her comment causes the hair to rise on my neck. "What do you mean, 'isn't like the farm'?" I ask, desperate for a peek into her past, but she's saved from answering when a short, plump woman approaches.

"Well, if it isn't Aiden Daniels," Carla, the woman who runs the care home, says before pulling me into an embrace.

"Nice to see you too, Carla."

"You must be Liliana," she says, bustling toward her and throwing her arms around her in a tight hug. "I've heard so many great things about you, dear. Thank you for coming."

"This place is incredible," Liliana replies when they break apart, and Carla's grin widens further.

She takes us through the house, giving a quick tour

for Liliana's sake before leading us into her office. She brings over a pitcher of lemonade and a tray of molasses cookies, then sits behind her desk.

We spend the next hour discussing their achievements over the last year, where most of their funding is going, and areas they've noticed need improvements. Liliana and Carla hit it off, sharing ideas back and forth until we have more plans and strategies than we could possibly implement in the next twelve months.

When the meeting ends, Lily hands her a business card and assures Carla that she can message anytime. Before we leave, Carla introduces us to some of the children in their care and I watch as Liliana practically blossoms before my eyes. She gets right down to their level, making them laugh and feel important. Maybe this is what haunted her earlier. Could it be as simple as not wanting to see a child sad, or was it more than that? The haunted expression in her eyes told me it was far worse, and I wish I could ask her more about her past. What happened at the farm that she hoped wouldn't happen here?

After another hour of visiting and a home-cooked meal, we say our goodbyes to Carla on the porch.

"Make sure you lock this one down, Aiden. A smart woman like her won't wait around forever." Carla lowers her voice, as if trying to whisper, but the bright red that now stains Liliana's features tells me she failed. *Time to get out of here.*

"I know. Thanks for having us, Carla," I shout back as we walk toward the car.

"I'm really glad I got to come today," Liliana says as we drive toward the bed-and-breakfast we're staying at. "We should open up more centers like this in other cities, too. If my sister or I had this type of help when we were growing up, things might have been different."

I glance at her from the corner of my eye and catch her wiping away a tear that slipped down her cheek. My heart breaks at the sight. I'm desperate to push, to find out more about what happened to make her this sad, but I hold back. As much as I want to help slay the demons currently tearing her apart, it's not my place. She doesn't owe me anything, certainly not her trauma.

Instead, I reach over and clasp her hand in mine. "I think that's a great idea. When we're back home, we can meet with Kaleb and put together a plan."

She squeezes my hand and whispers, "Thank you."

I thought she would pull away, take her hand back and end the moment, but to my surprise she keeps mine firmly in her grasp. Whatever she's dealing with right now must be bad enough for her to accept the comfort I offer. She hasn't exactly been avoiding me at work, but our relationship isn't as easy as the one she has with Kaleb.

I pull into a spot at a cozy-looking country home and unclasp my fingers from hers to park the car. Our eyes meet, but neither one of us speaks. Temptation surges through me at our closeness. What would she do if I leaned over and kissed her? Would she kiss me back, or would that one move ruin everything we've worked for these last few weeks.

Her phone vibrates in the center console, breaking the spell and stopping me from kissing her senseless.

"It's Calantha, do you mind?" she asks, sheepishly.

"Not at all. I'll go get us checked in." I grab our bags from the trunk and head inside the rustic-style house that's so refreshingly different from anything you'd find in New York.

A middle-aged woman wearing an apron with what must be flour dusted along her nose approaches. "Hi, honey, what can I do ya for?"

"Just checking in. There should be two rooms for Aiden Daniels and Liliana Sinclair."

The woman opens up a thick worn book and flips through it while Liliana approaches us with a smile. "There you are. Aiden and Liliana." Digging through a drawer, she pulls out a key and places it on the counter in front of us.

"This key will open both of our rooms?" Liliana asks politely.

"Oh no, dear. There's only one room."

Her face falls, though the woman in front of us doesn't seem to notice, or maybe she just doesn't care.

"What do you mean? When I called, I booked two rooms. No one mentioned there only being one available."

The woman's brows crease slightly. "I'm sorry, sugar. We only have the one, I'm afraid. Will you be taking it?"

Liliana turns her questioning gaze to me, and I shrug, careful to keep my expression neutral. She didn't need to know how fast my heart was beating at the thought of sharing a room with her. "If you're uncomfortable, I'm sure we can find another place to stay."

She hesitates, drawing her lower lip between her teeth and igniting a fire inside of me that I struggle to keep hidden.

"You'd best keep the room, dear. We've had to turn away several visitors looking for rooms already. With that marathon happening this week, all the hotels are booked right up."

Liliana takes a deep breath, straightening her back as she prepares for her next words. "It's fine. We'll make it work. Thank you so much for your help."

"Oh, good! Down the hall, last door on your left. I've got cookies baking in the oven now, and breakfast starts at eight. If you need anything, just holler."

When my new roommate for the night reaches for the handle of her bag, I shake my head. "I've got these if you can handle the door?"

"I think I can manage," she says sardonically. I follow her down the hall until we reach the last door on the left. Inside lies a cozy room with a king-sized bed as the focal point. The cushioned headboard and plush pillows look incredibly inviting, and I can't stop from picturing Liliana lying on top, clad in nothing but a smile as she invites me to join her. Fuck. Tonight is going to be harder than I thought. I avert my gaze, catching sight of a flat screen T.V. hanging on the wall opposite the bed with a compact dresser below it.

The room is small, but cozy. Certainly not meant for

two strangers to share, though that's not what we are. At least, not to me.

What the room lacks in size, the bathroom more than makes up for. A large soaker tub sits in one corner and a decently sized shower in the other. On the bathroom counter is a basket of handmade soap and other locally made toiletries. They might not be great with communication, but this place really knows how to class up a room.

Attempting to curb the desire in my veins, I set our bags on the floor by the window and turn to face the woman who holds every ounce of my attention.

Chapter Nineteen

Liliana

Awkward as hell.

That's the only way to describe my current evening. Aiden has been nothing but a gentleman, yet I can't help but stare at the bed and imagine all the things we could be doing in it. How was I supposed to sleep beside him after everything that's happened?

He had stepped away to make a few phone calls, and I'm struggling to compose myself while he's gone. I'm a grown woman. I should be able to handle sharing a bed with a man. Even if he's also my incredibly attractive boss who's already known me in the most intimate ways. *Not helping, Lil.*

As a distraction, I turn the television on and try to focus on a show. It's about a woman covered in tattoos who finds herself naked and alone in the middle of Times Square without a single memory of who she is. Under different circumstances, I'd likely be consumed by the plot, but not tonight.

Aiden returns to find me lounging on the bed, surrounded by pillows as I lean against the headboard.

He removes his shoes and suit jacket, loosens his tie, then matches my position on the bed. We sit in silence as we watch the Jane Doe character struggle to remember her past. I try so fucking hard to ignore the weight of the man beside me, especially when his arm brushes against mine and the warmth of him seeps into my skin.

He clears his throat. "This might not be the best time for us to discuss this, but I've put it off long enough already."

I don't bother looking at him. I can already guess what he wants to talk about, though I'm not against pretending I don't.

"Cryptic, but alright. What do you want to discuss?"

He grabs the remote off the bed, turning the volume down before setting it on the bedside table. I shift my attention to an invisible spot on the wall, not trusting myself to meet his gaze. I've never been very good with face-to-face confrontation, at least not for my benefit. If Calantha was involved, I had the strength of a thousand warriors and I would tear the universe apart to protect her. But for myself... hiding behind a phone or computer was so much easier than looking someone in the eye. *I know, I know. I'm a coward.*

"Club Rapture."

Those two words ring out through the room like gunshots. The naive part of me had hoped we'd never have to talk about it. If we could just pretend it didn't happen, we wouldn't have to have this awkward conversation. What if he felt the need to tell Kaleb? I wouldn't be able to face him again if that was the case. But maybe, if I truly opened up about it, we could clear the air and move on.

A small part of me didn't want to put it behind us — alright, so maybe it wasn't actually small, but I'm totally fine to live in denial. That part of me wanted it firmly in our path, in our future, because during that night at Club Rapture... I was free.

Shifting my body in his direction, I pull a pillow out from behind me and place it in my lap as a barrier. As if that might just save me from the uncomfortable conversation.

"I was kind of hoping you'd forgotten about that," I whisper, staring at my clasped hands.

"Sorry to disappoint." A smile seeps into his tone, providing all the confirmation I need to know that he isn't sorry at all.

I take a deep breath, solidifying my resolve to finally ask the question that's been on my mind for weeks. "Did you know who I was the whole time?"

"I did."

With his confirmation, my stomach drops. "Is that why you hired me? Was Kaleb in on it too?"

All this time, Exalta Solutions had felt like home, but if he'd only hired me because my name had been selected for the lock-in, I would have no choice but to leave.

"God, no. Your job has absolutely nothing to do with the events of the club. I never intended for you to see my face, but I lost control. The last thing I'd ever want to do is make you uncomfortable or second guess your role."

I nod, unsure of what to say. Questions fill my mind,

and I want to ask all of them. If he's so close with Kaleb, how come he doesn't know? Why is he bringing this up now, while we're alone in bed together? Thoughts race through me like an angry breeze, forcing words from my lips before I can stop them. "Do you participate at the club often?"

I catch the shock on his face for a moment before he covers it. "Occasionally, yes."

I'm fully prepared to ask him if Kaleb does too. The question sits on the tip of my tongue, begging to break free, but it gets stuck when he places his hand on mine, running his thumb back and forth against my skin and says, "But no one has ever consumed me like you have."

He moves closer slowly, giving me ample time to pull away in case this isn't what I want, but I don't move. When we're only inches apart, he stops. "There's never a moment that goes by that I don't think of you, of that night. And now that I've gotten to know you beyond just sex and pleasure, I'm even more captivated by you."

My heart races as he reaches up to trail his fingers across my cheek. I close my eyes and hold my breath, incapable of speaking even if I wanted to.

"Tell me you don't feel it too," he whispers, closing the space between us, but he halts before our lips touch, leaving the choice up to me.

But is it even a choice? An invisible energy tethers me to him, and the knowledge that he feels it too makes this moment between us almost impossible to fight.

My core ripples with need, spurring me to open my

eyes and stare deep into his gray depths. Without another thought, I press my lips to his.

His arms gather me close as his lips dance over mine until his tongue beckons my mouth open. I give in, needing more and knowing he can provide. My hands move around his neck, into his hair, pulling him against me with fervent movements. All his talk of being consumed by me when it's me who's been tormented. Thrust into a job where I'm forced to see him every day, to yearn for his touch without ever being able to act on it.

A moan escapes me as he fists my hair, changing the angle and deepening the kiss. I'm need and desire incarnate, hungry for more of his touch.

A loud knock reverberates through the small space. We stop moving, our breaths coming out hard and fast as yet another knock rattles the door.

"I've got cookies for you, as promised," the female voice singsongs from the other side.

A strangled laugh escapes me as I pull away from Aiden, from the promise of pleasure, and head toward the door. On the other side stands the owner with a tray of oatmeal chocolate chip cookies and two glasses of milk.

"Here you go, dear. Warm, ooey-gooey cookies to finish off the day. Are you two settling in okay?"

"Yes, thank you," I reply, as if on autopilot.

"Happy to hear it! I'll leave you two to rest and see you both in the morning. Sweet dreams!" With a swish of her apron strings, she walks back down the hall, leaving Aiden and me alone once more.

He strolls towards me with outstretched arms, taking

the tray from my hands and placing it carefully on the dresser. When he turns back, I shake my head.

"We can't," I whisper before he can touch me. "You're my boss, and I love this job. I don't want to fuck that up."

His gaze roams over my face, from my eyes to my mouth, where I'm chewing on my bottom lip. I immediately stop, not wanting to provoke him any further, because if he touches me again, I don't think I'll be able to stop him. Hell, I don't even want to stop him now. God, this is torture. I want him to throw me on the bed and make good on all the promises I see in his gray depths. *But could I handle that, or would I just end up jobless and brokenhearted?*

I have to be rational here. I can't give him what he needs long-term, and I'm realizing now that I don't know if I'm truly made for the short-term stuff. I can't do the whole physical thing without emotions. And if I'm truly honest with myself, what we're doing now doesn't feel right without Fitz, whoever he is. But I could never ask Aiden to introduce us. They were only working, after all.

He nods and picks up the tray again. "Come. Let's eat these and finish that episode you were watching."

I follow him to the bed, returning to my comfortable spot among the fluffy pillows. He puts the plate between us, letting me grab one first, and I wonder if he did that on purpose. Is he trying to avoid touching me? If he is, I'm grateful. This is far too much temptation for me as it is.

With that thought, he takes a bite of his cookie and

lets out a groan. I try not to let it affect me, even though I'd be lying if I said it didn't, and take a bite of my own.

"Holy shit," I say around a mouthful of soft cookie. Cooked to perfection.

"I might not agree with her banging on the door to give us these, but damn, they're good."

A giggle escapes me as I picture the other poor guests she might have disturbed with her knocking. We eat the rest of our snack in silence as we finish the episode of Blindspot. Since it's not the first episode, it's been hard to follow, but tonight that's a blessing. I'll do anything to distract my mind from the man lying beside me.

Cuddled up in the soft embrace of the bedding, I could easily fall asleep. I let out a yawn, stretching my limbs as I rise to my feet and grab my bag.

"I'm going to get ready for bed," I tell Aiden awkwardly before shutting the bathroom door with an internal facepalm. *And the award for the most awkward person goes to... Liliana Sinclair!*

I brush my teeth while I search for my pjs — the ones I thought I'd be wearing alone or else I'd have chosen another pair. After I rub my face cream on and relieve my bladder, I step back out into the room.

I'm frozen in place when my eyes land on Aiden's broad and bare muscular back as he closes the curtains. He wheels around, giving me a full display of his chest, and I have to physically stop myself from stepping toward him. I'd forgotten how fine a specimen he is, and now that I see him like this again, I can't stop the memories from resurfacing. Will he take off his pants too? If he sleeps next to me like that, I might just have to move to the bathtub if I want to get any rest.

His gaze drops to my chest as he reads my shirt. *Sometimes I wrestle with my demons. Sometimes we snuggle.*

"That's good to know, actually," he says, confusing me.

"What is?"

"That you snuggle your demons. If I feel someone big-spooning me later, I'll know who it is."

So surprised by his joke, I can't help the burst of laughter that escapes me. Between him and Kaleb, Aiden is usually the more subdued of the two, but I can't deny how nice it is to see this side of him.

He escapes into the bathroom while I settle into bed. I consider pushing a few of the pillows down the center like a barrier, but decide against it. It's not as if I don't trust him. He's already proved he wouldn't force anything when I shut down our earlier adventures — one that likely wouldn't have stopped if it wasn't for our nice cookie supplier.

I close my eyes and will myself to fall asleep. *You can do this, Lily. It's a gigantic bed. You won't even notice he's there.*

Every sound from the bathroom causes my heart rate to pick up as I expect him to come back into the room. After the fourth sound and still no open door, I smack myself internally. *Go. To. Sleep.*

Of course that's when the bathroom door opens, almost making me jump, but I keep my eyes closed. I'm half tempted to open them, curious to find out if he's taken off his pants, but I know that the answer to that question is better left unknown. If they're still on, I'll be disappointed, and if he's taken them off, my mind will run a goddamn marathon with middle of the night temptations.

Beneath the weight of the comforter, I start to sweat. *Okay, fine, so it probably had nothing to do with the blankets and more to do with the fact that behind my eyelids, all I can see is his sculpted chest. Shit. Maybe I should have put those pillows in between us. I might trust Aiden, but could I even trust myself?*

There's a soft click before the room darkens behind my closed lids at the same moment the covers shift and the bed dips slightly. With my back to the center of the bed, I'm safe to open my eyes now, though it's too dark to really see anything.

"Goodnight, Liliana."

"Goodnight, Aiden."

I'm sleeping in a cloud. I have to be. There's no way in hell this is the old couch I usually sleep on. I'm enveloped completely in the soft warmth of it, with a belt around my waist so I don't plummet to the ground.

Wait. What?

I open my eyes, blurred with sleep, to a tuft of white blankets. *I guess this must be the cloud.* With languid movements, I stretch out beneath the duvet when the belt I was dreaming about earlier tightens, and I freeze.

Careful not to shift too much, I lift the sheets and peer down at the arm currently wrapped tightly around my waist. A man's arm. *Aiden's arm.*

Immediately, I still. How the hell am I supposed to get out of this one? Before I can figure out a tactful way to escape, the arm around my middle moves upwards to palm my breast. Heat floods my core as the man behind me lets out a soft sigh of contentment.

I relax, giving myself over to the unforgettable sensation of being cherished. He shifts again, nuzzling his face against the crook of my neck and inhaling deeply as his fingers gently pinch my hardened nipple.

"I love your scent, Petal." His raspy voice gives away that he's not yet fully awake.

Like a fool, I'm frozen in place. Whatever happened to the smart woman yesterday who sucked face with this delectable man and then somehow shut it down? Shit. If his hand found its way beneath the band of my pants, I'd be a goner.

His teeth scrape against my ear, and his familiar hardness presses against my ass, causing my core to clench with need. I'm mere moments away from twisting toward him and letting myself have everything his body promises mine when his phone rings.

If the ringtone doesn't wake him up, the vibrations currently reverberating through the table surely will. But there's no way in hell I'll move before he does.

I can tell the moment he wakes up and realizes just

how close we came while sleeping. Like the heat that emanates off a shaft of light, I feel his gaze and force my eyelids not to move. With a tenderness I want to hold on to, he places a kiss on my head before extracting his arm from around me.

Acting like that kiss didn't just make my heart grow three sizes, I stretch and pretend I've just woken up, cracking my lids slowly.

"One second," he whispers into the phone before placing it on the bedside table and pulling his pants on.

"I'm sorry I woke you. Go back to sleep, Lily."

I say nothing as I watch him throw a shirt on and grab his phone before exiting the room.

As if I could go back to sleep now. Not with the way my stomach flutters with an ache only he can fill.

I slump back on the bed, letting out a disgruntled puff of air as Aiden's masculine scent surrounds me.

Shit. I'm so fucking screwed.

Chapter Twenty

Liliana

If I was wondering why my libido started raging over the past few months, I now know why. The sight of Aiden and Kaleb dressed in formal suits has me salivating.

It's okay to lust after your bosses, right? I'm sure everyone fantasized about it at some point in their lives. It couldn't just be me.

Between waking up in Aiden's arms and Kaleb holding me through the turbulence on the plane, I can't stop envisioning what might happen if we gave into this thing that plagued us. It's silly, really. I would never want to come between them, and that's exactly what would happen if I was forced to choose. But I'd rather have their friendship than nothing else.

Calantha had strong feelings about my choice, or rather, my lack of it. She didn't understand why I would rather keep things completely platonic with both of them than lose one, but I liked who I was around them. Kaleb made me feel like a carefree kid again, and Aiden instilled a sense of confidence in me that I never thought I'd feel again. I wouldn't risk losing either of them.

She dropped the argument eventually, but I saw the fire in her eyes tonight while she helped me get ready for the charity gala. If she couldn't convince me herself, she'd do all she could to make me as tempting as possible. Secretly, I loved her for it.

Whoever was in charge of setting up Guastavino's for this event had exceptional taste. Hell, whoever picked this venue to begin with was someone I'd like to meet. The main floor has three bars for guests to procure their cocktails, with random elevated tables scattered throughout the room to showcase auction items which would take up the latter part of the evening.

As much as I love the gorgeous red dress that Calantha and I picked out, I can't help but feel like an imposter. My attire is notably cheap compared to others in attendance tonight, my two bosses included. It feels weird to be in a room with this many people who probably have more money in their bank accounts than I'd ever see in my entire life.

How was I supposed to fit in with anyone here?

"Penny for your thoughts," Kaleb whispers in my ear as we wait for our drinks at the bar.

"They wouldn't even be worth that, I'm afraid."

He eyes me skeptically, but loses his chance to reply when the bartender brings us three glasses. We make room for the other guests to order, moving to the side of the bar as Aiden approaches and Kaleb hands him his drink.

Both of them lavished me with compliments when we met at the office earlier tonight so that we could arrive together, but I couldn't hold a flame to their elegance. They are breathtaking in their suits, and I wasn't the only one who noticed. All eyes were on them as we made our way toward the first table of auction items.

Based on the looks on the women's faces, it wasn't hard to figure out that they envied me. Which was silly. I was Kaleb and Aiden's employee. It wasn't as if I shared an intimate relationship with them both, regardless of how often my thoughts might have taken me there.

When I catch sight of the items up for auction, my mouth goes dry. Gorgeous paintings by some famous artists, week-long vacations on private islands, signed sports memorabilia, and even an instrument signed by some classical musician I'd never heard of. I definitely couldn't afford to bid on anything here.

"Wow," I say in a breath, more to myself than either of my two companions. They both look at me though, and Kaleb chuckles while Aiden only smirks.

"See something you like?" Aiden asks, making my face flush with heat. *Maybe wearing a red dress wasn't such a good idea.*

"Oh yes. The island looks quite charming, I do think," I reply with an accent that was supposed to portray a haughty British heiress but probably comes off more like the scullery maid. Being the gentleman that they are, they both only smile instead of poking fun at my failed accent.

As we make our way over to another table, two

elegantly dressed older women approach us with bright, almost unnaturally white smiles.

"Aiden. Kaleb. We're so glad you decided to come," the darker blonde woman coos, taking hold of Kaleb's arm.

The lighter blonde presses herself against Aiden before placing a kiss on his cheek and leaving a pink imprint behind when she pulls away. *Charming.* His lips turn down in a scowl as he grabs a napkin from a passing waiter to wipe the lipstick off. The woman seems totally oblivious, sticking close to his side.

Kaleb hides his discomfort better, but the tightness in his jaw gives away just how intolerable he finds these women to be. *When had I become so adept at reading their emotions? It was clear as day to me, and I couldn't understand how these two women could be so blind not to notice.*

Kaleb extracts his arm and places it on the small of my back. "Christine, Chantal, this is Liliana Sinclair."

"It's nice to meet you both," I tell them, trying to figure out which one is which. Both of them wear a wedding ring, and I wonder if their husbands know how they spend their time, or who exactly they hope to spend it with.

"The pleasure is all yours, I'm sure," the darker blonde says, while the other covers her mouth to hide a giggle. *Is she aware that covering her mouth does nothing to hide the actual sound that comes out?* Despite my dislike for them, I don't let it show and take a sip of my drink instead. As much as I want to fit in at events like these, I would never let myself become like they are.

"Actually," Aiden says, stepping up to my other side, "the pleasure is all ours." Then he dismisses them with a tilt of his head before both he and Kaleb pull me toward the next table.

"You didn't have to do that," I tell them, keeping a smile plastered on my face.

"And they didn't have to be such uptight old birds, but here we are," Kaleb replies with a soft pinch to my back.

I can't help the laugh that escapes my lips, causing a few guests to look over with interest. "Are these events always like this?"

"Unfortunately. Though not everyone is as ill-mannered as those two." Aiden scoffs distastefully as he looks back at the pair of women still staring after us.

Kaleb pulls me close, his warm breath moving the few soft curls left loose around my face. "We try to make it fun by using those awful moments to figure out if those women are married for love or money. When they act like that, it's usually because they're only in it for wealth and status."

We get another drink before Aiden and Kaleb introduce me to a few of their friends, all of which are much easier to tolerate than the women from earlier, and before long, it's time to take our seats for dinner before the silent auction starts.

Because charity galas were so far outside my comfort zone, I looked up cutlery rules before coming so that I wouldn't look like a complete fool when it came time to the meal, even if our table was strictly friends and colleagues. The food was exceptional and much too fancy. Tiny portion sizes must be how the rich stayed so thin, seeing as how even the salad was barely more than a mouthful.

Warmth spreads through my body as I ride the edge of a cheerful buzz. When the waiter comes with a pot of coffee, I jump at the chance. We still have an entire auction left to sit through, and if I drink any more, I'll no doubt make a fool of myself.

I wonder if Aiden and Kaleb plan to bid on anything. They don't strike me as sports fans, at least not enough to own a signed baseball. Maybe they're collectors of art and like to hang pretty pictures in the hall of their homes. It hit me then that I didn't know as much as I thought I did about my two bosses. In some ways, it felt like I'd known them for years, but in reality, I knew very little about them outside of work. Probably for the best.

We mingle a bit more while the auction gets under-way, starting with the signed violin which goes for an exuberant amount of money. Anyone looking closely would catch the astonishment on my face, despite my futile attempts to hide it. These people were bidding more money than I'd ever seen in my entire life on trin-kets and memorabilia. It's hard for me to understand splurging like that.

As the auctioneer announces the next bid for a one-of-a-kind painting, I excuse myself to the bathroom. With as tight as my dress was, I'm sure my full bladder had me looking extra bloated, and it wouldn't hurt to check that my makeup wasn't smeared under my eyes too. Having left Calantha in charge of my makeup, I wore way more than usual tonight. She'd tried to get me to wear fake lashes, but I put my foot down. With my luck, they'd unglue from my eyes at the worst moment and I'd be left looking like I had caterpillars climbing on my face. No thanks.

A sharp, pungent scent envelops me as I sashay past a crowded table, transporting me back in time. My heart hammers in my chest as I scan the room, searching for the source of it. Sweat forms on my upper lip and my palms turn clammy. *Breathe, Lil. You're in New York, not on the farm.*

I walk faster, needing to get away and even more determined to find the bathroom. Lady luck is on my side when I don't find a line or even another soul inside. Locking myself in a stall, I pull air into my lungs to steady my racing pulse. *You knew this could happen someday, Lily. It's only a scent. Tons of old men probably wear that brand. Calm. Down.*

The door to the bathroom opens, followed by the sound of several heels clicking against the tiled floor. Shit. There goes my peace.

I wait until I hear them enter the stalls on either side of mine before I flush and head out to wash my hands, blotting my face with a damp paper towel to cool down. Fear has a funny way of materializing. Sometimes it comes as a cold sweat, but other times, like tonight, it's as if the blood in your veins catches fire, searing you from the inside out. I just have to get back to the safety of Aiden and Kaleb.

With one final glance in the mirror, I exit the bathroom and take a different route back to the table, squeezing between a cluster of chairs until I catch sight of my men.

A smile spreads across my face and some of the panic seeps out of me as I take another step closer.

"Ah, my sweet Anna. I thought I saw you here."

Dread fills my lungs, suffocating me as I recognize the man blocking my path. My vision dims, blackening around the edges. The years haven't been kind to him, but there's no mistaking his cruel smile. How many nights had they forced me to attend to him? How many mornings had I thrown up after he'd left and the sedative wore off? It had never seemed to matter how much I scrubbed. The scent of him lingered for days.

I try to move, to get away, but it's as if every cell in my body has turned to ice. My heart thrashes wildly against my ribs, ringing in my ears.

"Visiting your uncle just hasn't been the same without you, you know. Why don't we go somewhere a little quieter to catch up?" He reaches his meaty hand toward me, placing it on my arm. Bile rises in my throat, and for a second, I fear I might actually throw up on him right here in the middle of this fancy party.

With the reminder that we're not locked in a room on my uncle's property, I tear my arm from his grip and stumble backwards. Directly into a server with a tray full of drinks. Glass shatters and liquid spills everywhere, but

I barely notice. All eyes turn to us, watching, scrutinizing. *I need to get out of here.*

"I'm so sorry," I whisper to the waiter, but I can't hear his response. I can't hear anything but my own thoughts. *Run, Lily. Get away from that vile man before it's too late.*

My arm burns where he touched me, this deep searing pain that makes my stomach roll. *Did he mark me? Can everyone else see what he's done to me?*

Without another thought, I kick off my shoes and run.

Chapter Twenty-One

Kaleb

For as many events that Aiden and I had attended, this was by far my favorite. Having Lily by our side made everything better. She was a beacon of light, keeping us safe against the dark forces around us. The dark forces being the money-hungry women of society, of course.

The night had been perfect until she left us.

When I'd seen her walking back toward our table with such a glorious smile on her face, it was like standing in the sun. All I wanted to do was bask in her warmth, but then Burt fucking Brandon cut her off and everything changed.

I'll never forget the look on her face. I don't think I'd ever seen such pure, unadulterated fear before. But I didn't have any time to figure out why she might be afraid of him because the glass shattered and everyone turned to watch as Lily, my perfect blossom, fled.

Aiden and I were already on our feet, ready to find out what the fuck was going on. "Go after her. I'll take care of things here," he says, his voice sharp and cold like steel.

He didn't need to tell me twice. It wasn't long before I caught sight of her, running barefoot down the hall toward the bright exit sign. She made it through the doors before I could reach her, thankfully slowing down once outside. Her wails echo off the concrete walls, making me want to turn around and take care of Burt myself.

What the fuck had he done to make her this afraid?

"Lily!" I shout as I catch up with her. She leans against the wall, bent over and breathing hard. Her long black hair hides her face as I step closer.

"Lily," I say again, softer this time as I reach out to touch her arm.

"No!" she screams, thrashing against me like a madwoman.

"It's Kaleb. He's gone. You're safe."

At the mention of my name, she settles a little, but her body continues to tremble. I move forward, embracing her tightly and whispering soft words of reassurance. That's when she truly falls apart.

She's no longer the strong woman I met at Club Rapture and worked with for these past few months. Seeing her like this feels like my heart's being ripped right from my chest

"Let me take you home," I whisper, knowing we need to get away from here. She needs to go somewhere she feels safe.

"I can't," she chokes out, hiccupping now. "Calantha."

Through her convulsive breathing, she says her sister's name as if it's three separate words. *What the fuck happened tonight?* Even though I'm desperate to know why she'd want to hide this from Calantha, I don't push her on it. She needs to be around people she trusts, people who love her.

"Alright, you'll come home with me then. I'll keep you safe, Lily. I promise."

She nods, her teeth chattering now. I pick her up, cradling her against my chest as I take out my phone and call our driver to bring the car around.

For the entire drive back to the penthouse, I hold her trembling body close. I throw my jacket over her, trying to give her back some of the warmth she always radiates.

Our building's doorman lets us through as I carry my woman to the elevator, holding her snugly against my chest until we reach our floor.

"What do you need?" I ask, willing to gift her the stars if that's what she asks for.

"Shower."

Striding through the apartment toward my ensuite bathroom, I hesitate. Do I leave her alone in this state? It's the last fucking thing I want to do right now, but I'm afraid that having me so close while she's this vulnerable will only make things worse. *Fuck! She deserves better than this.*

"I have to set you down. Can you stand?"

She nods, staring vacantly at an invisible spot on the tile floor. When I set her down, she strips naked and walks into the shower. Pain and anger flare white hot inside me while I watch as she scrubs her arm raw. *What the fuck had this man done to her?*

A strangled, gut-wrenching sound leaves her lips, urging me to step inside the shower.

"Lily..." I whisper, desperation clawing at my insides with the need to protect her from whatever demons currently race through her mind.

My heart stalls in my chest when her haunted eyes lock with mine. "I need him off me."

Those five little words will plague me for the rest of my life. "I've got you. He won't ever hurt you again." The words escape me, unbidden yet powerful. A promise. No matter what I must do, that motherfucker will never get another chance to hurt her.

Makeup trails down her cheeks, but I can't tell if it's from the water or her tears. Probably both. Her chest heaves as the frantic scrubbing of her arm stalls out, and for a second, I worry she might collapse.

With tentative movements, I cover her hand and slowly take the soap. She lets me wash her, cleanse the grime of Burt fucking Brandon from her flesh. Then I grab some shampoo, directing her to sit on the small stool carved into the shower while I massage her scalp.

Neither of us talk. By the time I smear conditioner into her hair, the sobbing has stopped. Now she appears numb, and somehow, this is worse. What cage in her mind is she trapped in and how can I help her break free?

Shutting off the shower, I grab a towel and direct her to sit on the toilet seat while I comb her hair. Whatever I can do to make sure she knows just how important she is, just how many people are in her corner, I'll do it.

She stares blankly at the wall, her eyes glassy and unfocused as I attempt to braid her long black hair. Having never braided hair in my life, the end result is messy and barely kept together, but at least it's tied back now.

"Come," I say, holding out my hand for her. She gazes at it for what feels like an eternity before finally placing her icy fingers in mine. With the towel still around her body, I sit her down on the edge of my bed.

"I'm going to grab you some clothes, alright?" When she doesn't acknowledge me, I turn and head toward the closet on the other side of the room. I grab two of everything, knowing I'll need to get out of these wet clothes before I can comfort her further, but as I walk back into the room, I find her snuggled beneath the blankets and her wet towel discarded on the floor.

I place the clothes on the bench at the foot of the bed and unbutton my wet shirt.

"Kaleb..." My name on her lips sounds like a prayer, causing my heart to crack further.

"I'm right here, baby." The endearment slips out, but I don't have it in me to feel ashamed. Tonight, I am her protector, and Aiden is her gladiator. Whoever thought they could hurt her would soon realize that they'd have to go through us first, and we were far scarier than any demons.

"Stay."

A command. A question. Yet what she doesn't seem

to realize is that I have no intention of leaving. I will be her light, her warmth, and I'll slay the devil if I have to.

"I'm not going anywhere, but these wet clothes aren't going to help you, baby."

"Please," she whispers, pulling back the blankets with an invitation, a plea.

I throw on a new pair of boxer briefs and crawl into bed beside her. She curls her body around mine, burying herself into my chest where her tears fall against my skin.

"I'm here, Lily. You're safe. We won't let anything happen to you." I repeat the words several times, stroking her back and promising her the world. We stay like this until her tears dry and my arm goes numb. She pulls away, peering up at me from beneath her dark lashes.

Slowly, I raise my hand to trace her face. Down her nose, her cheeks, her jaw. I do my best to ignore her nakedness because that's the last damn thing she needs right now. But to my surprise, she lifts her own hand and traces my face too. Over my lips, down my neck, across my chest. Her eyes roam over my body, flashing with a heat so potent it feels like I'm standing over a volcano, ready to sacrifice myself to this goddess.

Slowly, she closes the space between us, placing timid pecks of her lips against mine that cause a pang to resonate through me. I follow her lead, allowing her to control how far this goes. When her small hand trails lower, down over my briefs and grips my cock, I groan.

"Lily," I whisper, stopping her hand on my shaft. "Now might not be—"

"You... you don't want me."

"Does it feel like I don't want you?" I reply with a thrust into her palm. "But with what happened tonight, you're vulnerable. I don't want you to have regrets."

"I want it. I want you. And I... I need to forget. Please, Kaleb. Make me forget." Her lip wobbles, crushing my soul into dust.

"You're in control, Lily. Whatever you need, take it. I'll follow your every command. And if you change your mind, we'll stop. Okay, baby?" Whatever happened with Burt went far deeper than just tonight. It also didn't take a genius to figure out that what happened left her feeling completely without control. So tonight, I'd give her back that power.

She kisses me then, her lips tasting of pain and heartache, salty from her tears. I savor it. This moment. This gift she's giving me. I serve at the pleasure of my Blossom, my Lily. And I will do whatever is in my power to replace her spoiled memories with better ones.

I leave her lips, pressing my own down along her neck, over her collarbone, and to her incredibly sensitive nipples. Just like that night at Club Rapture, tonight isn't about me. It's about her. And I'll continue to cherish her for as long as she'll let me. Despite her demons, this woman shines a light on every single person she meets, choosing to keep her darkness hidden. She refuses to let her pain cast a shadow on anyone else.

In that moment, I make a vow to chase away that darkness, to illuminate every aspect of her life, just like she does for me, for Aiden, and for everyone else.

I flick one nipple with my tongue, gently pinching

the other with my fingers while she mews beneath me. It reminds me of that night all those weeks ago and how we thought we could bring her over the edge just from these two pebbled points.

She writhes on the bed, watching as I shift lower and let my fingers dance along her slit. This is what was missing from the club. Her eyes give everything away. Hooded with desire, they almost appear golden.

"You're so wet," I say, pressing kisses against her stomach and inserting one finger inside her slick heat.

"Kaleb," she moans, tilting her hips and riding my finger.

"What do you want, Lily?"

Instead of answering, she licks her lip and stares at me with contemplation. I extract my finger, bringing it up to her clit and making slow, gentle circles.

"What do you want?" I ask again, lightening the pressure even more until I barely touch her.

She licks her lips and looks away while I continue to kiss along her stomach, her ribs. Just when I think she's not going to answer, she says, "Taste me."

Blood rushes to my cock, hardening it further as I move to follow her direction. I lay between her thighs and stare at her glistening pussy.

"Spread your legs for me. Yes, just like that, baby." I whisper words of appreciation as I inch closer to her center and place small kisses on her inner thighs, her lips, her mound, until finally, I allow myself to taste the delicacy in front of me.

As my tongue delves inside her, she gasps. Her hands

move to my hair, her fingers curling around the strands and pressing me more firmly against her. I fuck her with my tongue as my cock throbs inside my boxers, then I lick my way up to her clit and suck it into my mouth.

"Kaleb!" she shrieks, holding tighter to my hair as I hum my enjoyment.

I add two fingers to the mix, dipping them inside her to graze against her g-spot and continue my onslaught, listening to the way her body speaks to me until she shatters. Even then, I don't let up, letting her ride out her pleasure just a little longer while I lap up her taste.

When she closes her legs, I pull back and give her a smile, happy to find color returning to her cheeks.

Leaving my home between her legs, I shuffle toward the pillows and plant a searing kiss to her lips that I hope will tell her everything I can't say with words.

"Let's get some rest, baby. Tomorrow's a new day."

"But—"

"No buts. You need to rest." I place a kiss on her forehead, and to my surprise, she doesn't fight me further. With her head on my chest and one of her legs tossed over my own, she falls asleep. Before I know it, I do too.

Chapter Twenty-Two

Aiden

Burt Brandon has been a thorn in our side for only a few weeks, but I already want him gone. Not only is he trying to leverage us for God knows what, he's also harming the woman Kaleb and I vowed to protect.

The event coordinator, Renaldo, intercepts me before I reach Burt.

"She was with you?" I nod in confirmation, so he continues, "Is she alright?"

"Kaleb is with her now. I will, of course, cover the damages for the broken glass, and I hope the server wasn't hurt. But I need to speak to Burt." We've been to several of Renaldo's events, and from every interaction I've had with him, he's a decent guy. He might tolerate the wealthy, and let's face it, he is one too, but it hasn't eaten away at his soul like it has for so many of the guests in attendance.

"Absolutely." He turns away with a flourish, addressing the onlookers with an easy smile on his face. "Now this is a true charity event, my friends. Let's all focus our attention back to the auction so that we may spend our exuberant amounts of money, shall we?" The crowd laughs, turning away from the broken glass while I hunt down the piece-of-shit councilman.

Unsurprisingly, I find Burt near the bar with a fresh drink in his hand and several men around him. I don't need to hear what he's saying to know he's talking about Liliana. That's the only reason a sniveling cockroach like him would have such an audience.

I enter the circle of men gossiping like housewives, and their laughter stops. For a second, I regret not eavesdropping on their conversation in case he let something slip that would help me understand. Was he bragging to his friends about what happened? Probably not entirely. It's more likely that any words coming out of his mouth are a lie, and I'm far too angry for his bullshit.

"May I have a word, Burt?" I ask, trying to keep the iron from my tone.

"I'm a little busy at the moment." He smirks, gesturing to the others around him. I follow his hand, glaring at each one until their smiles fall and they make an excuse to leave.

"It wasn't really a question." Everyone scurries away like the rats they are. Even the bartender disappears, likely sensing the tension between us. "Now, what the fuck did you do to my assistant?"

Burt scoffs, sipping on his scotch like he doesn't have a care in the world. "The fact that you think I did anything at all is highly offensive and only proves how very little you know your staff. That woman is far too unsophisticated for an event like this, but you brought her anyway. Do you even have a vetting system for new employees, or will you just take in any used mutt off the streets?"

This over-confident prick is on my last fucking nerve. I step closer, smiling as I notice the slight tremble in his jaw. Despite his attempt to hide it, apprehension replaces his bravado from only moments ago. It's obvious in the buildup of sweat on his brow and the way he leans back, attempting to create distance between us. Good. Be afraid, Burt. It's the only smart choice you've made since we've met. "Liliana has more class in one strand of her hair than you do in your entire disgusting body. I'll ask again—"

"That little slut should have stayed home."

Time seems to slow down as the air stills around us. "Mind your fucking words, Mr. Brandon. Or I will find a way to do it for you." In my mind, I'm strangling him, watching him fight for his last fucking breath. Heat explodes in my chest as I watch him suffer, and I'm desperate to end him right here.

But in reality, he's nearly untouchable. At least in our current state, surrounded by hundreds of the city's wealthiest. The slimy fucker from our first meeting with Burt at the Plaza steps closer, as if to intervene.

"I'd advise you to keep far away from my staff, Burt. Don't fucking test me." Giving myself one last moment to enjoy the trepidation on his face, I turn and head back to our table. I grab my jacket off the back of the chair, say my goodbyes, and make my way toward the exit. On the way, I check my phone to find a text from Kaleb letting me know they're at the penthouse and asking me to find her shoes.

While I search, I send a quick text to Renaldo to let him know my bid for one of the auction pieces and ask him to handle it in my absence. After I find her heels scattered along the hall, I pick them up and make a call to our driver.

What the fuck had happened between them to make Liliana react like this? Had he hurt her? How did they even know each other? Worries race through my mind like snowballs, growing larger with each unanswered question. By the time I arrive at our building, a little of the tension leaves me knowing that I'll see Liliana soon and can check for myself that she's alright.

The sounds of breathy moans and pleas reach my ears when I exit the elevator, and I can't stop the little pang of jealousy that shoots through me.

I pour myself a glass of whiskey and head to the balcony, shutting the door tight to drown out the delectable sounds coming from the bedroom. If this were any other night, I'd be pleased. Liliana is here, in our home. *Is it the events of tonight that sour this moment, or that she's chosen Kaleb?*

Not wanting to find out, I take a sip of my drink and enjoy the cool night air. I drain the glass in one go, wishing I'd brought the whole bottle. Temptation. That was my Liliana. But I couldn't just waltz into Kaleb's room and hope to join their lovemaking, could I? No, she was too vulnerable. Maybe if she'd come here under different circumstances I would, but not tonight. Maybe not ever.

Now I'm even more desperate to talk to him, to find out what pieces of the puzzle she might have exposed that could help us see the big picture. How were we supposed to protect her without knowing what darkness lurks beyond the light?

The sound of the door sliding open interrupts my pity party. Kaleb carries the bottle of whiskey and an empty glass. He leaves the screen door open in case Liliana needs us, then he sits and pours us each a healthy amount of whiskey.

We don't speak. Instead, we stare out at the city lights and sip our drinks.

"How is she?" I finally ask.

"She'll be alright, in time."

"Did she tell you what happened?"

"Not in so many words, though I have my suspicions," he growls. "What happened tonight... I don't think it was the primary cause. She knew Burt before the gala, and whatever transpired between them was bad enough to put her in a full-blown panic. He must have touched her tonight, because she scrubbed her arm so hard, I thought the flesh would fall right off. Then she asked me to make her forget."

His words cause my already dark mood to plummet. That disgusting piece of filth thought he could touch what was ours? We might not have been around in her past to protect her, but we sure as fuck were now.

"What did Burt have to say?" Kaleb asks, finishing his whiskey and pouring himself more.

"Nothing good. He did say something that was odd, though. He said, *'That little slut should have stayed home'*."

Kaleb's knuckles turn white as he grips the glass hard enough for it to shatter. "Please tell me you made him bleed for that."

"Unfortunately not, though the night isn't over yet. I was too angry to understand at the time, but now that I'm thinking about it, it doesn't make sense. She should have stayed home? As in, she shouldn't have come to the event, or is he talking about something more specific?" It didn't add up for him to mean the gala. I don't even think he knew she worked for us until tonight. A memory flashes, making me sit up straighter. "When we were in Massachusetts, she mentioned something about a farm. She seemed equal parts terrified and repulsed when she brought it up. Perhaps that's where he knows her from. Maybe that's what Calantha alluded to in the club application, where Liliana protected her?"

"I doubt Burt will tell us anything, though I'd be happy to try to get something out of him if we decide to go that route," Kaleb says, his voice shifting, turning darker with the taste of violence. "Message Elliott. If anyone can find a connection, it's him."

Liliana's high-pitched scream reverberates through the apartment as I unlock my phone.

Forgetting everything else, we jump to our feet and

race to his bedroom. Kaleb throws open the door, but all we find is Liliana fast asleep on the bed.

"No. No. No. Get off her!" She's tossing frantically, kicking and flailing like she's fighting a ghost. And that's exactly what she's doing.

"Lily," Kaleb says in a low voice, but it doesn't stop her thrashing.

I call her name, hoping she'll recognize our voices and settle because touching her in this state will skyrocket her fear. When she doesn't respond, I try another tactic.

Kaleb kneels on the bed now, inching toward her thrashing form.

"You're safe, Petal," I say soothingly.

Following my lead, Kaleb reassures her too. "We'll protect you, Blossom."

Her erratic movements ease until she stills, breathing deeply in a restful slumber. Neither one of us wants to leave her alone again, not while the demons wreak havoc in her mind. Kaleb curls beside her on the bed while I make myself comfortable on the plush chair in the corner.

Don't worry, Lily-love, your ghosts don't stand a chance against us.

Chapter Twenty-Three

Liliana

Five Days Later.

When we escaped the farm, I thought I'd left the past behind me, but I was wrong.

It's taken everything within me not to fold in on myself. I was making progress, becoming a new person, with friends and a job I loved. Now it feels tainted somehow. Even though the gala wasn't an official Exalta Solutions event, I was struggling not to fear every phone call or meeting request. Clearly, the man who used my body as a teen ran in the same circles. And now he knows where I work.

How long will it be before he tells my uncle?

In the days following the event, I kept my fears hidden, locked up tight in the corners of my mind. Aiden and Kaleb had been way more supportive than I could have imagined. When I woke up naked in Kaleb's bed the next morning, it was like waking up at the farm once the sedative wore off. I was drowsy, confused, and once again, afraid.

If it hadn't been for Kaleb sleeping beside me or

Aiden's nearby presence, I probably would have freaked. To my surprise, they hadn't demanded information, yet I could see in their eyes that they were curious. Something in my gut told me they wanted to know only because they cared, and maybe if I let them in, I'd discover that the world really isn't so shitty. Sadly, life isn't all rainbows and unicorns. I couldn't have told them even if I wanted to. Not when everything was so fresh and the memory of what transpired between Kaleb and I, here in his bed, came rushing back. So I ran instead.

To say things have been weird since is an understatement. My overactive brain probably isn't helping, but it's impossible not to notice the subtle differences. Somedays it feels like they're avoiding me, which only leads to me doing the same. Instead of speaking to them in person, I've resorted to emailing whenever necessary or leaving post-it notes on their desk when they step out. It's ridiculous.

Calantha assures me I'm not doing myself any favors by avoiding the subject. She says there's no way either of them know what we went through and if I'd just talk to them each about it, I'll know what they're thinking and can stop with the mental conversations. She's probably right. It's not as if they've treated me differently, at least not like they would if Burt had told them the sordid details of my past. *If he did, they'd surely find me repulsive.*

And that's how I find myself cornering Aiden before a meeting to apologize.

"Um, hi." *Great fucking start, Lil.*

"Liliana," Aiden replies, a smile curving his luscious lips.

"I'm sorry for causing a scene at the gala. And for acting all weird after, including right now. Yup, I'm definitely being weird. Okay, now I'm going to go hide or stew over this entire one-sided conversation." I turn to leave, needing to escape this dumpster fire of my own making, when Aiden's hand lands on my shoulder.

"You have nothing to apologize for. It's that idiot Burt who owes you an apology, though that wouldn't even begin to make things right. That night doesn't change a single thing between us, at least not in the way you're thinking."

"You say that now, but you've been avoiding me. Deny it all you want, but I did have to corner you in order to have this conversation."

He grins. "You're right, I was. But it was only because I didn't want to smother you. I was only trying to give you space. I never meant to make you think you'd lost a friend."

"Is that what we are then, friends?" I ask, gazing at my fingers like a coward. My emotions have been all over the place as of late. Between the kiss I shared with Aiden in Massachusetts and the way I fell apart for Kaleb after the gala, my lady bits were giving me all sorts of wild ideas.

At night, I'm plagued with bad dreams. Burt has Calantha in my old room, the one my uncle gave me to please his guests, and I'm trapped in the wall, forced to watch him defile her. But during the day, I relive the soft moments with Aiden and Kaleb, wanting to feel their touch more than anything else. *What the hell is wrong with me? What kind of person does that make me, to want them after everything I've endured?*

"If that's what you wish, then yes. I would very much like to be friends."

I give him a bright smile as I finally bring my eyes up to meet his. *Friends is what we should be. Friends is all I can really handle at the moment, anyway.* "Good. It's settled."

I walk back to my desk, knowing I need to have a similar conversation with Kaleb later today but happy that at least one of them is over with.

Work picks up, keeping me busy until somehow, it's the end of the day. Aiden is on a call in the office, but Kaleb is just returning from a meeting with Karl from marketing.

"Heading out?" he asks as I grab my purse and jacket.

"I was hoping we could talk first."

He tries and fails to hide the surprise from his face, but it quickly turns to delight as he pulls me into a nearby empty boardroom. "Is everything alright, Lily?"

"Oh. Yes, everything's good. Sorry, I didn't mean to worry you. I just wanted to apologize for the scene I caused and make sure we were okay after what happened. It was very unprofessional of me, and I just hope you'll give me another chance to prove that I won't be a problem." Being in this closed room makes everything more potent. His nearness, the woody scent of his cologne, and the way he looks at me, like I placed every star in the night's sky. It's hard not to get lost in it. In him.

"No way. Nope. I don't accept your apology because there's no need for it. What happened at the gala was not your fault, and what happened after... that was something I'd been wanting to do for a very long time." He steps closer, brushing the hair from my face with such tenderness that tears threaten to build behind my eyes.

"Oh." I sound like a fool, and maybe I am, but I can't help feeling like I've finally found people who truly get me. Both of my two incredibly attractive bosses are telling me it's not my fault when they don't even have the full story. Knowing they have such faith in me is more than I could have ever hoped for. Not everyone would have felt the same way. *Am I just going to ignore the rest of his comment? Oh, hell yeah. I can't let myself think about it or I'll melt into a puddle right here on the boardroom floor.*

Kaleb's phone vibrates, interrupting the tender moment. "I'm sorry, Lily, but I have to get this."

"Of course. Thanks for what you said. I'll see you tomorrow!" With a little skip to my step, I head home.

Hands glide over my bare flesh, firm and demanding as I writhe on the bed at Club Rapture. I open my eyes, expecting to find only an inky darkness behind the blindfold, but to my surprise, I'm not wearing one.

There's a head of dark curls between my thighs, licking and sucking on my aching clit. Aiden catapults me to the edge of orgasm but never fully lets me crash over it. How often had he done this that night while pretending to be Wes? More times than I could remember.

He pulls away, bringing his gray eyes to mine. "My colleague, Kaleb, and I will take excellent care of you tonight, Petal."

Footsteps approach, and I turn my head to find Kaleb striding toward us with a wide grin on his face. His naturally tanned skin glows beneath the candlelight. When he reaches the bed, he leans down and kisses me deeply. Aiden's torturous tongue starts up again, somehow seeming to match the rhythm of our kiss.

I'm close, teetering on the edge, and as if he can sense it, Kaleb shifts to lavish his attention on my nipples. He kisses one, twirling his tongue around one sensitive peak while pinching the other until I'm arching off the bed in bliss.

My eyes snap open, then fall shut again as bright light filters in through the living room curtains. I'm not actually at Club Rapture. Kaleb was never there, and I've just had what might be my very first sex dream that just happened to feature my two bosses. "No," I groan, burying my face in the pillow.

Fuck. I really am screwed up, aren't I? Between the kiss I shared with Aiden and the oral sex Kaleb gave me after the gala, how do I still have a job?

Did they know what I'd done with each of them? Was it only a game? I knew the answer to that. These men, the ones I've started considering my champions, would never treat me as if I were a toy to be fought over.

My core aches with the need for release. I can't exactly touch myself on the couch with my sister sleeping in the bedroom only a few feet away. After checking the time, I discover that it's not as early as I originally thought and clamber out of bed toward the bathroom.

I stand beneath the spray of hot water and let it wash over me. Every nerve is on fire, electrified with arousal, and with my eyes closed, I can almost picture them here with me. My fingers skim down my body into the wetness between my thighs. With each beat of my heart, my clit throbs a desperate rhythm, and before long, I shatter, whispering their names like a plea.

A little thrill goes through me as I think about Aiden and Kaleb. Would they be able to tell what I'd done this morning, how I'd touched myself to the memory of their caresses in my dream? I'll probably only feel embarrassed about it later, but for now, all I feel is complete satisfaction.

Chapter Twenty-Four

Kaleb

"Thank you all for coming. Aiden and I are thrilled to have you at our fifth annual backyard BBQ. Since this is NYC and none of us have backyards big enough for everyone, we're grateful to 620 Loft and Garden for hosting us this year. You can't get views much better than this." I stand along the ridge of the fountain, staring down at a hundred or so staff members and their family. Behind me, the fading sun casts stunning beams of light on the high-rise buildings around us and throws a shadow on St. Patrick's cathedral.

"We hope you enjoy the evening and know that we wouldn't be here without each and every one of you. Your dedication and drive push us forward, bringing peace of mind to thousands of people around the world. Thank you!" He lifts his glass in a toast and the rest of our guests follow suit, clapping as Aiden steps down from the makeshift podium.

Instead of following along, I have one final announcement to make. "While I'm up here, I'd also like to give a huge shout-out to Liliana Sinclair. Where is she... Oh, there she is." Lily stands next to a woman who must be her sister. They share the same black hair, though Calantha's is cut into a stylish bob.

"Liliana made all the arrangements for this gathering, so if it's lame, you know who to blame." The crowd laughs while my beautiful Blossom tries to disappear into the bush beside her. "All jokes aside, let's give Ms. Sinclair a warm round of applause for one kick-ass party!"

I'm sure Lily will give me shit for that later, but I couldn't let the moment pass me by. It wasn't like our previous parties sucked, but our prior assistants never even bothered to learn about the other employees enough to plan something they'd enjoy, and we struggled to stay on top of arrangements between our schedules.

This, along with everything else we'd seen from her so far, was something she thrived at. I honestly can't think of an area where she wouldn't.

Aiden and I mingle, meeting the family members of our newest employees and reuniting with old ones. These events always prove just how much of a damn good job our talent team does with hiring. We've created a culture here that goes beyond the mundane transaction between employee and employer. We're a family. Our employees don't just come to work to get a paycheck. They show up every single day to enrich the lives of so many.

Instead of a sit-down meal, servers walk around the large terrace with trays of sandwiches and other finger foods. I wasn't sure how not having a seating chart would go, but it looks like our guests are loving it. They'll be in for more of a treat later once the buffet opens up.

I spot Aiden trapped in a conversation with one of our scientists and Lily by the small pool. She laughs at something Calantha says, her face practically glowing beneath the final shafts of sunlight peaking between the buildings. Not wanting to lose my shot at getting closer to her and finally meeting the sister who submitted her club application, I stride toward them.

Lily darts her gaze in my direction as I approach. Desire flashes in her eyes but it disappears quickly, making me wonder if I made it all up in my head. The dark purple of her dress brings out the mossy green in her eyes until I swear they aren't hazel anymore. *Damn. I could get lost in those eyes.*

Calantha wheels around and stares at me with curiosity.

"Lily, I hope you liked my speech," I say, giving her a wolfish grin.

"You live to embarrass me, I swear," she replies, feigning exasperation before turning to her sister. "Calantha, this is Kaleb Fitzgerald. Kaleb, this is my sister."

"I'm glad you could make it. Lily talks a lot about you, and with much nicer things than usual for siblings, at least in my experience."

"The good stuff you can believe. The rest is all a bunch of lies." Calantha winks. "My sister talks about you too, actually. All good things, sometimes *really* good things." She nudges her sister, whose ears have turned pink beneath the attention.

"I didn't—" she starts, but I cut her off.

"Oh really? Has she been talking about my fantastic espresso skills? It always makes her steamy when I start frothing."

"Oh my God," Lily sighs, covering her eyes. Calantha laughs, enjoying the discomfort on her sister's face, but something tells me it's not malicious. A person doesn't sign their sister up for a sex club only to turn around months later and enjoy their embarrassment.

"You know, she has mentioned that once or twice, actually."

"Kill me now," Lily whispers, taking a large drink of the cocktail she's holding.

Calantha throws an arm around her sister, giving her a reassuring smile.

Aiden joins our little circle, diverting the attention from Liliana to him. "What are we talking about?"

"Only my death," she replies. If she's hoping to change the subject, she'll soon find out that particular answer will have the opposite effect.

"I was only explaining to Kaleb how fond my sister is of him. Of you both. She mentioned your—"

"Nope! Aren't there other people you have to mingle with? Or can we talk about literally anything else?" Lily runs a hand over her hair, looking like she'd rather be anywhere but here.

"As you wish," Aiden replies before turning toward Calantha. "We haven't been officially introduced. I'm Aiden Daniels."

"Calantha. It's nice to meet you. I've only been to

your building a few times, but damn, that place is a dream. Was it always the plan to have a pool on site?"

With the change in conversation, Lily exhales a sigh of relief. The four of us talk for what seems like hours before Aiden's phone rings and he steps away.

"I should probably go say hi to the rest of the guests. Enjoy your evening, ladies. I'll see you both in a bit."

I talk casually with a few guests until I catch sight of Aiden beckoning me inside. He presses his lips into a grim line, making me wonder what might have ruined his good mood.

"What is it?"

He doesn't answer, only pulls me down the hall toward the kitchen. *This can't be good.*

"Elliott called. He apologized for the delay, I guess he's in the middle of a crisis in Blackstone Creek, but he confirmed our suspicions. Burt Brandon not only knows Liliana's uncle, but he also spent a good deal of time with him over the years."

"So that's what he meant by saying she should have stayed home. But why? What was her uncle promising him?"

"I have a feeling we know what Burt got out of the deal, but what I can't figure out is what her uncle would have gotten in return. Elliott's going to dig deeper, try to find other known associates, but whoever's working with them is adept enough to mostly cover their tracks. Not as good as Elliott, but still good."

"Fuck. Well, if anyone can find something, it's him. At least if we have names, we can avoid causing further discomfort to Lily. Though I'd like to make a visit to this uncle myself." Aiden's eyes darken, mirroring my own lust for vengeance. Instead of acting on it, we return to the party as if we didn't just peel back another layer of Liliana Sinclair's past.

I catch sight of her standing alone near the edge, staring off into the fading sunset. All I want to do is hold her close and protect her from everyone. Whatever Burt did to her, he has to pay. And if what we suspect is true, nothing would stop me from avenging the beautiful woman who now held my heart.

We'll get justice for Lily come hell or high water. And whoever threatens her will soon realize that Aiden and I are both the hell *and* the high water.

Chapter Twenty-Five

Liliana

I could stare at this view every single day and not tire of it.

There's something about this city that sets my heart alight, and I'm once again grateful that Calantha and I decided to come here after we escaped the farm.

As the last ray of sunlight disappears, twinkling fairy lights turn on around the open area until the entire loft illuminates beneath the soft glow. Despite the gentle breeze blowing a few curls free from my pinned hair, I'm not cold. It feels as if a furnace rages inside of me, fueling me toward something I can't quite figure out.

"Alright, I can't keep my mouth shut anymore," Calantha says, handing me a glass of water before taking a sip of her own.

When my sister says things like that, it's hard to guess what will come out of her mouth next. To my surprise, she doesn't mention Kaleb or Aiden at all.

"Exalta Solutions is ten times better than that textile company you worked for. Look at this freaking party, Lil."

She's not wrong. My old job didn't have half the perks this one does. *Or two incredibly hot bosses that make me ache like no other.*

"Do you think the pool is warm?" I ask, seriously considering sitting on the edge and letting my feet dangle inside.

Calantha's smile grows as she pulls me toward the water. The crowd isn't as full as it was earlier, a sure sign that the night is almost over, even though I don't want it to be. Dipping our toes in the cool water, I entwine my fingers with Calantha's and cherish this moment.

We're here. We're safe. And things are finally turning around.

"It's nice to see you so happy," my sister says, gazing at me intently. "And I already know you understand what I mean, so don't try to play coy. It's okay to let them make you happy, Lil. That's what they want to do, you know. It's written all over their faces when they look at you. This mix of possession and need, but not in a bad way."

"That's not—"

"Oh, please. If either of them had the chance to whisk you into a dark corner and ravish you completely, they would. Hell, I bet they'd even work together to help get the task done, if you know what I mean." She wiggles her eyebrows at me until my annoyed look turns into laughter.

"It's not that simple, Calla. Forgetting the fact that they're my bosses, which already complicates things, they don't know just how much my past defines me.

What if they find out how tainted I am and don't want me? Or what if they know someone else who traded favors for flesh with our uncle? I barely survived running into that guy at the gala... I don't think I will a second time."

"You can't truly believe they'd kick you to the curb over what happened when you were a teenager. It was beyond your control. What our uncle did to you doesn't define who you are. You protected me, for God's sake, Lil. Something I will never be able to repay you for but will do my best to."

"Oh, Calantha."

"It's true. And I'm right about this. Stop making excuses for why this won't work and talk to them. Even if you don't want to open up about the farm, at least find out where they see things going between you. That's the only way you'll be comfortable to move forward."

I don't respond, letting her words seep into my skin. Was I sabotaging this already? Fear of the unknown, of rejection and abandonment, weighs me down whenever I think about wanting them both. But if I push all of that aside and truly examine my relationships with Aiden and Kaleb, the truth is obvious. They both want me, and maybe, just maybe, they'd both be happy to claim me as well.

As another hour passes, I try to focus on the people around me, but everything Calantha and I discussed earlier stays at the forefront of my mind. Night descends around us as more people take their leave, and before I know it, my sister says her goodbye.

She hugs me tight, refusing my offer to leave with her before nodding to the men beside me.

"Thanks for having me! Best company party ever," she tells Aiden and Kaleb, who smile at her warmly. "Make sure she gets home safely, okay? I'm counting on you both to take care of her."

I don't miss the slight shift in her voice or the innuendo, and I'm positive my bosses don't either. Heat flares beneath my cheeks at the eagerness behind their eyes as they nod and say goodbye to my sister. I really should be more annoyed with her meddling, but I can't help the zing of excitement that flows through me. Could this really be happening?

For some people, the hour is still early and the nightlife of the city beckons them to play. They make their way toward us, praising us for a great time before departing until it's only the three of us left.

Without speaking, we gather up our things and thank the wait staff for all of their hard work before heading to the exit.

"Would you like to come back to the penthouse for another drink?' Kaleb asks, stopping at the entrance. I look between the two, wondering if this might be a test. If I say yes to Kaleb, what does that mean for Aiden?

As if sensing my dilemma, a smile grows on Aiden's face. "The penthouse is ours, in case that helps you decide."

"You live together?" I ask, startled at the news. I knew they were close, but I never would have suspected these two grown men shared a home. After the gala, I thought we were at Kaleb's house, and that Aiden had only shown up to make sure I was safe. Why else would he have slept on a chair in Kaleb's room?

"Come with us, and I'll tell you all about it on the drive over," Kaleb replies, throwing me a hopeful smile.

For once, I don't hesitate. I tamp down the fear and worries threatening to flood my body and do something I want to. Could it all blow up in my face? Possibly. But it's just as likely that it won't, and if I don't give myself this moment to find out, I'll regret it.

"Okay."

I sit between them in the backseat with the heat of their thighs pressed against mine and the brush of their shoulders keeping me still as we drive through the city streets. It's intoxicating. I feel trapped between them, a fly caught in their web, but I don't think they'll eat me. At least, not in a way I won't like.

Kaleb keeps the conversation going, doing exactly as he promised and sharing the story of how they came to live together after college. Even after they started earning enough to live alone, neither of them wanted to. It wasn't anything I didn't expect, and to be honest, it made a whole hell of a lot of sense. His words help distract me from the ache in my lower belly, the one urging me to put one hand on each of their thighs, to have them crowd me further and take whatever it is they want from me right here in this car.

Always the coward, I don't do any of that, and before I know it, the driver has parked in front of a tall building and Aiden holds the door open for me. I take his offered hand, unsurprised by the electricity that passes through our skin at the contact. His gray eyes darken to slate, holding on a moment longer than necessary once I'm free from the car.

He lets me go, heading toward a doorman who smiles at each of us as we pass. *Of course they'd have a doorman. Didn't every rich family in the show Gossip Girl have one?*

We pass what must be the concierge desk for the resident's of this building, and he waves us toward the elevators with a "have a good night." Once inside, Aiden inserts a key into a little hole above the buttons before pressing P4. I don't remember this from my last visit, but I hadn't exactly been myself when we arrived, and when I'd finally left the next morning, my only focus was on getting out of there as quickly as possible.

As the elevator begins its ascent, the sexual tension radiating off the three of us builds. It's palpable, heady, consuming every single one of my fears for tomorrow. I keep my gaze on the floor, my hands, anything but their faces, because if I see the same lust mirrored in their eyes, I won't be able to stop myself. And I want to be at least a little smart about all of this.

The doors part to reveal a large foyer with a walk-in closet and views of the open space living room. I let Kaleb take my jacket and step out of my wedge sandals, setting them on the little tray just inside the closet.

Aiden flicks a light switch, illuminating the space until I can see that the room opens up further into a masculine kitchen with dark cabinets and appliances and a pop of white in the backsplash. The living room has the same theme with dark gray sectionals, a black rug, and floor-to-ceiling windows that overlook the city.

"Wow." I step closer to the windows, staring out at the skyline lit up beneath the darkness of night. It feels like freedom being so high up and far away from everyone. Like I can finally breathe again.

"Beautiful," Kaleb whispers, but when I turn to him, he isn't looking beyond the glass. He's staring at me. I feel a blush creep up my face, but I don't shy away from his gaze.

"Can we get you anything?" Aiden asks. I consider asking him for something strong, something that might help smother the overactive parts of my brain that are constantly worrying about everything and nothing all at once. But I already had enough to drink at the party and ask for water instead.

As Aiden strolls to the kitchen, Kaleb takes my arm. "You didn't really get a full tour last time you were here. Would you like one now?"

I nod, following him down a hall past the kitchen and living room. There's a bathroom to my right, another small closet on the other side of the hall, and three doors at the end.

Vague memories spark as we head toward the room on the right, and as Kaleb flicks on the light, the images turn crystal clear. Here is where he soothed me after the gala.

What I didn't notice then was the second door on the

opposite side of the room. The one that connects to the bedroom on the other side of the hall. Aiden's room.

Kaleb lets me peek inside, though without Aiden here, it feels almost like an invasion of privacy. The layout is the same, but where Kaleb's room looks lived in, Aiden's is pristine. The heady scent of his cologne tickles my nose as we walk back toward the hall, and in my mind, I'm transported back to the kiss we shared at that little bed-and-breakfast all those weeks ago.

Shit. I have to get my feelings together. They only invited me here for a drink. Thinking anything else might happen would only cause problems. *Or disappointment.*

As we make our way back to the kitchen, Aiden hands me a glass of water with four pieces of ice inside, more like icicles than cubes. His fingers graze mine as I take the glass, and I absentmindedly thank him while trying to ignore the spark of heat zipping its way to my core from his touch.

Kaleb beckons me over to the couch. Soft music plays in the background from speakers I can't see, and they've kept the lights off, so the view from outside is our only source. I don't particularly mind it though, as it means my blushes will be hidden.

"Aiden and I have been talking," Kaleb starts as I sit down beside him. Aiden sits on my other side, slightly turned inward on the chaise part of the sectional.

"Oh?" My voice comes out too breathy, so I bring the glass to my mouth and hope they didn't notice. The moment the ice cold water passes my lips, Aiden speaks.

"We want you." His dark, sensual voice does

wonderful things to my body, but his words make me choke on my drink.

Both of them are silent as I splutter, though they each reach out to rub my back while I cough. This can't be what I think it is, right?

Aiden takes the glass from me, setting it on the coffee table in front of us before returning to my side. I avert my gaze, and after a steadying breath, I peer up into his eyes and see the truth of his words.

When I look over to Kaleb, he gives me a bright and buoyant smile, calming the raging storm battering against my mind, but still I can't get the words out. The lustful, carefree woman inside of me, the one that itches to get out every single day since Club Rapture, screams at me. *Say yes, Lil. Say. Yes. But how do I know they won't harm me?*

I push them both away, not letting either of them decide for me as I assess Aiden and Kaleb's faces, replaying every moment we've shared together. I know I could say no and leave, and neither of them would stop me. But saying no means losing what I had with both of them, and that thought hurts too much.

With images of the confident woman who walked out of Club Rapture clear in my mind, I open my mouth and let one word slip out.

"Yes."

Chapter Twenty-Six

Aiden

Her answer replays in my mind like my favorite song, reverberating through my limbs until I'm wired with the need to act. Kaleb and I don't say a word. It's like we're both holding our breath, waiting to see if she'll change her mind, but as the moments pass and she doesn't, I know I need to confirm she means yes to both of us.

He and I had already discussed the possibility that she'd choose. If she wanted to explore a relationship with only one of us, physical or otherwise, we'd accept it. Neither of us would stand in the way because we understand. We both shared a deep connection with Liliana, one that transcended all else, and though it would be hard to stand by and watch my best friend claim the woman I cared for, I would do it, just as he would.

I place my hand on her knee, circling my fingers on her soft skin. "I need you to be explicitly clear, Liliana. Are you saying yes to us both?"

Before she can answer, Kaleb reaches out to put his hand on her other knee, mimicking my actions. "We want to share you, physically and more than that, if you're interested. But we'll understand if that's not something you want."

Liliana bites her lip, inviting me in with her delectable fucking mouth and making my anxiety skyrocket as she continues not saying a word. She sucks in a deep breath, holding it for one beat and then another before she replies.

"Both."

It's only one simple word, but it changes everything. Had she given another word in its place, things would have gone differently. But now that she's agreeing to this with the two of us, my muscles go weak as all tension drains from my body.

She unclasps her hands, letting them fall on top of ours without looking at us. With her lower lip clamped between her teeth, she focuses solely on the skyline.

"You know what that does to me," I tell her, keeping my voice low. I don't dare speak too loud. I want her to feel safe, to fully understand what we're offering her and what we're asking for in return.

With my free hand, I cup her jaw, letting my thumb rest on her bottom lip, and her eyes finally flash to mine. The heat I find within them scorches me, branding me as hers. Shifting her head toward Kaleb, she ensnares him with the same lust-filled gaze. He leans in slowly, tentatively, but waits for her to close the last few inches between their lips.

I watch them, fascinated and rock fucking hard. I drop my hand, rearranging the erection straining to break free as their lips finally lock together. She opens for him, their tongues twirling through the kiss.

Kaleb brings his hand up, tucking it against her jaw and tilting her head just enough to deepen the kiss. I want to touch her, taste her, but part of me is worried that it's too soon. If I act now, will she get frightened and leave? If she changed her mind and chose neither one of us, could we survive it?

Deciding to risk it, I lean in to press a kiss to her collarbone, then another one slightly higher on her neck. She breaks off from Kaleb, turning toward me, and my breath stops. What she does next will determine how the rest of this night will go. Will she turn me away?

Her hazel eyes flash amber a moment before she kisses me. Her lips are soft on mine, following the demands of my own. The scent of cherry blossoms surrounds me, both relaxing and invigorating.

When she pulls away, she's breathless. She looks between Kaleb and me, and I can see the hesitation on her face before she says, "How will this work?"

"Just like this," I tell her, trailing a hand up her thighs and over one of her breasts, squeezing gently. Kaleb does the same on her other side, causing her eyes to close briefly.

"If you ever feel it's too much or you don't like something we're doing, you only have to say so," Kaleb says, gaining her attention.

I stand, grabbing her hand and pulling her to her feet. She wobbles slightly as she catches her balance, but I distract her with another kiss as Kaleb trails one hand up her dress. I swallow her gasp, using it to deepen the kiss while he teases her.

"She's soaked for us." Kaleb stands, cupping her cheek and pulling her face toward his. While she's distracted, I sink to my knees so that I can worship her exactly the way that I've been dreaming of.

I slip her panties down slowly, tucking the wet fabric into my pocket while I place kisses along her thigh. Goosebumps rise on her flesh as she trembles in our hands. She moans, and I look up to find that Kaleb has freed her breasts. He tweaks one nipple and then the other while he kisses her.

Reaching up, I unzip the rest of her dress and slip it down her body until it pools at her feet. She steps out of it, her eyes shining like the sun as she stands completely naked while we're both fully clothed. Instead of the shy girl I expect to find, I see the confident woman from Club Rapture. Kaleb pulls her back into a kiss, distracting her enough she doesn't see what I've grabbed from the table until I run it along her flesh.

She gasps when I press the ice to her chest, over her nipple, which pebbles further under the cold water, and down to her core. I tease her with it, letting it graze against her seam while I lick the path the icicle just traveled.

Feeling her gaze on me, I look up to find her watching me with eyes half closed as Kaleb sucks a hardened nipple into his mouth. Slowly, I press the ice to her clit, and she cries out, her body jerking at the change in temperature. Then I lean forward, letting my tongue slide over her sensitive nub, warming up the area before backing away to repeat the same movement.

I do this several times, waiting until she's comfortable and expecting the motion before I change it up. When I remove the ice once more, I don't pull away and instead, press it up inside her as I lean forward to suck her clit into my mouth.

Her legs tremble as a delicious moan gives way to her first orgasm. When her tremors subside, I pull what's left of the icicle out of her pussy and place it in my mouth. The taste of her arousal is heady, urging me to take her and claim her as ours before anymore time passes.

Kaleb and I stand on either side of her, caging her between us, but she doesn't act like she's trapped. This isn't a wild animal begging to be free. She's a woman who finds freedom in our captivity.

She reaches out a hand to each of us, fingering the buttons of our shirts. "Take these off, please. I want to feel you."

A groan rumbles up from Kaleb's throat as we both follow her request. But while she waits, she doesn't simply watch. Instead, she trails a hand down each of our stomachs until she's stroking both of us through the fabric of our jeans. Her touch is gentle, exploratory, and fuck if that doesn't make me harder.

At Club Rapture, we made sure the entire focus was on her. That's how we preferred it. Each of us took pleasure in bringing someone else to new heights, though I also enjoyed commanding exactly how they got there, but knowing just how much she wanted to give us pleasure in return made my cock thicken and pre-cum bead on the tip.

"Be careful, Petal. I'm having a hard enough time not freeing my cock and fucking you right here," I growl.

My words don't deter her like I expect and instead seem to embolden her. The pressure of her hand shifts, growing more needy, almost like she wants me to act on my warning.

"That's exactly what you want, isn't it, baby? You want us to stretch out that sweet little pussy right here on this couch while the rest of the city sleeps?" Kaleb tosses his shirt to the side, then unbuttons his pants.

"Yes," she sighs before dipping her hand beneath the waistband of his boxer briefs and gripping his hard length.

"Fuck," Kaleb hisses, his word drawn out.

"Let's see if we can please our girl enough to wake up the whole fucking city, shall we?" I ask Kaleb, whose grin turns almost feral. Turning to Liliana, I say, "Why don't you help Kaleb get out of his pants. He's been eager to get inside you for months."

Without hesitating, she does as I ask. I strip out of my own clothes while I watch her eyes light up with each inch of skin she reveals of Kaleb's body, and his own gaze, hooded with desire, as he struggles not to bend her over and take her before she's finished with her task.

She looks back to me when she's done and bites her lip as she notices I'm also fully naked. Kaleb and I might be busy with work but we make time to work out, and at a moment like this, I'm thankful for it. Liliana looks at us like she might devour us whole, and fuck, would I like her to give it a try.

"I want to watch you ride him." As I say the words, images flash through my mind of all the ways we could share her in that position, how we could stretch and fill her completely, and my God, do I want to. But not tonight. This is all so new to her, and I don't want to scare her.

"Like this?" she asks bashfully, reminding us both just how inexperienced she is.

"You're perfect," Kaleb replies, pulling her in for a kiss and guiding her hips to grind against him as he lounges on the couch.

I palm my cock, watching their fevered movements and wanting nothing more than to bend her over and sink my cock in beside Kaleb's. Before I let it get too far, I unhand my cock, even though it aches.

"Fill her up, Kal. I want to see that tight little cunt swallow you to the hilt."

She moans at my words, lifting slightly higher on her knees before sinking down slowly onto his rigid length. His groan and her gasp mingle as she shifts slightly, getting used to the position.

"Do you feel how deep he is, Petal?"

"Yes."

"That's a good girl. Now I want you to use him. Ride him like the hearty stallion he is until you cross the finish line."

She only nods, dipping her head down to kiss him as she starts to bounce on his cock. Whatever unease she might have felt before is gone now. She might be out of her depth but god-fucking-dammit, she is eager to learn, and we'll be more than happy to teach her.

Her tits jiggle with her movements, bouncing in a way that has me entirely captivated. She breaks the kiss, leaning back enough to rest her hands on Kaleb's thighs as she climbs higher toward her release.

She teeters there on the edge of bliss but can't seem to let go.

"Let me," Kaleb says, halting her movements as he grips her hips and thrusts his own upward. His movements are forceful, filling the space with the slapping of their bodies and the angelic cries from her lips.

My balls clench as if screaming at me to fuck her, please her, and take from her too.

Instead of acting on that want, I wait until her release dies down and she's slumped forward to rest against Kaleb, then I stand.

I straddle his legs behind her, my cock pressed against her ass as she sits up more fully.

"You feel so fucking good, Blossom," Kaleb tells her, and I try so fucking hard not to let the panic of his words show on my face. What the hell is he thinking using that nickname? Luckily, she doesn't seem to notice, too distracted by the feel of me behind her.

"Someday we'll have you like this, both of us filling you at once. Would you like that?"

"Yes," she whimpers, and Kaleb moans.

"From the way she just clenched around my cock, I think she would."

With my hands around her waist, I wrap one gently around her neck and press the other against her low belly as I thrust my hips, forcing her to grind against Kaleb's pelvis. She turns her head, capturing my lips with hers in an all-consuming kiss that has me groaning.

"Imagine us both inside you, baby," Kaleb says through gritted teeth as he tries to hold back his own release. "You'd take us so well."

"Please," she whines, breathless.

"There are so many ways we've fantasized about having you, Petal. Let us show you one of them." I stand, brushing the curls off her shoulder and reaching for her hand. She takes it gingerly, lifting herself until she's almost off Kaleb's dick before sliding back down once more.

When she gets up, she mewls softly at the emptiness, causing both of us to chuckle.

"On your hands and knees, baby." Kaleb directs her on the couch so that she's facing me before moving behind her and dipping back inside her wet pussy. "God damn, you feel like home."

He seats himself inside her, sheathed to the hilt, but doesn't move. Her eyes shift to mine as I approach with my cock standing proudly before her.

"I'm going to claim your mouth while Kaleb fucks that tight little cunt of yours."

The look on her face is pure hunger as she licks her lips. Balancing herself on one hand, she reaches out to stroke me and fuck. It feels like I might just pass out with the need to come.

Without needing my direction, she guides my cock to her lips and traces her tongue around the head. Kaleb thrusts slow and deep, not wanting to jostle her too much while she explores the taste and feel of me.

She wraps her lips around the tip, twirling her tongue again before taking more of me until I feel her gag reflex kick in and she pulls back.

"You're perfect," I coo, leisurely thrusting into her mouth, her cheeks hollowing out with each pump of my hips.

I glance up at Kaleb who nods at me, and we both pick up our pace until Liliana moans around my cock, the vibrations of it nearly throwing me over the edge.

A scream erupts from her throat seconds before she shatters, Kaleb following close behind her.

"Fuck, Lily," Kaleb whispers as he finally gets his breathing back under control.

Her lips leave my cock with a resounding pop as she looks up at me, the lust and want not diminished at all from her eyes. It's the same look from the club, but this time, there's something more, something that gives me hope for a future with Liliana between us like this.

I fist my cock, watching as Kaleb pulls his own out of our girl, and she whimpers at the loss of him. "Why don't we give New York a show, hmm?"

She stands and immediately presses her thighs together. They're slick with Kaleb's cum, and her eyes widen as she looks between us.

"Good girl," Kaleb tells her. "Try not to lose any. I

want to watch Aiden push it back up inside you before he fills you with his own."

My balls tighten as I watch her reaction. She sucks in a deep breath, her eyes widening before a desperate whine leaves her parted lips. *God-fucking-dammit, she's so perfect for us.*

Kaleb leads her to the wall of windows, kissing her once deeply before turning her to face the dark skyline. It's late enough now that some of the lights are off, but the view is spectacular nonetheless.

I press her against the glass and she inhales sharply as her heated flesh meets the chilled window. Kaleb spreads her legs for me, shifting her stance enough that I can see his cum leaking from her pussy. I guide my fingers down her back, over the feather tattoo on her spine, and in between her legs until I feel it. Their mixed releases coat my fingers as I press them deep inside her, pushing it back in where it belongs.

Kaleb kisses her again, and as I position my tip to her entrance, she presses into me and gasps. Her pussy stresses around me, strangling me until I'm positive I won't be able to fit anymore.

"Relax, baby. He'll fit." Kaleb moves a hand down to play with her clit, distracting her enough that I can finally press all the way inside.

Fuck, this woman. Filling her like this, it's as if her cunt is a goddamn portal to another universe. One where our pleasures are combined, flowing between our veins like they're connected.

I thrust slowly once, twice, three times before I lose

control. Savage. My inner beast takes over, driving into her with a wild abandon. She's slick around my cock, gripping me with her heat until I'm positive I'm going to explode. But not without her.

Her moans get louder, echoing against the glass as she teeters on the edge of the world.

"That's it, Petal. Let the city know you're ours."

"I'm going to..." she whimpers, before a shriek leaves her lips and her pussy clenches hard around my cock, forcing my own orgasm.

With shallow thrusts, I fill her with every ounce of my seed until I'm sure we've claimed her inside and out.

Liliana Sinclair is ours. And I'll spend the rest of my life making sure she knows it.

Chapter Twenty-Seven

Liliana

Sunlight filters in through the window like a spotlight.

As my eyes peel open, I panic. This isn't my bed, and this sure as hell isn't my living room. My heart races, throat closing as I look around for anything familiar.

My body aches as I shift, reminding me of what transpired with my two sexy-as-fuck bosses. Kaleb lays sprawled beside me, and I can't help but stare at his innocent face. But where is Aiden?

Memories flash of last night. We all ended up in Aiden's bed, one man on either side of me, but the right side is empty now.

With one more lingering look at Kaleb, I tiptoe out of the room on silent feet, careful not to wake him up. The urge to empty my bladder spurs me into grabbing a dress shirt, and I make it to the bathroom by the kitchen without being spotted. As I wash my hands, I stare at my reflection.

Sure, so maybe there's makeup smeared across my

face, but it's still me looking back. Just a little different. There's a confidence in my gaze that hasn't been there before, not like this. Is it the sex making me this way, or is it Aiden and Kaleb who do this to me?

As I exit the bathroom, the scent of coffee leads me to the kitchen, where I find Aiden pouring me a cup.

"I thought that was you," he says. "How did you sleep?"

I take the coffee, blowing on the hot liquid and hoping it'll hide my flustered state. I've never been in a situation like this before, how the hell am I supposed to answer him?

"Fine," I reply, and Aiden smiles like he can see right through me. "Yeah, okay, better than fine. You?"

He reaches out to cup my face, his hand warmed by the heat of his mug. "I've never slept better than with you by my side."

My lips tilt into a smile as if on their own, but I remain silent. What the hell would I even say? 'Yeah, I know what you mean. The nightmares usually ruin any semblance of sleep I might have, but snuggled up between you two after a night of fucking sure scares the demons away.' It might all be true, but there's no damn way I'd voice it. He'd only have more questions if I did.

Things had been changing with me for a while now, ever since Calantha signed me up for that sinful lock-in. Where before I might have been terrified of sex, now I craved it. Even after everything that happened at the gala, coming face to face with a man who sexually abused me, I should be a total mess. But somehow I'm doing alright.

"I'm not normally like this," I blurt out, immediately regretting the words.

"I know."

Of course he does. Aiden isn't some stranger I pulled in off the street. He was there at Club Rapture, and he's worked alongside me these past few months. I wonder if Kaleb knows about the night I spent with Aiden and another man. Would he change his mind about me if he knew? Would he think any less of me?

"Hey," Aiden tilts my head until I have no choice but to look at him. He smells clean, freshly showered, and my skin heats as I picture him lathering up beneath the hot spray. His hand comes up, smoothing out the slight v that formed between my brows.

I smile, unable to control the reaction as I watch my smokey-eyed god care for me.

"This thing between us... there's nothing to be ashamed of. We're all consenting adults, and it's so much more than just sex. Kaleb and I want to give this a real shot with you, but we'll understand if it's too much. Whatever you decide won't affect your job or our interactions." He dips his head low, pressing his lips against mine gently. "Mostly, anyway. I wouldn't be able to do that in front of Sharon, I suppose."

I chuckle, throwing my arms around his shoulders and kissing him again. Aiden lifts me up and sets me down on the counter as he crowds between my legs. The cold marble bites the back of my thighs, causing goose-bumps to rise on my arms. He presses his hard cock against my center, making me forget the aches and pains coursing through my body.

Through the kiss, I sense someone watching me, and when I open my eyes, it's not Aiden I find staring back. Kaleb rests against the wall, watching us with a passionate hunger in his gaze. Embarrassment sizzles through my veins as if I've been caught with my hand in the cookie jar. What if they only like to share at the same time? Fuck this was confusing.

"Damn," Kaleb says, stepping forward and letting out a long, low whistle. "I get why you like to watch now." He adjusts the bulge in his navy sweats before coming to stand beside us at the counter. God damn. Sweatpants on these two had to be a crime. If they wore these in public, there's no doubt in my mind that it would start a riot.

I watch him, unsure what he's going to do or how he's going to react, and when he does, it's not what I expect.

"Kiss her again."

My gaze darts between the two of them, but Aiden doesn't give me a second more to wonder before he claims my lips. No longer a delicate kiss, this one is demanding, filled with a fiery heat that brands my very soul. I feel Kaleb's hands on me, lightly trailing up my arm mere seconds before his lips follow the same path.

Tingles shoot down to my clit as he nips and licks his way up my neck, stopping to tug on my lobe gently.

"This is real, Lily. We've never wanted anyone more,

never craved a woman like this before. And now that we have a taste... I don't think we can stop."

As if on cue, they both shift back an inch, just enough so that we're still touching but they're giving me space to breathe. To think.

What they're offering is more than I'd ever expected. Hell, I don't even know what I expected at this point. I always thought my life would be dull and lonely. Something I was absolutely fine with after everything Calantha and I had gone through at the farm. Boring was the safe choice, one far better than the pain of abuse. I should have realized by now that my sister is stronger than me. She doesn't harbor self-doubt and hatred for what happened. She just moved on.

But for the first time, things are different. Aiden and Kaleb make me feel like I'm worthy of their attention and the craziest part of all is that I'm starting to believe them.

***

A few blissful hours later, I walk through the door to my apartment. While I might have hoped to sneak home and keep the events of last night to myself for just a little longer, my sister had other ideas.

Kaleb found a way to let her know I wouldn't be home until later today, so I'm surprised to find her patiently waiting for me when I get back.

Part of me is scared to tell her. Not because she'd judge me — Calantha is hands down my biggest supporter — but because saying it out loud makes it undeniably real.

She's curled up on the couch with her Oodie on — I know, I know. They might be expensive as hell, but damn did they spruce up our Sister Sundays — watching The Proposal. She pauses it when she hears me, and I breathe a sigh of relief that she hasn't gotten very far into it yet. Thank God I didn't miss all of Sister Sunday.

"Sorry I'm late! I promise it won't happen again, okay? Give me six minutes, and I'll be ready." My good mood plummets as I begin to spiral. Did I really choose Aiden and Kaleb over my own sister? What kind of crappy sibling does that make me? If my relationship with them is already causing issues, maybe I should just—

Arms wrap around me from behind as Calantha hugs me tight. "Oh, no you don't, missy. I'm not mad, upset, or any other emotion other than fucking ecstatic, so throw away whatever nonsensical fears are flowing through your head right now."

"But how can you even say that? Sister Sundays are our tradition, and I'm already making other things a priority. Maybe—"

"No. No *maybe*. I love our Sister Sundays, Lil, but I love seeing you happy more. And it's not as if I'm a total hermit without friends. I rather like my own company, in fact, so I am perfectly capable of taking care of myself." Calantha pulls back, keeping her hands on my shoulders as she assesses me. "Besides, it's obvious you're in excellent hands, so I really have nothing to be worried about."

A weight seems to lift from my shoulders with her

words, and I let out a chuckle. "Don't think for a second that I missed the glint in your eyes when you said 'friends', Calla. We're coming back to that."

"You first," she replies with a devilish smile. "Go get changed, then I want to know everything."

Chapter Twenty-Eight

Kaleb

"Do you really think calling her Blossom is a good idea?"

Aiden stands in the living room, looking out at the city. From his question, it's clear he's remembering our night with Lily. Taking her right here against the glass would be an entirely different experience in the light of day, and I hope we'll get to experience it for ourselves.

As much as I might want to, I can't ignore his comment. "Oh, it's not a good idea. More of a hellishly stupid one, I think. I'll work on it. But I also think we need to discuss telling her."

"No. You know how much of a struggle it was at work when she found out I was at the club that night. If she knew we both were, there's no way she'd forgive us. It would only make her uncomfortable, and by the sounds of it, she's had enough of that in her life already."

This entire situation has been eating me up inside. I want her to know I was there the night of the lock-in, but I can also see where Aiden's coming from. Whatever her past might be, it's clear that she went through some shit.

The last thing I want to do is add more to it. As much as I want her to know, it's not worth hurting her. She deserves so much more from life, and Aiden and I plan to give her everything. What's one little lie in the face of all that?

"Alright. I'll try harder. Now what else did you want to tell me?" It's only been thirty minutes since Lily left and already the penthouse seems empty. She's spent one night with us, the real us, and already she's like a permanent fixture in our lives.

"Elliott called earlier this morning. He has the call logs for Burt's phone, but without knowing what we're looking for, it might take a while."

"Shit. Let's have him focus on the day surrounding the gala. If Burt has some sordid connection to Lily, then it's possible he'd have contacted someone after seeing her. If that doesn't pan out, we can try another tactic."

Aiden nods. "Already done. Now we only need to wait."

Three days pass with no word from Elliott. Three excruciating days without a solid plan to protect the woman who dominates my every waking thought. To make matters worse, I've been out of the city all week for work. Allegiance Medical, the company we recently won a contract with, had their warehouse burned down.

At first, we thought it was an accident, but from what the investigators are saying, the fire was premeditated. This is the part of owning a business that no one ever talks about. It's common knowledge that when running a business, you have to deal with competitors, but what do you do when that turns sour? When your rivals make it an unfair fight, what's the protocol? Do you fight fire with fire or step back and let them win?

With what happened to Allegiance Medical, Aiden and I have to determine if the cause relates to us or with them. After everything that happened with Burt, something tells me we can't rule out that he might have had a role in this.

As it is, we went up against several companies in order to get this contract, so the list of suspects is far larger than we'd hoped.

The hardest part has been dealing with all of this without Lily at my side. It feels like I abandoned her. I promised her we'd figure out a relationship between the three of us, and then I just left. Granted, it wasn't entirely of my own choosing, but now I'm stuck hours away with no end to my suffering in sight.

My phone rings, breaking me out of my miserable thoughts. When I glance at the screen, I'm surprised to find Lily's name. I swipe to answer without another thought.

"Lily. I was just thinking about you."

She laughs, and I can already picture the rosy hue of her cheeks. "I've been thinking about you too. How are things in Pittsburgh?"

"Slow. Allegiance Medical lost a lot of their supplies, so if I'm not fielding questions on that, I'm talking with the police department about trying to find the asshole who did this. Hearing your voice has been the highlight of my week, actually. How are things at the office?"

"Chaotic. Though I'm sure it's not nearly as bad as what you're dealing with. Did the owner show up yet? Aiden mentioned they were sending someone from their national team to help spearhead the issue."

"We met an hour ago. They've added a few more names to the list of suspects and got rid of even more, so at least we're getting somewhere. I'd give anything to be back home. After Saturday night, I'll admit that it's harder to be apart from you than I expected."

For a few seconds, I'm only met with silence, and part of me worries that I've been too forward. Maybe she's having second thoughts? Fuck. It's too complicated to figure out from so far away. I really should be there. But before I can say anything more, she responds.

"I feel the same, actually. Even though traveling isn't unusual for either of you, this time it feels different."

Relief floods me as her words sink in, washing away every single doubt. Reassurance is a funny thing. Such a small gesture, but shit, does it make a world of difference.

My phone beeps, and I pull away to check it.

"Shit. Aiden's calling. I've got to take this. I'll call you later?"

"Of course! I hope he comes bearing good news."

"Me too," I reply with a smile. "Chat soon, Lily." I press the button to switch the call, more hopeful than I've been all day.

I fill Aiden in on the reports from the police, explaining my conversation with the representative from

Allegiance Medical. Apparently, their top suspect is the company we competed with just a few months ago, the one that lost out on the contract. HealthRx. Having never heard of them before our bid, I was shocked to find their name come up again.

"What do we know about them?" Aiden asks, his question the same one I had earlier.

"Not much. They're fairly new, only operating in the last two to three years. Most of their contracts are small, and their reach is fairly similar. To be honest, I don't understand how they've stayed afloat so long."

"Hmm. As much as I want to get Elliott involved, he's better off focusing on our Burt problem. I'll see what I can find and keep you posted."

"Of course. I've got another meeting with the lead investigator in twenty minutes, though I'm not expecting any new information, but I'll keep you posted either way."

"Did Liliana call you?"

"She did. Despite her reassurance, I won't last much longer being so far away from her."

"I don't envy you, that's for sure. Once you're back, we might want to rethink our current travel schedule. I'm not sure about you, but I don't want to go very far without her."

"Agreed. Whatever happens here, I'll be back on Friday. Then we can ravage our girl and figure out how to make this thing work."

Chapter Twenty-Nine

Liliana

Cool morning air whips my long, dark hair around as I walk toward the main entrance of Exalta Solutions with a smile on my face. I can't seem to keep one off nowadays.

I usually catch a ride to work with Aiden and Kaleb, but I was running out of outfits, and it was time I spent a night in my own bed. Of course, I regretted that decision immediately. The couch in our apartment was basically a boulder compared to the luxurious mattresses they've spoiled me with at their penthouse. But it was worth it to see Calantha.

She's been more supportive of my weird three-way relationship than I ever could have expected, and although I was worried what my absence would do to her, I really shouldn't have been. She's thriving. I try not to take it personally, but from where I stand now, I realize that my constant worrying was only smothering her.

I'll see her again tonight. We're having dinner together at home while I grab a few more outfits to bring to the penthouse. Sometimes it feels like I'm rushing things with Aiden and Kaleb. Already I have clothes there, ones that I hang up in the closet and get washed amidst their own. Yet I don't think I could slow down even if I tried. Being with them feels right. Like my entire life before now was only a shitty movie, one I needed to live through for character development before I could turn me on the right path.

I nod my head, feeling silly, and check my phone in the elevator. There's a text from Aiden.

This whole sleeping away from us thing doesn't work for me. We're waiting for you in the office.

My stomach flutters, remembering the evening two nights ago when I was alone with them after hours. We'd been so exhausted after dealing with a massive crisis that the elation we should have felt at resolving it never came. Kaleb didn't let the win go to waste, though. Ever the optimist, he made sure Aiden and I took the time to celebrate — which had me spread open on their desks and feasted on like the rarest delicacy.

Rushing to my desk, I drop my purse and jacket haphazardly on top, then head toward their office door. Before entering, I take a moment to calm myself. As excited as I am, it wouldn't hurt to at least feign some nonchalance. My two men were already cocky enough with the reminder of my eagerness.

I knock and hear Kaleb call me in. They sit on the edge of their desks when I enter, both watching me with similar expressions on their faces. As usual, Kaleb's face holds more playfulness than Aiden's, but there's a charge in the air, something dark and demanding that puts my body on high alert.

"You wanted to see me," I say before shutting the door.

They exchange a look, but neither of them moves as I approach. I pull the chair in front of Kaleb's desk to the middle of the room and sit down, crossing my legs as I wait. Their eyes trail over me, lighting a fire low in my belly.

"Last night was awful." Kaleb breaks the silence but stays glued to the side of his desk. I risk a glance over at Aiden to find him gripping the table tightly. A heady rush pulses through me as I realize how much power I have over them. They're fighting to keep their distance because if they don't, who knows what sort of fun we could get up to? Maybe I should test this out a bit.

"I know, I'm sorry. Calantha and I had a long chat about it, and I was considering staying with her again." I cross my legs, lifting my skirt slightly but pretending I don't notice. They do, though. *God, how did I go my entire life without knowing how intoxicating this was?*

"Why doesn't she come stay with us instead?" Aiden asks, his knuckles white with tension.

"If I thought she'd say yes, I'd ask her." Pulling my hair over my shoulder, I twist it casually between my fingers. "Besides, wouldn't that limit our... fun?"

Kaleb stares at my neck, one of his favorite spots on my body, and Aiden can't seem to take his eyes off the sight of my thigh-high stockings. My pulse quickens, beating a steady thrum straight to my clit as I imagine all the ways this meeting could turn.

"There are other places to have fun, baby. You know that."

A knock reverberates through the space, dousing my fire. Someone from the Project Management team apparently has a crisis big enough to bother the bosses over. Before I can stand and fix my skirt, Aiden practically growls one single word.

"Sit."

I fall back into the chair at his command, my panties drowning with the need for more.

Kaleb hasn't moved from the desk. He looks at me like a man in the desert would look at a watery oasis. His gaze his hungry, desperate, and fuck, does it turn me on.

Aiden fists my hair from behind, pulling on it so I'm forced to tilt my head back. "We can't survive without you," he whispers in my ear, taking my lobe between his teeth when he's done. He loosens his hold on my hair enough for me to look forward and catch sight of Kaleb.

He stands in front of me, his hard length evident through his slacks. Reaching out, he cups my cheek in the most tender manner, causing my heart to flutter right along with my clit. "We can't stand being away from you, baby."

"I hate it too." And I did. Nothing could compare to the way I felt nestled safely between them.

With his grip still on my hair, Aiden moves to stand beside me. I let my eyes slowly trail up his body. From his thick erection, up over his button-up shirt, until I reach his eyes. What I find there almost knocks the wind out of me. Sensual promise mixed with something else I can't name.

"Before you leave this office, why don't you make it up to us?" he asks, palming his cock.

At his words I salivate, and in this instance, I'm not sure I've ever wanted anything more in my life.

I glance to the door, finding it locked and the blinds pulled down to cover the glass walls.

Kaleb grabs my chin and turns my face toward him. "What do you say, baby? Think you can handle it?"

His words light a fire inside me. Oh, I can handle it alright.

Instead of answering, I only smirk. He's going to eat his damn words once I'm done choking on his cock. I unbuckle his belt and free his cock, placing a playful kiss on the tip before I turn to do the same with Aiden.

Neither man speaks as they watch me, and when I finally have them both free, I wrap my hands around their cocks and stroke.

I'd never paid much attention to dicks before now, totally happy never to see one again, but now that I'm face-to-face with two of them, I can't help but stare.

Kaleb's has less girth than Aiden's, only by a little, but their length is similar. And fuck, do they both feel good.

I lean forward as if to lick Aiden's tip, but then I backtrack and swirl my tongue around Kaleb's. My pussy pulses with need, soaking through my panties as I continue my little game, going back and forth but never truly tasting Aiden.

With my eyes trained on them, I can't help but notice their reactions to my playfulness, and it comes as no surprise when Aiden finally snaps. "Petal," he growls, his voice deep and sultry.

"Be a good sport and wait your turn." I ignore him and wrap my lips around the head of Kaleb's dick, taking him deeper until I gag. His blue eyes sparkle brilliantly, filled with desire and a hint of laughter as I tease his friend.

With one final pull, his dick pops out of my mouth and I turn to Aiden. He looks entirely unimpressed but maybe I can turn that frown upside down with a little sucking magic.

I don't hesitate, licking and sucking on his tip before taking as much as I can in my mouth. My lips stretch to accommodate his girth, but thankfully they've already had a warmup. Fuck, this is hard work. How do people manage this with more than two dicks? *Stop thinking and start sucking, Lily.*

Before I get the chance to play, Aiden pulls back, fisting my hair gently and directing me toward Kaleb's cock. "You have to finish him off first before you can have me. I want to watch you swallow every last drop of his cum. Can you do that, Petal?"

Fucking hell. I could probably build a damn rocketship if he asked me like that. Nodding, I let my mind go blank and focus on pleasing my bosses. I reach out, gripping Aiden's cock and stroking him in tandem to the bobbing of my head. Their groans of pleasure send jolts of electricity straight to my clit until I can't help but clench my thighs together and wish I had more friction.

Aiden fucks my hand while I suck Kaleb's dick like I'm trying to win a medal. *And let's be honest, I totally am.*

I gaze up at him, seeing the exact moment he loses control before hot jets of cum slide down my throat. I swallow every drop, sucking gently on his dick while his orgasm fades.

"You're perfect," Kaleb says, leaning down to kiss me and taste himself on my tongue.

"Now, let's see how well you take me," Aiden says, fisting his cock. His eyes, now a deep charcoal gray, shine with need.

Like an excited golden retriever, I pounce. He continues stroking his shaft while I explore, but the moment I take him fully into my mouth, he takes control. Holding my head, he fucks my mouth slowly as I peer up at him beneath my lashes.

Leave it to Aiden to find some way to claim me when it should be I who's claiming him. I can't even pretend I don't like it though. Not when he's fucking me like this. *Now if only I could get Kaleb to fuck me at the same time.*

Just then, Kaleb gets on his knees beside me, kissing my cheek and whispering in my ear. "That's it, baby. You look so fucking good with a cock in your mouth. Don't you feel how hard he is for you? How much we miss filling your every hole? Fuck, Blossom, you're all we fucking think about."

I can't help the moan that escapes me at his words.

My eyes roll back into my head, and it feels like with just a little friction, I could be coming alongside my men too.

I swallow, causing Aiden to groan. "Fuck. Eyes on me, Petal."

The moment I follow his command, I'm trapped in his gaze.

"Those pretty lips of hers look so fucking good around our cocks, don't they?"

"Prettiest thing I've ever seen," Aiden grits out. He's close, and God I want nothing more than to taste him falling apart.

As if sensing my plea, Kaleb takes both of my hands in his. "This'll do the trick," he whispers to me before wrapping my hand around the base of Aiden's cock and bringing my other one to cup his balls. Together, we match the rhythm of his thrusts until he thickens and I swallow down his release.

Kaleb presses a kiss to my forehead before stepping away to let Aiden claim one of his own. I'm aching for my own release, nearly at the point of begging, but even my sex-crazed brain knows we can't do it here. With them, I have no self control, and short of gagging me, there's no way I'd be quiet. *Now that's an idea.*

Both men retreat to their desks, settling into the same position as earlier like I didn't just successfully get them both off in this office. *Wait, wasn't there a reason I came in here?*

Taking pity on me, Kaleb breaks the silence.

"How do you feel about Hawaii?"

They have a private jet. A private jet! What kind of world am I living in that I get to fly to Hawaii in such luxury? Never in my life had I expected to string those specific words together, yet here I am.

We left the office rather quickly, and to my surprise, Calantha had sneakily packed a few island essentials into my bag before I left. When I called her to make sure she didn't feel like I was abandoning her, which I suppose I already knew the answer to after our talk last night, she only laughed. Then I had tried to get her to join us, but she only sighed and told me there was no way she was crashing my sex-cation.

Now, I'm miles high in the sky on plush leather seats with a glass of champagne in my hand. The captain told us it would be just over eleven hours of flying before we'd arrive. Eleven! I wonder if people actually do this on commercial flights. I can't imagine flying anywhere over ten hours with strangers or babies beside me.

At least I'm in good company. I look over to where Aiden and Kaleb sit on the opposite side of the plane with their laptops open, answering emails and sending flirty glances my way. I don't want their flirty glances though. I want their hands and cocks and tongues so I can finally deal with the ache inside me. After our little escapade at the office, I'm certainly due an orgasm or two.

Feeling a rush of excitement, I decide to start up my fun from earlier. They can give me all the sexy little looks they want, but three can play at that game.

With their eyes on their laptop screens, they don't notice my reposition, and they definitely don't notice as I shimmy the lacy thong down my thighs. Once removed, I ball it up and place it into the pocket of my blazer before removing that, too.

Both men look up from their computers as I stand to take off my jacket, though I play it off as being too warm, which isn't technically a lie. But the reason I'm so hot has nothing to do with the air on this plane. It's far more carnal than that.

I grab a magazine from the aisle seat beside me and flip through, barely paying attention to anything on the pages. How can I focus on anything when the heat of their gaze all but sears my flesh?

I cross my legs, thankful when my skirt rises with no help from me but they continue to stay oblivious. After a few more minutes, I shift again, kicking off my shoes.

Each time they try to focus back on work, I move. And each time, their focus returns to me. The rush of it goes from my head down to my core as I control them with only the slightest movements. How did I not know it could be like this? A laugh bubbles up from my throat as I realize that's a foolish question. The last thing my aunt or uncle would have wanted was for me to know how much better things could be.

I feel safe with Kaleb and Aiden, but it's so much more than that. They make me feel worthy and supported, like I matter for more than just how I look or what they can use me for. And despite our current relationship, everything at work is the same. I feel valued there, just like I did in the beginning. My opinion matters, and fuck, does it feel good.

Both of my men look at me with a question in their gaze, but there's no way in hell I'll tell them why I laughed, so instead I just flip another page. Across from me are two empty chairs and a long table latched to the side of the wall.

Extending my legs, I prop them up on the seat and bite my lip as I feign interest in my magazine. I can feel their gazes roaming over me, and my clit pulses with every beat of my racing heart. Has anyone ever come just from their clit throbbing? Because damn I might be about to.

"What are you doing, Petal?" Aiden asks, closing his laptop.

I look up at him, pretending to be both startled and confused. "Just reading this article," I tell him, and I see Kaleb close his laptop too. He and Aiden share a knowing look before they stand and approach me. I widen my legs infinitesimally, hoping they don't notice.

"Is it good?" Kaleb questions, sitting in the aisle seat across from me.

Shit. He's so fucking sexy. "Is what good?" *What were we talking about again?*

"The article you're reading."

Fuck. I swallow past the lump in my throat, feeling the steady pulse at the base of my neck. "Fascinating."

Aiden moves to sit in the chair directly across from me, and when I attempt to move my legs, he picks them up and places them in his lap.

"Your magazine is upside down."

My eyes widen as I glance to my lap with apprehension coiling in my belly, but the magazine is right side up. When I lift my gaze back to them, they stare at me with smug expressions on their stupidly handsome faces. Shit. The jig is up.

Heat flares low in my belly as they watch me intently, and I'm hit with a need so forceful that I can't help but press my thighs together. I stifle a moan at the tiny amount of friction, but Aiden stops me.

He passes one of my legs to Kaleb before they each stretch them wide. My face heats as I realize what they must see. Me, completely bare and spread open for them. I glance up at the door behind them, anticipation making me tremble as I consider the fact that anyone could come through those doors and find us like this.

"Is this what you wanted?" Aiden asks, sitting forward and rubbing a hand up the inside of my thigh while Kaleb does the same. Neither of them stops until they reach my core, finding my thighs slick with arousal. I whimper as I feel both of their fingers touch me, not knowing whose is whose, but still, I don't respond.

"Such a naughty little thing," Kaleb replies, pulling my leg even wider. I gasp as someone presses a finger inside of me before pulling it out and bringing the wet digit to my aching clit. Another finger replaces the one inside me, and I can't do anything but gasp and moan.

I cover my mouth, trying to quiet my sounds in case anyone hears. The last thing I want is for someone to see us like this, but I can't deny the little flutter of pleasure at the idea that someone could.

"Do you want this, baby?" Kaleb asks, and I nod.

"Use your words, Petal," Aiden demands. "Tell us what you want."

"Touch me."

Both of my men remove their hands from in between my legs and trail them up and down my thighs. I let out an exasperated sigh, knowing full well they know what I was asking for. But I guess if I think about it, I knew what they were asking for too, and I took the coward's way out.

Taking a deep breath, I tell them exactly what I want. "Taste me," I say to Aiden before turning my attention to Kaleb. "While you fuck me with your fingers."

"Good girl," Aiden whispers, before moving to the floor at my feet.

Instead of Kaleb joining him though, he moves to the door I'd been eying in fear and excitement. Before he can slide a lock into place, I stop him with only two words.

"Leave it."

Both of them look at me, their eyes ablaze with desire.

After this, I don't think I'll ever be able to fly commercial again.

Chapter Thirty

Liliana

"You little bitch! Stop avoiding me and spill; I need all the details," Calantha practically squeals over the phone.

She and I haven't been able to talk much in the week since I got back from Hawaii with Aiden and Kaleb. Her new job was keeping her busy, which I'd be worried about if I didn't know how much she loved the work. But it meant we're long overdue for some girl time.

"I'm at work," I hiss out, glancing to make sure no one's around. "You busy tonight? I can come by, maybe pick up some takeout and wine so we can dish in style."

"You bring the food. I'll pick up the wine. Oh, shit. I've gotta go. There's a raging pussy in the lobby. Love you!"

I laugh, unable to stop the images from popping up in my mind, though what I picture sure as hell isn't an angry cat. With all the changes happening in my life, it really puts into perspective just how much I miss my sister. The space has been good for us both, but after relying on her for so much of my life, this distance feels like a cavernous hole right in the center of my chest.

She's going to freak when she sees what I brought back for her from Maui. A charm bracelet complete with beach glass, animal charms, and even a best sister one too. It feels good to finally be able to afford actual gifts. Birthdays before working for Exalta Solutions were still special, or at least I tried to make sure they were, but now that we have more freedom, I don't want to waste any of it.

A stranger approaches wearing slacks and a pressed white shirt with the sleeves rolled up. He has a jacket slung over his arm, sporting blond hair that's cropped short and left messy, though he pulls it off.

This must be the friend Kaleb expected a visit from. He reaches my desk, his ten-watt smile set to full as he looks down at me. "I'm here to see Kaleb Fitzgerald."

"Of course. And your name?"

"Jasper Donnelley."

"Perfect. Come with me. He's waiting for you in the boardroom." Jasper follows me down the hall until we reach the closed door of the boardroom. I knock once before opening.

"Jasper is here to see you. Is there anything else I can do for you?"

He smiles, and it's like watching the sunrise in the dead of winter as warmth seeps through my skin and chases away the cold. He must notice the figure behind me because all he says is, "Nothing more, Ms. Sinclair. Thank you."

I turn to Jasper. "You may go in. It was nice to meet you."

He offers me the same platitudes then heads into the boardroom. Before the door fully shuts, I hear something that halts me in my tracks. *Fitz.*

I lean in, resting my ear on the door. They're laughing now, likely catching up or whatever it is that men do. Shit, I must be losing it. What if someone were to catch me eavesdropping? It's not like I can tell them about the elusive Fitz from my sexual awakening. I shake my head and make my way to the bathroom.

Why the hell am I even thinking about Fitz, anyway? I'm perfectly happy in this new, slightly odd relationship I have with Kaleb and Aiden, and there's no way I'd want to add another member. I'm sure some people can juggle more than two partners, but I am not one of them. *What the hell was a woman supposed to do with four dicks? Is it like visiting the DMV where you take a number and wait for a hole to free up?*

When I walk past the boardroom on my way back, I'm tempted to listen but force myself to keep moving. No. Only a crazy person would listen in on their boss's private conversation.

At my desk, I keep busy answering emails and phone calls, jotting down ideas I have for the layout of the Restorative Care App's new space. Aiden is in his office locked on a call with the contractors who apparently fucked up on the floor we're renovating. It sounds like a mess, but if anyone can find a solution, it's him.

A notification pops up on my screen from Dean,

asking me to come to his office. When I pass the board-room that Kaleb and Jasper were using earlier, I find it empty. A little further ahead I hear voices, one of which is distinctly Kaleb, and a smile passes my lips as I approach.

I'm hidden in the hall when I hear the elevator doors open, but before I can rush forward to wave goodbye, Jasper's voice stops me in my tracks.

"Shit, man. I can't believe you and Aiden own this place. The Fitz I knew in college was more likely to hit the stage with a standup comedy act than own something like this."

Kaleb chuckles. "Oh, I'm still hilarious, don't you worry."

The rest of his words muffle as the elevator doors close, but I barely notice. I stand frozen, rooted to the spot as a cold chill sweeps over me. So I wasn't crazy earlier. But if Kaleb's friends call him Fitz, why have I not heard about it before?

Thoughts battle their way through my mind as every single worry and doubt flashes brightly behind my eyes. I can't breathe as understanding grows deep inside, rising to the surface until I feel like I might throw up.

A little voice inside my head screams at me to calm down. Aiden doesn't call him Fitz, and they've been best friends for years. Who cares if that was his college nick-name? Even Jasper said he was different.

But as hard as I try to think rationally, the realistic part of my brain won't let me accept those excuses. If Kaleb really is Fitz, the other guy from Club Rapture, it just makes sense. I feel foolish for not realizing it sooner. Aiden was there as Wes, but he couldn't hide that fact. He even introduced Fitz as his colleague. *Shit, shit, shit.*

A memory rises to the forefront of my mind, making the ugly truth impossible to ignore. That night at the penthouse, when I slept with Kaleb and Aiden for the first time, Kaleb called me Blossom. Just like Fitz did.

The room seems to spin as I gasp for air. How could they keep this from me? Was any of it real, or was it all just a game to them?

My eyes burn with the need to cry as anger and betrayal seep into my bones, but I hold them back. Not here. They don't deserve my tears.

I rush back to my desk, glad to find the door to Aiden and Kaleb's office still closed. Then I remember the entire goddamn reason I went down the hall to begin with. Shit. I send a quick message to Dean, letting him know that something has come up and I won't be able to meet him. If it's important, he'll email. Though it's not like I'm in the right headspace to deal with anything right now.

I take all of my belongings from the desk, stuffing them into my purse before logging out and shutting down my computer. Rage grows inside me, festering like a wound with every passing second.

Without another moment's hesitation, I grab my things and walk out.

It isn't any easier at home.

Thankfully, Calantha is still at work, so I don't have to explain the tear stains on my blouse or why I've spent the last fifteen minutes updating my resume. It took longer than I thought it would to decide if I'd include Exalta Solutions as a workplace, but in the end, I decided not to.

I didn't trust that they wouldn't share the details of our personal life, and the one thing I want is to get far away from it. From them and their lies.

Aiden had emailed an hour ago to ask where I was and make sure I was okay. Checking on his little toy, I bet. Instead of exploding at him like I wanted, I just told him I was sick and turned him down when he offered to come by. My heart had squeezed at the kind gesture I now knew was nothing more than a ploy to keep me useful.

He probably only wanted to get me healthy so I'd continue to be their plaything. Either way, I told him I'd be napping and locked the doors.

How many nights had I stayed with them, nestled between them both, and neither one said a goddamn thing? They lied to me, used my body just like my uncle did, except they were cowards about it. As awful as my uncle was, at least he owned his shitty behavior.

I stop my pacing as a thought smacks me right in the face. The gala. Had running into someone from my past truly been a coincidence, or had they planned it all along? Shivers race up my spine and sweat forms on the back of my neck as I try to shake off the thought.

Fuck. A sob escapes me, and I crumple to the floor.

How could I have been so blind? Was I that defective that I couldn't see what was glaringly obvious? *Liliana Sinclair, a woman so bereft of love that she'll debase herself just to have it.*

The laptop I share with Calantha dings, signaling a new email. I hesitate for a moment, unsure if I want to read it. What if it's Kaleb or Aiden?

Pushing past the doubt, I open the browser to find an interview invite from HealthRx. *Shit. That was fast. I'd sent my resume out barely an hour ago and already they wanted to meet.*

The company name sounds somewhat familiar, but I hope it isn't someone I've dealt with while working for Exalta.

They want to interview today in forty-five minutes. I quickly type the address into Google Maps, finding that I have just enough time to freshen up and rush out the door.

Emotions war within me as I wash my face and race to catch the bus. I feel hopeful that I'll get the job and never have to see Aiden and Kaleb again; satisfaction, because by the time they realize why I've left, it'll be too late. But the most prominent of them all is loss. There's this paralyzing sense of homesickness worming its way through me, and I can't make it go away. I actually loved my job, and if I'm honest with myself, I was falling for my bosses too.

They made me feel alive, wanted, and despite what I now know, those feelings won't just disappear. If only feelings were like a chalkboard, erased with just one swipe and replaced with something new.

I don't even realize I'm at my stop until someone bumps into me. With only ten minutes to spare and still an eight-minute walk, I hurry off the bus and down the street. The building isn't as tall and luxurious as Exalta Solutions, but it's new and clean, which is enough for me. The woman at the front desk smiles brightly as I walk in, telling me to sit and that Mr. Stuart will be right down.

As quickly as I can, I search the company website on my phone to familiarize myself a bit with their values and mission statement. From my experience, most employers like it if you know at least a little about their business.

The elevator chimes, and I look up to find a vaguely familiar-looking man walking toward me with a smile that doesn't quite reach his eyes. It's more deranged than genuine, but I brush it off as my usual worries and stand to meet him.

"Liliana." He says my name on a sigh, as if we're long-lost friends finally reuniting.

"It's nice to meet you. I'm thrilled you were able to interview me so quickly."

"We are quite eager to get our hands on you. Please, come with me."

Alarm bells go off in my head at his words, but I push them aside and follow him through the doors, down a hall, and into what must be his office. On the main floor, it's a bit small as far as offices go, with barely any furniture and no personal photos. To the right of his desk is a door outside, providing access to a small patio and the back parking lot.

The chair he directs me to is one of those cheap, black folding chairs that are rickety and entirely uncomfortable, but I sit anyway. As much as I want to leave Exalta Solutions, maybe this isn't my finest decision. This place screams bankruptcy, and as much as I love a challenge, even I'm not foolish enough to think I could save a place like this. Not when Calantha relies on me. *Isn't this why you never rush into things, Lil?*

"Your resume states you left the textile company almost six months ago. Where have you been since?" he asks, diving us straight into the deep end.

"I've been working for a company in the health sector, but as I'd only been there for a short time, I didn't see the point in including them." Okay, so that's a lame excuse, but the more I sit here, the more I realize I don't want to work here. I might be desperate, but I'm not *this* desperate. Kaleb and Aiden may have lied to me, but at least they never made me this creeped out. Maybe everything will be fine if I just give them the chance to explain. *Would have been great if I had thought of that earlier.*

His smile grows, reminding me of a jaguar about to pounce on its prey, and I swear I've seen it before. "Exalta Solutions, correct?"

"Yes," I stammer, trying to keep the shock from my face. How the hell does he know that, and why does he look so familiar?

"That company is rather large and growing fast. Why would you want to leave?"

"I'm just keeping my options open."

"Are they not satisfying you?"

"Excuse me?" My pulse thrums fast as I wait for him to respond.

He makes me wait an entire minute before he does. "Usually when someone keeps their options open, it's because they aren't finding joy in their current position. Is that the case? Are you hoping to find satisfaction somewhere else?"

Unease crawls up my spine as I realize that I'm alone in a room with this man who doesn't seem the least bit professional and much too creepy for my liking. If they truly are going bankrupt under his leadership, it's no surprise. "Mr. Stuart, I think this might have been a mistake. If you'll excuse me."

He doesn't move to stop me like I expect, allowing me to walk to the door, all the while watching me with a terrifying glint in his eyes.

When I twist the knob, it doesn't budge. *It's locked.*

Before I can disengage the deadbolt, I hear a rustle of clothing behind me and turn. The last thing I see is him standing close, his arm cocked back, before pain lances through me and it all goes dark.

Chapter Thirty-One

Aiden

What the fuck is going on?

Liliana didn't show up for work today, and while I might not be shocked by that alone, she also didn't call in sick. It's so unlike her to bail like this without an explanation. Just how sick was she yesterday?

She hasn't answered a single text, email, or call from either of us since yesterday, which leaves us with only one option. Calantha.

With Kaleb beside me, I dial her number and put the call on speaker phone. It rings three times before she picks up with the sound of howling dogs and mewling cats in the background.

"Hey, Aiden. I'm a bit busy right now." A cat hisses in the background and she yelps.

"I'm sorry, I'll keep it brief. We just wanted to know if Liliana was feeling better. She went home sick yesterday, but she isn't answering our calls."

There's a pause before Calantha whispers to someone. A door creaks and then the animal sounds fade away. "She didn't stay with you last night?" she asks, fear clouding her voice.

"No... Did she not stay with you?"

"No. She was supposed to come over to catch up, but when she didn't show, I figured she'd been dickmatized by you guys. She was definitely at the apartment yesterday afternoon, though. The laptop was on the coffee table. I just assumed she stopped by to pick something up. Hold on." Another door opens and there's a few thumps before Calantha comes back. "Let me see if she left anything open on the laptop. This isn't like her."

Fear settles in the pit of my stomach while we wait, and I scour my mind for what might have caused this. Maybe it was our new shared relationship that made her run, though that didn't seem likely. Liliana seemed happy with us. Hell, even Calantha had mentioned how content she seemed. But then, what could it be? I wouldn't let myself think of the worst yet. If I did, if I considered for even a second that she didn't go willingly, I wouldn't be able to function.

"Hmm," Calantha breathes through the phone. "Did something happen between you guys? It looks like she sent out resumes yesterday and even had an interview."

Kaleb and I glance at each other, confusion and alarm lining our faces. "Not that I'm aware of. Everything seemed fine before my meeting with the contractor yesterday. When I came out, she was gone."

"Ah, shit," Kaleb mumbles.

"What?" Calantha and I ask simultaneously.

"I think I know why she's upset, but that still doesn't

explain where the hell she is. Who was the interview with yesterday?"

I consider pressing Kaleb for more details, but whatever it is, he must not want to share it with Calantha, so I hold back.

"She interviewed around four pm with a company called HealthRx. Have you heard of them?"

"We have, but..." Kaleb tells her before looking at me.

HealthRX is the top suspect in the fire incident at Allegiance Medical. Fuck! We should have told her more about the investigation. But why would Liliana interview there? Why would she want to leave at all?

"We don't have anything concrete, but from what we know so far, they aren't good."

Calantha starts freaking out on the phone, even more worried about her sister since clearly we have no goddamn tact. Kaleb interrupts her, his voice soothing. "We're going to look into this, Calantha. We won't let anything happen to her. You have our word. The moment we know anything, we'll let you know."

"In the meantime, be normal. Go to work, save the animals, and don't look into this on your own. This is important, Calantha. Not just for Liliana's safety but for yours, as well." I'm half tempted to explain further, but even though she might not think so now, my cryptic answer is much better than the truth.

"I'll try," she replies unconvincingly before hanging up.

"What happened?" I ask Kaleb, unsure if I want to hear the answer but knowing I need to.

"Look, I don't even know if this is why she ran, but it's the only thing I can think of. Jasper stopped by here for a visit yesterday, and he called me Fitz a few times. She wasn't with us when he did, at least not that I'm aware of, but we both know sometimes this office can be a maze. I was out of the office for about an hour, so I didn't even consider it an option yesterday when she went home sick, but now..."

"Now she knows you were at the club too and that we lied to cover it up."

We're both silent for a minute when suddenly Kaleb's face pales. "That report we got back from Elliott about Burt's call logs... Wasn't there someone listed there who worked for HealthRX?"

My stomach drops, practically hitting the floor as I process what he just said. "Fuck. Shit!"

Turing to my laptop, I open up the report and scan for any mention of that goddamn fucking company. I find it next to the name Hank Stuart, along with a list of calls between him and Burt that are practically a mile long.

"Do you think he has her?" Kaleb asks, his voice hard.

"If he does, he'll pay."

It didn't take us long to arrive at the HealthRX head office and even shorter still to find out that despite the shabby-looking building and lack of funds, the receptionist was loyal. If things were different, I'd be impressed, but with Liliana missing, it only pissed me off.

Other than finding out that Hank didn't show up to work today, she wouldn't give us any information about his interview from yesterday or where he might be today. Kaleb and I knew how to get what we wanted, but we didn't have time for blackmail or schemes. We just had to hope she'd accept a bribe.

Taking a wad of bills from the pocket of my coat, I slide it across the desk. "Look, Sarah, it's imperative that we speak with him today. Life or death, even. Do you know anything that could help us find him?"

She hesitates, then takes the cash and starts flipping through, counting each bill until her eyes grow wide as she notices I've just dropped a thousand dollars for information. What she doesn't realize is that I'd drop way more than that to find my Petal.

Even though our girl might hate us right now, she's ours. No one will take her from us, and we sure as fuck won't let anyone harm her. Even if she chooses never to see us again.

"Life or death, you said?" Sarah asks, and when we both nod, she opens the drawer of her desk and slips the cash into her purse. "Hank's got a little log cabin in the woods outside of town. If I had to guess, that's where he'd be."

If she had to guess? It dawns on me that this woman didn't have a fucking clue where Hank was, but before I can open my mouth and tell her exactly what I think of her little act, Kaleb stops me. With his hand on my arm, he only shakes his head. I jerk away from him but keep quiet until Sarah slides a post-it note across the desk.

Kaleb takes the note, reads it once, and then hands it to me. I don't bother reading it, not with this bitch watching, and head for the door instead. Kaleb doesn't follow. As I walk toward the exit, I hear his steady voice.

"You never even knew where he was, did you?"

At her startled expression, he doesn't bother waiting for an answer and just walks off to join me on the sidewalk. His face is set into a scowl, the determination I see there matching my own as we step into the car. Hank Stuart better fucking be there.

"Let's go save our girl."

Chapter Thirty-Two

Liliana

Drip. Drip. Drip.

Something warm brushes against my chest, but I keep my eyes closed. It happens again, and I giggle. "Kaleb, Aiden, it's too early." The touching stops, but neither of my men respond, and I slip back to sleep.

Drip. Drip. Drip.

A cold chill seeps into my body, all the way down to my bones. Where did my blankets go, and where is that breeze coming from? I wrap my arms around my torso, huddling into myself when I feel it. A wet patch on my blouse. What the fuck?

My eyes pop open to find darkness. There's a broken window to my left that lets in enough light for me to understand that I have no fucking clue where I am.

A match flares somewhere close behind me, and I jolt, turning around to find Mr. Stuart lighting a long-stemmed candle.

I scramble back, shaking with cold. "Wh-where the hell are we?"

"Liliana," he sneers before lighting another candle

with the same match. "You can try to class up the name, *Anna*, but it doesn't make you any less of a slut."

My back hits the wall below the broken window, and I'm grateful for the light. I only wish the breeze was warmer as another shiver streaks through my body.

Holding tightly to the lit match, he stalks towards me, seeming completely oblivious to the flame growing closer to his fingers. He seems deranged, but beneath the glow of the candle, I find something familiar. His words finally break past the fear, and I realize what he said. Anna. Slut. *Could he really be—*

Without warning, he thrusts his hand forward, holding the match close to my face until I feel the heat of it against my cheek.

"You're really going to sit there and pretend you don't know me, Anna? Like we didn't spend our youth fighting for the same scraps of attention? Though, it wasn't as if you ever had to try very hard, was it? Perfect little Anna."

"Hank," I whisper, unsure if I can believe him. Hank Stuart was a year or two older than me and had been at the farm long before Calantha and I ever got there. He was my uncle's pet, the protege, or so the other kids said, but that all changed when I arrived. For whatever reason, he hated me and was always trying to compete for my uncle's recognition even though I never wanted it.

The flame extinguishes against his fingers, thrusting us into darkness. He doesn't make a sound. Not of pain from the fire licking against his flesh or movement away from me. The light shafting in from the broken window behind me is my only salvation, and as my eyes adjust, I find him standing exactly where he was. Too fucking close.

"I was happy when you left," he states, still unmoving. "I figured with you gone, things would go back to the way they were. And they did. Everything was fucking perfect. After I turned twenty-two, your uncle promoted me. He relied on me and praised me for a job well done. I supplied him with troubled teens, and he gave me the one thing he always saved for you. His love."

His words crash into me, making me forget that I'm trapped here in this darkened cabin with a demented man. Hank had been jealous of me? After everything we'd been through at the farm, how could he not realize there were no better ends to that shitty stick? "He never loved me. He used me, just like he's using you," I say softly.

"You shut your fucking mouth," he growls, gripping my jaw in his fist and making me flinch. "You lost the right to speak about him when you hightailed it out of there all those years ago. And you lost your chance at his love, too. Like the bitch you are, you stole my contract with Allegiance Medical, along with every chance I had to prove my worth. You jeopardized my shot of becoming a real member of the family with the man you never fucking cared about. How could you do that? I've been on the outs for months, but when he learns that I've secured his precious fucking Anna, I'll be back in his good graces."

I don't move, unable to speak with the tight grip he has on my jaw, but I wouldn't know what to say anyway.

Pieces start falling together. Allegiance Medical and the contract I helped Aiden and Kaleb secure... HealthRX must have been the other company vying for that contract. But it wasn't as if I knew that. I didn't help them just to screw Hank over. If I'm completely honest, I'd forgotten about him entirely until today.

Just then, the light glints off something in Hank's other hand. *A knife.* Reality crashes down around me. Hank intends to send me back, gifting me to my uncle like the prized turkey at a country fair, right before they break my neck. I can't survive the farm again. I won't make it out of there a second time. Not alive, anyway.

He lets go of my jaw, stepping back toward the candles and pulling a phone from his pocket. I watch him dial, listening as it rings and rings. Part of me hopes whoever he's calling doesn't pick up, but even I know I'm not that lucky.

"Hank, I thought I told you not to call me anymore," I catch my uncle say through the speaker.

"You'll want to hear this, I promise."

"Well, spit it out already. I'm very busy."

"I have her." The words rush out of Hank's mouth in one breath, sounding almost irreverent. "I have Anna."

There's silence on the other line and for a second, I think I might be safe. It's been so long that I'm sure my uncle won't care. Why would he? The only reason I ever behaved was because he threatened Calantha, and without her, there's no way I'll do what he wants.

"You have Anna," I hear my uncle repeat skeptically. "Right now?"

"Yes. It was easy, actually. I—"

"Never mind all that. Bring her home, Hank. I want my niece back where she belongs. There might be hope for you yet, son." With that, the call goes dead.

My vision blurs as the words repeat in my head. Home. Back where I belong. The farm... He wants to trap me there again.

I close my eyelids, pressing them tight as if I can erase everything with enough force. But when I open them again, stars fading from my vision, I realize nothing's changed. I can't go back.

To my surprise, Hank falls silent. His back is to me so I can't see his face, but the hand holding the knife trembles. The truth of my current situation registers in the back of my mind. I've been so scared of having to go back to the farm that I never even considered the fact that I might not make it there at all.

I'd rather die here, alone in this cabin with only the cool breeze and the rustle of the trees outside, than be stuck beneath my uncle's heel. My mind flashes quickly to Aiden and Kaleb, the only men who ever made me feel truly loved. I wish I had done things differently. Maybe if I had, I wouldn't be staring death in the face.

When Hank turns around, I'm surprised to find his features drawn tight. He holds a candle in one hand, the hot wax dripping over his unprotected flesh while still holding the knife in his other one. The flame flickers in the breeze, illuminating the glint in his eyes and making the blood freeze in my veins.

I take a breath, then speak. "Well, you should be happy then. It sounds like you're back in his good graces."

He lets out a hollow laugh, stepping closer. "And it sounds like you never left them," he mumbles under his breath. Louder, he says, "You know he banished me after what happened with Allegiance Medical? Do you have any idea what it's like not to be allowed back to the place you grew up?"

As he grows closer, I move, shuffling to the side as fast as I can to get away from him. I try to stand, my limbs feeling numb as he continues speaking.

"No, but I guess you wouldn't," he sneers, his face turned down in disgust. "You left of your own accord, and even after you abandoned him all those years ago, he'll still accept you with open arms. What makes you so fucking special?"

"Nothing. I'm not." I try to placate him even though I know it's useless. He's not in his right mind anymore, and whatever anger he's feeling right now, he should really direct it at my uncle. He's the reason for all of this, not me. It hits me then, a sad fact I hadn't considered before now. Hank and I are the same. Victims of my uncle's abuse. The only difference is how we used it. All I wanted was to be free, to make a life for myself and Calantha somewhere we could be safe and loved with no strings or demands. But Hank... He fell deeper into the games my uncle played, always believing there was love to gain.

"You're right. All you are is a pretty piece of meat we used to curry favor." Stepping forward, he stands in front of me, pointing the knife at my belly. I search behind me for anything I can use as a weapon, but all I find is the cold wood of the wall.

The sharp tip of the blade presses against my wet blouse, and I suck in a breath as Hank leans forward. "Why don't we find out once and for all what all the fuss is about?"

Chapter Thirty-Three

Kaleb

Despite the late afternoon sun, it appears more like dusk beneath the dense crop of trees.

Aiden and I hadn't passed a single vehicle in the mile or so since we'd turned onto the dirt path, so we had our driver stay with the car while we went ahead on foot. If Hank Stuart was as shitty a person as I expected, we'd want the element of surprise on our side. The last thing we wanted to do was spook him, not while he had Lily so close.

We just had to hope she was okay. If she'd been with him since yesterday, who knew what kind of shit he'd forced her to do? Rage simmered beneath my flesh, hot and fierce, until I'm sure steam will start billowing from my ears. After her reaction to Burt at the gala, I'm terrified. Was Hank a part of her past too, and if he was, had he hurt her just like Burt had?

"It should be just up ahead," Aiden whispers before tucking his phone back into his pocket.

Instead of staying on the trail, we trek through the forest, slipping between trees while being careful to stay silent. In hindsight, this might not have been the best move, but staying on the only noticeable path seemed like an even worse one.

We find a banged up jeep parked by the front deck of the cabin, and I consider slashing the tires, but the fear of what's coming stops me. While I don't want fucking Hank to get away, I wouldn't be able to live with myself if I took away her chance to escape. If things go sideways...

It's not a very large cabin and would have been beautiful once upon a time, but now it's more of a rundown shack. Boards cover the front windows and the door looks like it's barely hanging on. Definitely not the place I'd choose to go to unwind, but maybe roughing it is exactly what Hank likes.

Aiden signals that he's going to check the perimeter before heading off to the left of the house while I make my way around the right side. The windows are boarded up here too, but just as I spot a broken board and what just might be the only view inside, I catch sight of Aiden.

I can't help the hopeful look on my face, but he only shakes his head. Fuck. This hole might be our only chance of finding out what's happened without being detected. Otherwise, I have no issues going in half cocked and ready to take down this son of a bitch.

I signal for him to be quiet, then point toward the window. We both step forward as quietly as possible, noticing it's not just the board that's broken but the glass too. What I see inside traps my breath in my lungs.

A man stands tall with a melting candle in one hand and a survival knife in the other. His hair is greasy, standing up on all sides, and he has dirt smeared on top of his five o'clock shadow like he's been thinking, but it's the look in his eyes that nearly has me risking the sharp glass to rush inside. He looks totally fucking crazed.

I hear Lily then, thank fuck, and it sounds like she's close. "Well, you should be happy then. It sounds like you're back in his good graces."

The man who must be Hank lets out a humorless laugh, mumbling something I can't make out before he says, "You know he banished me after what happened with Allegiance Medical? Do you have any idea what it's like not to be allowed back to the place you grew up?"

Allegiance Medical? Was this the piece of shit who burned down their warehouse? If he's willing to go that far in retaliation, I can only imagine what he's willing to do to our girl.

There's a commotion inside, and I'm half a step from rushing to the front door when I finally see her. She looks exhausted. Her blouse is wet, and there's dirt streaked down her face, but it's her shivering I can't look away from.

"No, but I guess you wouldn't," Hank continues, looking disgusted. "You left of your own accord, and even after you abandoned him all those years ago, he'll still accept you with open arms. What makes you so fucking special?"

"Nothing. I'm not," I hear Lily reassure him, but that only seems to piss him off further.

"You're right. All you are is a pretty piece of meat we used to curry favor." In a flash, he's in front of her, holding the knife to her stomach, and I share one last frenzied look with Aiden.

We don't bother waiting to see what he does next, but as we move away from the window, Hank's words seep out into the forest. "Why don't we find out once and for all what all the fuss is about?"

Over my fucking dead body.

Aiden rushes to the jeep where he must have seen the keys left inside because he reaches in to push the alarm button. Suddenly, the car blares to life. He ducks behind the wheel while I stay hidden in my spot at the side of the house.

"What the fuck?" Hank says before the door opens. Lily is still trapped in his hold with the knife pressed to her belly. There's a small red spot blooming beneath it, and I fight the need to kill him. He deserves more than death for what he's done to our woman.

He pulls her with him but doesn't force her off the last step of the deck while he reaches inside the jeep for his keys.

She bolts barefoot into the forest, but before he can follow her, I step out from beside the house.

"Your third mistake was leaving her on the deck," I say, startling him. He turns on me, brandishing the knife while still trying to look for Lily through the trees.

"Your second mistake was leaving your keys in the car," Aiden taunts, standing and walking toward Hank on his other side but not bothering to turn off the alarm. It's fucking loud and distracting, but that might just work out in our favor.

"Who the fuck are you, and what the hell are you doing on my property?" he yells, thrusting the knife toward each of us. "I'll have you assholes arrested for trespassing!"

"Don't you want to know what your first mistake was?" I ask, stepping forward. He swallows tightly, his Adam's apple bobbing with the movement. With his focus on me, Aiden grabs him from behind, pressing on the pressure points on his wrist until he drops the knife.

"Your first fucking mistake," Aiden whispers with all the ferocity of a goddamn lion as he twists Hank's arm behind his back. "Was thinking you'd get away with kidnapping the woman we love."

I rear back and punch the asshole in the gut, watching him collapse on the ground in a heap. Aiden lets him fall, moving toward the jeep in search of something to tie him up with, and I turn to the forest. "Lily!" I call out, hoping she's not lost.

The car alarm turns off, but I don't hear her calling back to me. Being held captive in a cabin with Hank was bad enough. Now she's stuck outside in a forest she doesn't know with night closing in. Fuck!

Just then, I hear a rustle in the trees, followed by footsteps, and I see her. Her eyes, filled with panic, almost distract me from the heavy log in her hands as she sprints toward me. "Behind you!" she yells, and I turn to find Hank on his feet, about to lunge toward Aiden.

Expecting Lily to rush into my arms, I'm shocked when she moves past me and raises the log like a weapon.

"Hey! It's me you want, isn't it? I guess I do always win," she challenges.

But just as he turns around, she smashes the log into the side of his face with surprising strength, knocking Hank out cold. Aiden turns to us with a pack of zip ties in his hand and a smile on his face that says he's going to enjoy tying this piece of shit up.

"Thank fuck you're okay." I pull her into my arms, gripping her fiercely and never wanting to let go. Seeing her again is like getting a straight shot of oxygen after not being able to breathe properly.

Aiden approaches us after securing Hank but doesn't touch her. "Did he hurt you?"

"Not like that, no. The rest will heal. I'm just glad you both showed up in time. Thank you. I'm sorry, I—"

Finally Aiden reaches out, gripping her face beneath his muscular hands. "You have nothing to be sorry for. But we do."

My phone rings, vibrating in my pocket, and I step away while Aiden and Lily stare into each other's eyes. I know Aiden won't go on without me, and it's not like this is exactly the place to put all of our cards on the table, but I only answer because it's a blocked call.

"Hello."

"Nice of you to finally pick up," Burt all but growls. "It's time for you and Aiden to realize who calls the shots around here. As it is, there's so much at stake."

I'm about to laugh, to throw it in his face that his little ploy with Hank didn't work because Lily is safe with us and there's no way in hell we'll be letting her out of our sight now that she is, but I don't get the words out.

Burt softens his voice as he speaks to someone else, the sound diminished slightly like he's moved the phone away from his mouth. "Calantha, my dear, you truly have grown into such a beautiful woman. Dare I say, you're even more attractive than that sister of yours. But don't worry, she'll be here soon too. Maybe then I'll be able to compare how you both taste."

Jesus fucking Christ, he has Calantha? I barely have a moment to process before his angry tone is back, and it's clear that he's not fucking around.

"I grow tired of playing this foolish game. I'm in charge now, Kaleb. You might be the face of Exalta Solutions, but it's no longer under your ownership. Do as we say and the girls live. You have three hours to decide." Then the line goes dead.

"Who was that?" Aiden asks, likely seeing the look of horror on my face.

My gaze flashes to Lily, unsure if I want her to know about this. She's already been through enough tonight, hasn't she? But it's lies and secrets that got us into this mess in the first place. It's time we put everything in the light.

"That was Burt," I say, wincing at the flash of pain on Lily's face. "I'm so sorry, Blossom. Sorry that we lied and didn't protect you when it mattered most, but now…"

"Thank you. I'm sorry too, for the part I played. It doesn't mean I forgive you, either of you, but I'd really like to get home." She gives us a weak smile, and she hugs herself as she shivers. Aiden and I both notice at the same time, and he gives her his jacket.

"What is it?" he asks, knowing there's more.

"Burt has Calantha, and we have three hours to submit to his demands or she dies."

Chapter Thirty-Four

Liliana

It's funny how nightmares work. Creeping up only once you're asleep and breaking down your defenses. But when you wake up in a cold sweat with the taste of fear coating your tongue, it still doesn't go away. Like a dark fucking cloud, it lingers.

Ever since leaving the farm, I'd had this horrible dream that Calantha and I traded places. Sometimes my uncle's friends got tired of me and wanted something fresh to whet their appetite, and other times it was a punishment for something I'd done. In the dream, I'd scream and fight, but I'd never been able to save her. The only way I'd gotten through those nightmares was the fact that it hadn't truly happened. She escaped with me and never had to know what it felt like to be sexually abused. *Now my nightmares were becoming reality.*

I watch country fields pass by through the window as we head toward the very place I swore I'd never go back to. My uncle's farm. It's where he wanted Hank to take me, and I would bet everything I had on Calantha being there too. Though the nausea churned in my stomach, I'd do anything, go anywhere, to get my sister back safely.

What a fucking disaster. I should have been more open with her. She knew enough about what I'd gone through, but there was just some things you didn't share with your little sister. Maybe if I had, she wouldn't have gotten caught. *Fuck, who was I kidding? All of this was my fault.*

I'd acted like a child ever since I learned Kaleb was Fitz. I let them all down.

"Take the next left. We'll park there and sneak up by the lake," I tell Aiden, thankful that neither of them mentions the hitch in my voice.

They'd called the cops on Hank and left their driver to handle the details, promising that we'd come back and make our official statements tomorrow. With anyone else, I was positive that shit didn't fly, but being Aiden Daniels and Kaleb Fitzgerald sure had its advantages. I'm just lucky they let me tag along. *Okay, scratch that. A million overbearing bosses couldn't keep me away from this mission. They were lucky to have me since I knew this place inside and out. Never in a million years had I thought that knowledge would be helpful, but here we are.*

Aiden parks the car, but when I reach for the handle, Kaleb stops me. "You've dealt with enough shit for one night, Lily. We wouldn't judge you if you wanted to stay back."

"Hell no. I know my way around this place better than anyone, and as much as it may haunt me to be back here, they have my fucking sister in there. I'm going." I ignore them and step out of the car into the chilly night air.

"We're running out of time," Aiden whispers as he checks his watch.

"Well then, let's get going. This way."

They follow me through tall grass that tickles my calves. I'm still wearing my skirt and blouse from yesterday, but luckily, I've got on flats instead of heels, or else this trek would be a whole hell of a lot harder. The lake comes into view, practically glowing beneath the rising moon. It's bright tonight, an almost full moon that seems to light up the entire sky. Good for us in some ways but bad in others.

"Stick with me and stay quiet," I whisper. "We're about to pass where they keep the foster kids, and the last thing we need is to be spotted by a cabin full of children who want to earn favor with my uncle."

Like my personal shadows, Kaleb and Aiden follow behind me as silent as the wind, adding confidence to my every step as we approach the converted barn. Before Calantha and I escaped, renovations on the barn had already started. My uncle was calling it a guest house, but I knew better. He was tired of keeping the sex slaves under the same roof where he slept and wanted us gone. We'd tried to burn it down when we left all those years ago, but it looks like we didn't succeed.

I motion for the guys to stop and hide behind a thick oak tree. Someone stands guard in front of the barn door. He looks younger than me by a few years, though it's too hard to tell for sure with only the light of the moon.

"One of you has to pretend you're Hank, and we'll just have to hope this guy wasn't friends with him. Kaleb, your coloring is about as close as we'll get. Just act like you're hauling me home, okay?"

"I don't like this," Aiden replies.

"Well, if you have another idea, I'm all ears." To my surprise, he says nothing, and I don't get even a peep of disagreement from Kaleb. The Liliana of last week would never have talked to them this way. She might have been comfortable around them, but she'd rather someone else call the shots. Not this time. Calantha was *my* sister, and I'd storm the gates of hell to save her.

Without another moment to think it through, I whisper, "Aiden, be ready to strike when he's distracted. We don't want him notifying anyone that I'm here before we're long gone with Calantha."

Still wearing Kaleb's jacket, I move out from behind the bush and let him lead me toward the barn doors. I try to pull away, scowling at him over my shoulder as I act like a sullen child that's been caught escaping their chores.

"Hank, man, it's been a while," the guard says, and I inwardly cringe. *Shit.*

Instead of answering, Kaleb moves to pass him and open the door, but the guard gets in our way.

"Hold up. Is this the infamous Anna?" His eyes roam over my body, staring at my chest far longer than I'm comfortable. "Well, fuck me. Even when she's a drowned rat, she's sexy."

Kaleb remains silent and tries to pass him once more,

but it doesn't seem like this asshole can take the hint. "Hey, why don't I take her upstairs? Give me five minutes with her." He skates his gaze down to my ass and says, "Better yet, make it ten."

"I'll kill you before I let you lay a fucking finger on me," I say, practically growling. I don't know if it's the confidence I get from having Aiden and Kaleb close by, or if my protective big sister genes are kicking in, but I'm done letting these assholes get away unscathed.

It would seem that my boys are too, because the moment the guard grabs my arm, Aiden comes out of nowhere and wraps him in a choke hold. Once he's out cold, we move through the door and stuff his body in a small coat closet. Before we manage to close the door, his walkie-talkie goes off.

"All clear at the house. Anything at the barn?"

Kaleb slips it from its holster, brings it to his lips, and with an almost terrifyingly similar voice to the guard says, "All clear at the barn."

He hooks the device to the belt loop of his pants while I just stare at him, shocked. He and the guard sound nothing alike, so how the hell did he mimic him so well?

"I've got talents you don't even know about, baby," he says with a wink, and I can't help the smile that spreads across my face. It doesn't last, of course, as we make our way through the renovated barn on the hunt to find my sister.

We pass by four bedrooms, their doors open to reveal empty rooms, before we make it to the end of the hallway where it opens into a comfortable kitchen. When we step inside, Aiden immediately hauls me behind him while Kaleb steps up to stand shoulder to shoulder with him.

What the hell?

Then I hear it. The settling of a teacup in its saucer. The sound rings through my ears, bouncing around my mind and bringing up all the memories of being here. My aunt drank tea like it was going out of style. Sometimes it's how she'd sedate me, under the guise of spending quality time together, feeding me yummy sandwiches and cakes like we were upper fucking class. It never ended well for me.

"My sweet Anna, is that you?" Her voice is as delicate as I remember, far too soft for someone married to my uncle.

I try to move out from behind Aiden and Kaleb, but they're as solid as fucking mountains, completely unmovable. As much as I love their protection, this is one battle I need to fight on my own. I'm done cowering in the dark. They took it too fucking far when they involved Calantha, and I wouldn't let them get away with it. She was fucking pure, a beautiful light amidst the darkness of my youth, and they'd have to kill me before they stole that from her.

To Kaleb and Aiden, I whisper, "Please. I need to speak with her." When they let me through, I turn my sights on my aunt. Her hair is completely gray, pulled back into a low bun on the back of her neck. Other than a few extra lines around her eyes and mouth, she looks exactly the same.

"Where is she? Where's Calantha?" I ask her, standing straight and unafraid.

"It was never meant to go this far, you know," she says quietly. Her eyes are unfocused, like she's a million miles away instead of sitting in the kitchen with us. "I tried to fight back when the abuse started, but he's a harder man to control than you'd think and knows far more ways to hurt someone than I do."

She rubs her forearm then, and I'm reminded of the time she broke it, falling off the loft in the storage shed. My eyes widen as I consider that maybe that wasn't the truth at all. My uncle had always seemed to love her, doting on her whenever possible. And she'd always followed along with his plans as if they were her own. *Had all of that been a lie?*

"You have a chance to change things now," I say, swallowing down the taste of fear and approaching her. "Help save Calantha. She's better than any of us. We can't let him take that from her. Hell, I'll even take her place if that's what it takes."

Both men behind me snarl at those words, and my aunt lifts her gaze briefly to them before dropping them back to me. "I swore to myself that if he ever succeeded in bringing you back, I'd finally take a stand."

She picks something up from the chair next to her and hands it to me. Hesitation keeps me still as I recall all the ways she used to manipulate me into doing what she wanted. *Was this another of those times?*

Even if it was, we didn't have the luxury of waiting to find out. I untie the leather string and unwind it from a soft bundle of fabric. Unrolling the soft material, I find three needles inside. Just like the ones she would use to sedate me with.

Noticing the look on my face, she says, "I really thought I was helping, but I realize now that there was far more I could have been doing. I'm sorry I let you and your mother down." A tear falls down her cheek, but she wipes it away and curves her lips into a small smile. "She's on the second floor, but there's a guard in front of her door and another man inside. The spiked tea I gave the guard twenty minutes ago should be kicking in by now, but it's up to you to get past the man inside before he can talk to your uncle."

"You were going to help her by yourself?"

She nods. "I realized a long time ago how much I'd fucked up. I swore I'd never make the same mistakes again. Now go, quickly."

"Thank you," I whisper, holding on tightly to the bundle in my arms. An odd sense of calm rushes through me, and I can almost hear a door to my past closing in my mind. Is this what closure feels like? Not that I'm truly there yet, but maybe someday.

Aiden takes the pack of needles from me as we walk up the stairs, then passes something to Kaleb. I expect it to be one of the needles, but when I look down, it's the hat the guard was wearing outside.

Kaleb nods, putting it on and pulling it low over his brow. I don't like the look of it on him, though I can't decide if it was because that sleazeball had owned it or just that I'd never seen him wearing a ball cap. *Those beautiful curls of his should never be tamped down by a hat.*

"Be careful," I mouth to Kaleb as he takes the last step to the second floor on his own. With someone inside the room, we can't afford to cause a scene. After five minutes, I'm seriously considering going out there when Kaleb finally returns, giving us both a thumbs up. I smile and find that I rather like the look of this powerful man taking down my foe and then signaling with something as simple as that.

Aiden distributes the needles, reluctantly giving me one when I glare at him. Clearly he doesn't realize I'll have no fucking qualms about shoving this into whoever's in there with my sister. I'm angry at my uncle, his friends, and every sick piece of shit working for him. *This ends tonight.*

The hallway is the same on the second floor as it is on the first, with several open doors leading up to what must be the master bedroom at the end. We listen by the doorway for any signs of life, but they must have sound-proofed these rooms or something, because I hear nothing.

I look to Aiden and Kaleb for some sign of what to do, and it's like they've been having a silent conversation this whole goddamn time because they're prepared. Kaleb opens the door quickly and we follow him inside. What we stumble upon makes me want to fucking vomit.

Bile rises in my throat as we catch Burt fucking Brandon fisting his cock while my sister sleeps on the bed. The top three buttons of her shirt are open and her skirt's risen to her thighs, but otherwise, she's covered. Then I notice how still she is. Why the fuck isn't she moving?

Panic claws at my insides, and with Burt's nasty-ass dick out, I might actually throw up all over this goddamn room. *With my luck, though, that disgusting pig would only use it as lube.*

Kaleb has already poked him with the needle, the plunger firmly pressed down with the syringe empty, but Burt isn't down yet. He fumbles to get up, tripping over the pants bunched up around his ankles. I leave him for my avenging angels and focus on the only person who's ever loved me unconditionally. *Please be okay.*

Her skin is warm, and I breathe a sigh of relief when I find a pulse. It's thrumming erratically, but it's there. Wrapping my arms around her, I hold her tightly as tears stream down my face.

"Lily," she croaks.

When I pull back, she stares at me with glassy eyes. "I'm here, Calla. We've got you." She holds onto me, squeezing hard when a thump echoes from the corner of the room. Twisting around, we find Burt collapsed on the floor, his now-soft dick resting on the floor, and I don't even fucking think. I stand up, walk toward him, and press the heel of my foot onto his limp dick.

He sports two black eyes and a bloody nose, and I hope his fucking penis never works again after tonight.

Aiden picks up Calantha from the bed, and we're off, rushing downstairs to freedom. I stop when I glimpse my aunt, her face set with relief at the sight of Calantha.

Taking a deep breath, I reach my hand out to her and invite her to come with us, but she only shakes her head.

"It's time I do what I should have done all those years ago. Go, be safe."

With one last glance in her direction, we exit the barn and rush out into the night.

Free at last.

Chapter Thirty-Five

Liliana

One *ne week later.*

Birds chirp softly through the open window and light shines on the bed where Calantha and I sleep. I haven't wanted to leave her side, not until I know without a doubt that she's okay, but she's almost back to her old self.

I stretch and turn to find her sitting up against the wall with a magazine in her hand.

"I love you, Lil, but if it's all the same to you, I'd like my bed back."

"Decapitate my heart, why don't you. I'm in agony!" I yell, feigning upset as I head to the bathroom. Turning on the shower, I let the water get hot while I use the toilet and get undressed. I've been avoiding the mirror, but if Calantha has made such progress, maybe I can do this.

As I look at my reflection, my eyes zero in on the small wound on my abdomen. Thankfully, it hadn't needed stitches and the doctor didn't think it would scar, so that's a relief. I don't want any physical reminders of what Hank or Burt did to my family. It'll heal, and so will we.

While I want to say this week has been a chance for us to unwind, it hasn't. Between dealing with the cops over what happened with Hank at the cabin, my sister and I had been called in to testify against my uncle. Apparently, my aunt had finally come clean about what he was up to, and now my uncle and his powerful, repulsive friends would be thrown in jail. Or at least that was the hope. Who knew there was so much red tape for this type of shit?

Kaleb and Aiden had given me my space, only checking in a few times to make sure we were okay and to see if we needed anything. I was grateful to them. Not just for giving me this time, but also for being there. Things would have ended differently if they hadn't come looking for me.

The three of us have a lot to talk about, and I'd put it off long enough. I wasn't sure what I'd even say, since all of this was my fault. Okay, maybe not all, but most of it. They'd lied to me, but I hadn't been completely honest with them either.

After getting dressed and braiding my wet hair, I head out to the kitchen. Kaleb and Aiden sit on the couch with my sister, holding a coffee from my favorite cafe around the corner. Calantha passes one to me.

"What are you guys doing here?" I ask, wincing at my lack of decorum. But what do they expect when they spring this on me before I've had my energizing nectar?

Instead of a male voice, I get Calantha's soft one.

"You've put off this conversation long enough. You can either go with them to discuss at their place, or I can go out and let you have the apartment. The choice is yours."

"Sheesh, who knew you were so damn bossy?" I mutter before taking a sip of my salted caramel macchiato. "I'll go with them. You stay here."

The ride to the penthouse might go down in history as the most awkward drive ever. Maybe it would have been easier to have Calantha go out, but she'd been through enough already, and until things were solidified with my uncle and his deplorable friends, I didn't trust her going out alone.

Over the last week, I had a lot of time to think about everything that happened, but one thing kept popping up more than anything else. When we were at the cabin and I was trying to find a suitable weapon to take Hank down with, I overheard Aiden say something that almost had me running back into their arms.

Your first fucking mistake was thinking you'd get away with kidnapping the woman we love.

Had he been caught up in the moment of my rescue? Love seems like such a strong word for him to throw around after the short time we've been together, even more so when they'd both been lying to me. But I couldn't deny my own feelings before everything went down. I'd been falling for them too. It was all such a fucking disaster now, and I couldn't figure out how the chips might fall.

When we're settled around the table in their penthouse, I decide to start this little chat with gratitude. "I can't express how glad I am that you showed up at that cabin. Just in the nick of time too." I reach down, feeling the spot Hank cut me beneath my oversized black t-shirt.

"We'll always show up for you, Lily, regardless of where things stand between us," Kaleb says, and something about the way he holds himself makes me think he's trying really hard not to reach across the table and take my hand.

"Though, in the future, we'd much rather you just talk to us instead of taking risks like that. If you truly want to leave Exalta Solutions, we'll happily find you a suitable place to work." Aiden clasps his hands in front of him, tilting his mouth down almost in a frown, but his eyes give everything away. Normally a storm cloud gray, in the kitchen's light they almost look silver.

As we sit here, I take in their words. Is that what I want, to leave the company? No, not really. But I don't know how I'll be able to trust them again.

"Did you mean what you said to Hank?" I blurt out, and I want to slap myself. *This isn't what you practiced, Lily!* "His first mistake... I heard it when I was trying to find something to whack him with."

"That we love you?" Aiden asks, and I can't help but hold my breath as I nod.

"Admittedly, it's not quite how we pictured you

would find out, but it's the truth," Kaleb chimes in, shifting in his chair like a little kid.

"I don't know what to say."

Finally, Kaleb reaches a hand across the table and lays it palm up, giving me a choice. "You don't have to say anything, not yet. We didn't keep my involvement at Club Rapture a secret to harm you, but we saw how hard it was for you to handle Aiden at the office, and we couldn't risk losing you."

"We'd love it if you stayed on as our assistant and hope that someday you'll forgive us enough to give us a second chance, but in the end, we'll respect your decision." Aiden stretches a hand across the table in a similar position to Kaleb.

I swallow past the lump in my throat, my mind whirling a mile a minute as I try to process everything. The pros and cons, possible scenarios, and everything that could go wrong, when I recall something Calantha had said to me before Club Rapture. *Don't give up because you're scared.*

That's exactly what I'd been doing. Giving up on the chance for love and acceptance, to be cherished at work and at home by two men who had more than proved themselves. Yes, they lied, and yes, I'd have to deal with it, but that didn't mean they were shitty people. In fact, I knew deep down in my very soul that they were two of the best people I'd ever met. Just like I did with Club Rapture, it's time I jumped in with both feet.

"Okay," I whisper, not trusting my voice to be steady if I speak any louder.

Silence rings loud and clear from across the table until finally, Aiden speaks. "You'll have to be a bit more specific, Petal."

"I don't want to leave the company. And..."

"And?" Kaleb asks, standing up like he's ready to pounce on me. I'd chuckle if my heart wasn't beating like war drums.

"And although I still have to work through the pain of being lied to, I'd like to figure out this thing between us." Their faces darken until I can almost feel the sexual tension in the air. "Slowly," I tack on. As much as I want to be sucked into the pleasure I know they can provide, I want this to work. Jumping into sex won't give us the time to work through our emotions.

Both men approach me, taking languid steps around the table until they stand on either side of me. Aiden tilts my head toward him and places a gentle kiss on my lips.

"Oh, we can take it slow, Blossom," Kaleb says, pressing a finger to my chin until I face him before kissing me softly.

My body burns as if on fire, making me regret the decision to take it slow.

Fuck. Me and my big mouth.

Chapter Thirty-Six

Liliana

Three weeks later.

I finish taping up the last box of stuff from the apartment Calantha and I have lived in these last few years. It feels strange to say goodbye to the place that was our home after the farm but not in a bad way.

As much as I tried to pretend I wanted things to move slowly with my new boyfriends, I ended up agreeing to move in with them and have finally convinced Calantha to come live in their building.

Apparently, Aiden and Kaleb got the landlord to reduce her rent to match the old building, but I have a sneaky suspicion they're covering the difference. They might be big shot business men, but even they couldn't have that much sway.

"The end of an era," Calantha says wistfully as she sets a box down.

"And the start of a new one," I reply.

She laughs, wrapping her arm around my waist as we look around the apartment. "Optimism looks good on you, Lil."

"Well, I learned from the best." I squeeze her tight, not wanting this moment to end because then it'll be real. My sister and I will no longer live together. I can't help the tears from building behind my eyes, but I don't let them fall. This chapter of our lives might be closing, but the future is bright.

"Are you sure you have time to help me get these last few boxes over? I'd understand if you bailed, ya know, what with your hot date and all," she teases.

"Oh, shut up. It'll be fine. I've got plenty of time to pamper myself after you're settled." It's been three weeks since I told the guys we'd take things slow, and they've taken my words to heart. Maybe too much, since neither of them has done more than kiss me, and I'm starting to go crazy. *It's time to speed things up.*

I made a reservation at DANIEL, the posh restaurant they took me to after my first week at work, and they aren't going to know what hit them. My cheeks flush as I think about the special purchases I made in preparation.

"You minx." Calantha slaps me playfully. "These boys have ruined you in the best possible way, and if I didn't love you so much, I'd hate you."

"Oh, Calla, don't you know? Your own ruination is just around the corner."

I arrive at the restaurant early, wanting to check out our table before the guys arrive. This reservation was a bitch to get because apparently the Skybox is notoriously booked for months in advance. It took me having to name drop both Kaleb and Aiden to get it, but I'm sure they won't mind. Not once they see what I have in store for them.

The Skybox is a private table with a view of the bustling kitchen via a window that I'm happy to find has curtains. If we can see into the kitchen, surely that would mean they could see us as well, and what I have planned for tonight is only for the three of us.

I get settled into the plush bench and order us each a drink - an old-fashioned for Aiden, a negroni for Kaleb, and I decide to get the white cosmopolitan again for myself because, holy shit, it's tasty.

I shuffle on the seat as I get used to the odd sensations from my surprise gifts. The remote-controlled vibrating panties aren't turned on, but I can still feel the little device against my already sensitive nub, and the buttplug I put in before coming here has my blood pumping harder with every move I make. *Fuck. Maybe this was a bad idea.*

There's no time to think about it further though, because I catch sight of Kaleb and Aiden as they're led into our private room with shocked smiles on their faces.

Once settled, the waiter leaves without taking our order. The Skybox comes with a very special eight course meal and will essentially use up my entire bonus from work, but I didn't want it, anyway. Not without deserving it.

"You look ravishing," Kaleb tells me, leaning in to place a kiss on my cheek.

"Quite," Aiden agrees, following suit with a kiss on my other cheek. "Though I hope you realize the only thing we're hungry for isn't on the menu."

At his words, my clit throbs against the little toy in my panties, and I feel myself grow wet beneath their heated gazes. "Well, actually," I start, but at that moment, someone comes in with our first plate of food.

I unfold my napkin and place it on my lap, feeling their eyes on me. My face heats, whether from the alcohol or desire, I can't be sure. "While I appreciate that you've followed my wishes of taking things slow, I was hoping we could, uh... speed things up."

A grin spreads across Kaleb's face and Aiden's gray eyes shift down my body with such intensity that I can almost feel it.

"Would now be too fast?" Kaleb asks, standing as if to leave.

I chuckle, loving that he wants me just as much. Maybe this is why they both sat on the opposite side of the booth. *Do they find me that tempting?* "Let's enjoy the food. I even brought a gift, though you'll have to share."

As I reach into the pocket of my dress and pull out the small remote, I feel Aiden's leg brush against mine. The soft feel of his pants rubbing against my smooth, sensitive flesh has me shifting and heightening my already rampant arousal.

I place the small device on the table between us and watch as both sets of eyes zero in on it. My embarrassment gets to me then as I worry that maybe I've gone too far and they aren't going to want this. "It was just a silly idea I had, but if you're not into it, that's totally fine."

My desire starts to plummet, but these two men I adore don't let me worry a second longer. Kaleb grabs the remote while Aiden slips from his side of the booth over to mine. He doesn't talk as he moves his food and cutlery with him, taking a sip of his drink before he puts that down on my side of the table as well. I'm crushed between him and a bookshelf, with Kaleb opposite us, flipping the remote between his fingers.

"Do you know," Aiden starts, putting a bite of food on my fork and bringing it to my lips. I hesitate for only a moment before letting him slip it into my mouth. "That we're both at your mercy, Petal? Just being in your presence has our cocks rock fucking hard, but then you do something like this. It's taking everything we have not to fuck you right here."

He continues to feed me tiny bites of the food on my plate until the server comes with our next course. The moment he steps in with fresh plates, my panties start to vibrate. It's low, barely more than a tease, but I'm thankful it isn't loud as a gasp escapes me.

"Is everything okay, miss?" the waiter asks, causing heat to rise on my cheeks.

"Yes, of course. The food is just so good," I manage to squeak out as Kaleb plays with the buttons. When the waiter leaves, I turn to him, fully intent on chiding him, when he turns it up higher, and I have to grip Aiden's leg to stop from moaning.

Just before I can hurdle over the edge, he turns it

back down to a low hum and Aiden pops another piece of food in my mouth. At this point, I can't even tell what it is I'm eating, let alone if it's any good or not, because my mind is frazzled.

As we eat, they keep the conversation going and I try to stay active, but holy fucking shit. I can't focus on anything but the need to come. I should have known they'd take control. *If they want to play this little game, so can I.*

My hand still rests on Aiden's leg and I casually move it, focusing my attention on the feel of his pants beneath my palm instead of the soft vibration on my clit. At this low of a speed, I don't think I can finish anyway, and I have a feeling I'll be waiting a while before I see oblivion.

When he takes a bite of his own food, I move my hand up to caress his hard length through his slacks. He chokes a bit on his food as I squeeze, and I can't help the smile that spreads across my face.

"Did I mention that I'm wearing another surprise?" I ask, rubbing my high heel-covered foot on the inside of Kaleb's thigh while still stroking Aiden's dick. A rush goes through me as I watch desire darken their gazes. "Would you like to guess what it is, or should I just tell you?"

"You're playing a dangerous game, Petal," Aiden whispers in my ear while Kaleb practically shakes across from us. It must take everything he has not to climb across this table and join us.

I pout at Aiden, feeling victorious. "Don't you want to play with me?"

The men share a look but don't speak as they move in tandem. Aiden trails a finger down my neck and over the thin material of my dress.

"Is the surprise here?" he asks, just as Kaleb turns the vibrator up a notch.

"No," I gasp as he pinches my nipple.

Aiden feeds me another bite of food before the server brings us a new dish, and I have to stop myself from growling at him. All I want is to be left alone with my men. Screw the fucking meal.

After he departs, the guys each try their food and ignore our earlier conversation. Kaleb hasn't turned down the vibrator, and I'm finding it harder and harder to stay still as little tremors crash through me. I must be soaked by now. Probably leaving a fucking mess on this nice cushion, but I don't even care.

I'm given another bite of food that I don't even want, but I chew and swallow it like a good girl. I grab my drink, needing something to cool me down, and the moment I set it back on the table, Kaleb hits another button.

"Are you making room for us both to have you at once?" Kaleb asks as both men watch me writhe on the booth.

I press my knees together, trying to add friction so that I can finally see stars, but once again, the vibrations lessen. Now I do growl. "Yes, just let me come already."

"Not yet, Blossom. Soon."

The rest of the meal passes in a blur of almost orgasms, and by the time dessert arrives, I'm afraid they won't ever let me finish. My mind is mush, zeroed in on the only thing it wants until everything else is a blur.

On the plate in front of me sits a delicate chocolate concoction that should have my mouth watering for a taste, but it's not what I'm hungry for. To my surprise, neither of my companions eat theirs either, though Kaleb moves to grab his fork but accidentally drops it on the floor. Before I can offer him mine, he's already crouched beneath the table to get it.

Instead of popping back up though, I feel his hand wrap around my calf, and I jump at the contact.

"Kaleb," I whisper, worried that someone will come in, but he only ignores me and spreads my legs apart.

Aiden stands, somehow holding onto the remote now, and leaves the Skybox entirely. I can't worry about where he went though because Kaleb is pressing kisses along my inner thighs, getting closer and closer to my center. With my legs spread, the vibrations feel even fainter than before, and I almost weep with the need to come.

Aiden returns, shutting the door and making sure the blinds are closed before he sits back down next to me.

"Eat your dessert, Liliana. You don't want to leave hungry." Aiden lifts the fork to my mouth and I close my lips around it. Creamy chocolate mousse hits my tongue just as the vibrator speeds up. Whatever setting he's using now is sporadic, pulsing in indeterminable lengths and driving me wild.

I feel a finger press into me, and I cry out, covering my mouth to hide the sound.

"Do you want a taste of my dessert?" Kaleb asks,

lifting his hand up from beneath the table. I'm shocked silent when Aiden licks my wetness from Kaleb's finger and releases a delighted hum when he's done.

Kaleb's kisses return as his tongue spears into me.

"Please," I beg desperately.

As if answering my call, Aiden presses another button on the remote, and my body seizes beneath the pleasure. His mouth finds mine, muffling my cries as I'm catapulted into the stars, light dancing behind my closed eyelids.

Beneath the table, Kaleb laps up my juices as the vibrator turns off. I sit in the booth, twitching as I come back into my body, and a little giggle escapes me.

"Holy shit," I whisper, checking to make sure the door is still shut.

Kaleb comes up from under the table, his lips glistening beneath the soft light. He licks them, tasting me again before groaning. "Fuck, you taste so good, baby."

Aiden stands, holding his hand out for me. I take it, confused but not caring. My legs are wobbly as I stand, and my thighs are slick with the events of our night. I should be embarrassed, but somehow, I'm not. There's something about these two that makes it almost impossible to care about what anyone else thinks.

"Here's what's going to happen," Aiden says, lifting my dress and cupping my pussy. "You're going to come for us again on the drive home, and then we're going to stretch you out and fill you up."

He fingers my pussy, and I clench around him. Kaleb grabs my ass, pressing against the plug so it feels like he's fucking me, too. Then, like flipping a switch, they both remove their hands and fix my dress before exiting the room.

I follow along mindlessly, not paying attention to anything but them as we head out of the restaurant and into the waiting car. Their usual driver smiles as we climb in the back, and embarrassment floods my cheeks as I remember Aiden's words. He wants me to have an orgasm with someone else driving the car? No fucking way. *I couldn't...*

It's dark out as we begin the short drive to the penthouse. I'm boxed in between both men, trying to ignore the wetness between my thighs and the anticipation of what's coming.

"Did you enjoy the food?" Kaleb asks. I turn my head and look at him to answer when the vibrator comes to life again, not giving me any chance to prepare or ease into it. I swear it has to be set to full blast.

On my other side, Aiden shifts slightly, whispering, "Oh, your seatbelt is twisted. Let me fix that."

What the hell?

But instead of even touching my seatbelt, he moves his hand beneath my dress and shoves two fingers inside me.

"So, did you have a good time?" Kaleb asks again, but all I can do is nod. I can't help but look in the rearview mirror, wondering if their driver will look back and catch me falling apart. As much as it scares me, I can't deny just how much I love the thrill.

"Is it fixed yet?" Kaleb asks Aiden, whose fingers are pulsing inside me, pressing against my sweet spot.

"Almost got it," he replies darkly

"Let me see if I can help." Kaleb then presses another button, and I realize how wrong I was. It hadn't been set to full blast. Until now. My legs shake as I convulse beneath the onslaught, and the walls of my pussy clench around Aiden's fingers tight as I finally come in what might just be the best fucking orgasm of my life. I try to keep quiet, do my very fucking best not to let any sound out, but by the way I'm breathing, there's no chance in hell the driver doesn't know exactly what we're doing back here. It's both pleasure and pain, my clit is so over-stimulated that even hitting bumps in the car causes little spasms to erupt within me.

The lights of the city pass us by, or maybe those are just the stars in my vision from such an intense orgasm, but finally Aiden removes his hand and sits back.

"Got it," he says with a chuckle, and I almost want to smack him. The driver comes to his rescue when he announces that we've arrived.

"You'll be the death of me, I swear," I whisper as we enter the penthouse elevator a moment later.

"Well, the French call it *la petite mort* for a reason." Kaleb chuckles, planting a scorching kiss on my lips as we ascend toward the penthouse.

I barely have time to enter the house before they take my clothes off, not that I mind. I've craved this for so long but never felt confident enough to have it. Their love for me has opened my heart to so much more than I was ever letting myself feel.

When I'm stripped bare, I watch as their eyes heat at the sight of me. I should feel exhausted after such a long night, but instead, I'm rejuvenated.

"I need you both inside me, please."

Aiden lets out what I can only describe as a roar before lifting me off my feet and carrying me toward his bedroom. I wrap my legs around his hips, disappointed when I find jeans pressed against me instead of the heat of his bare flesh.

He tosses me on the bed, and I watch as both men get undressed. They're mesmerizing. Such incredible bodies, sexy in their own way.

"If you're uncomfortable at any point, you just have to tell us, and we'll stop. Do you understand?" Aiden asks while Kaleb pulls out a bottle of lube from the bedside table.

"Just fuck me already, will ya?" I demand.

Aiden climbs onto the bed, laying down and pulling me on top. I straddle him, grinding against his cock. He kisses me, twirling his tongue against mine in a dance we've perfected over these last few weeks.

His cock nudges against my entrance, teasing me mercilessly. When Kaleb starts playing with the plug in my ass, I almost break down and beg. He leaves it in as Aiden presses his thick cock inside me, and I let out a whoosh of air at how full I feel. Fuck. Will I even be able to take them both? Kaleb twirls the plug around, fucking me with it a few times, and I gasp at the sensation. If it'll feel like this, I'll suffer any discomfort to have them both claim me.

It's over far too soon though as Kaleb removes the plug and places it in the bathroom sink. I whimper, desperate for them both to hurry up and possess me already.

Aiden thrusts slowly while Kaleb spreads the lube over my ass, fucking me with his fingers a few times to stretch me out.

"Are you ready?" Kaleb asks, walking around the side of the bed with his lubed-up dick in his hands and plants a kiss on my lips.

"I'm ready."

Then he's behind me, nudging against my tight hole. He takes it slow, entering me little by little as my body struggles to accept them both. It burns as they stretch me out, but Aiden's fingers dancing along my clit and his mouth on mine help distract me until finally I feel Kaleb fully seated inside me.

"Fuck, Blossom," he grits out. "You're so fucking tight."

Aiden moves first, fucking me in slow, deep strokes, and it feels like my body might disintegrate into tiny particles. When Kaleb adds his thrusts, it's not long before I shatter into a million pieces, my screams of pleasure echoing off the walls.

I clench around them, my body gripping their cocks tight until I feel Kaleb pull out and hot jets of his cum coat my back. Aiden grabs my hips, spearing into me with an intensity so fierce, I can't help but lie there and take it.

I feel it when he comes, his dick pulsing inside me, filling me to the brim.

Kaleb cleans my back with a warm towel while I lay half dead on top of Aiden. Once my back is clean, Aiden slips out and lays me back down.

They both stand at the end of the bed, staring in awe at Aiden's cum as it seeps out of my pussy.

"I love you both," I tell them, desperate for them to know just how much my heart has grown since I've known them. "You've shown me how to be free and gifted me with a love that I feel in the very depths of my soul. I hope to one day do the same for you."

"We love you too, Blossom," Kaleb replies, climbing up beside me and scooping me into his arms.

"And we'll cherish you always, Petal," Aiden says as he lies on my other side, placing his hand on my hip.

As I lay between my two men, I think back on the night that started it all and smile as the moment seems oddly familiar. But it wasn't that night or the sex that strengthened me. It was these two men who, without even knowing it, changed my life forever.

And I don't plan on ever letting them go.

Acknowledgements

Thank you for taking a chance on this book. I hope Liliana and her men brought you as much joy as they did me.

To my close friend and PA, Megan... There aren't enough words in the English language to describe how grateful I am for your friendship. I wouldn't be able to do this without you. Hopefully someday we can meet in person!

Thank you so much to my beta reader, Lillie. This book wouldn't be what it is without your comments and friendship.

I'd also like to thank my editor, Telisha. You're the real MVP with this book. Thank you for making this story shine!

A huge shoutout to my chicken nugget bestie, Cici Reads, without whom I'd have far fewer smiles on my face. Thank you for being a light in this sometimes dark world. I hope someday we can meet in person over a massive batch of nuggets.

Lastly, I'd like to thank Indie Black for running such an awesome shared world. Vices and Hedonism contains incredible stories with such kick-ass authors. I'm so glad to have been a part of it.

Love,
Victoria

About the Author

Victoria is a Canadian girl with a love for travel, music, and mayonnaise.

When she's not writing, she's likely reading, researching her next vacation destination, or playing games with her family.

If you want to stay up to date with everything she writes, come hang out in her Facebook reader group: Victoria's Villainous Queens, or visit her website www.victoriapauley.com for all available pre-orders and release dates.

Also by Victoria Pauley

Creating Destiny Duet

(Double MF Fantasy Romance)

Guided by the Stars

Fighting for the Stars

Standalones

Caged *(MF Gang Romance)*